RAYESSA AND THE SPACE PIRATES OMINIBUS

INCLUDES RAE AND ESSA'S SPACE ADVENTURES

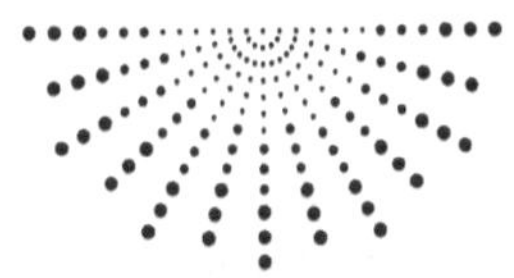

DONNA MAREE HANSON

RAYESSA AND THE SPACE PIRATES

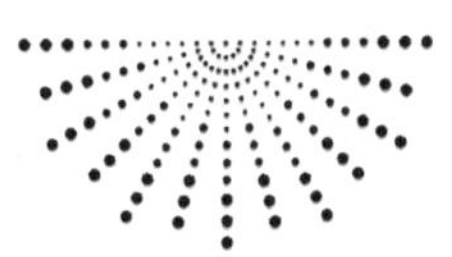

For Matthew, who believed...and still does

1

OUTPOST 311

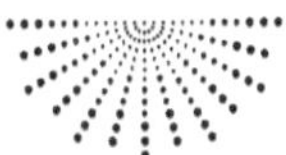

My throat itched as I connected the power relay above my head. The torch clipped to my belt jerked light beams from floor to ceiling doing little to help me see clearly. I groaned and when I lowered my arms, knives of pain dug into my shoulders. As I wiped sweat from my forehead and eyes, I wished I was watching a vid instead of doing this. With a snort of disgust, I left the cords dangling while I took a sniff of oxygen. Then I turned the respirator off with a snap.

I breathed in the thick, gluggy gas that passed for air in this corridor and felt an ache arrive just behind my left eyebrow. That's what you got when you lived in a forgotten, hollowed-out asteroid.

I looked up at the dangling cords and thought of Gris topside trying to align the solar sail and sighed. No choice but to get the darn thing fixed before the plants died in the hydroponics bay. Besides providing a small of amount of food, the plants converted carbon dioxide to oxygen, something the air filters couldn't do. Even I knew that.

I stretched upwards to place the cables back in the conduit and groaned when I heard my ragged body-stocking tear again.

'Rats,' I said, as I eased the piece of metal plating I used for a shirt.

What I wouldn't give for a nice, new, sleek ship suit. Then, I inhaled a mouthful of air so thick I could feel it clog my lungs and coughed. There was a crackle of static and I groped for the commlink hanging off my belt.

'Rae?'

'Gris?' I said into my commlink, which was taped together and had its power cell exposed.

Gris' familiar slurred speech sounded in my ear. 'Sail…is…up…Rae,' he said, from the surface of the asteroid.

Gris, a towering hulk of flesh, had been injured in a pirate attack a few years before. I had nursed him back to health with the aid of the dilapidated med unit but something wasn't right in his head. He had never been the same man again.

Often I dreamed that my life had all been a mistake and that I was actually living on a Class Five Space Station with floor-to-ceiling view ports, overlooking the rings of Saturn or the storms of Jupiter, enjoying all the modern conveniences of the 2050s. I fantasized that I had friends my own age and we hung out at the vidmovie arcade and talked about our favorite actors. I frowned as I went back to work.

I checked the alignment. The sail was slightly off, although some power was being converted by the superconductor. I checked the solar radiation levels in the hydroponics bay. Better, but not perfect.

I took another snort of air and said into the commlink, 'Gris, can you shift the sail to the left another half a centimeter? Yep that's it.'

I checked the monitor. The power levels were up. 'Okay, head back now. Meet you at the control center. I think I can scrounge up some de-molded hard tack and a tin of beans.'

Gris' guffaw reached me over the crackle of static. Our shared joke. The only food we had was hardtack and beans.

After replacing the ceiling panel, I walked along the hexagon-shaped corridors. I passed the signs of our scrapping operation, the gaping rents in the wall where the metal planking curled away from the bulkhead, leaving the superstructure and conduits exposed. I headed back to the control center, taking another snort of oxygen to keep me going.

Around the corner at a junction, I paused. A curse burst out of me. I had to stop here and work out how to get back. We'd sold the signs for food. I looked for an identifier, shining the torch along the edge. The corridors linking the bay to the main service areas were out. We couldn't afford the power or the oxygen to keep them useable all the time. Only one was safe to use. My torch revealed the squiggle dash I had etched into the rim. That was the way back to the control center.

My head was feeling a bit fuzzy from the lack of clean air by the time I made it to the main corridor. I shoved the door to slide it back, but it was stuck. I unhitched a power cell from my belt and attached the switch cable. The door slid open jerkily. Stepping through, it slid shut as I pulled my hand and the precious power cell through. The air was cleaner here closer to the center, and I breathed it in deeply. The headache that had begun in the service corridor would fade eventually.

Bending down, I retied my handmade boots and adjusted the shin plating over my leggings. Gris had made these clothes for me, using scrap and wiring to hold together the rotting remains of my body-stocking.

When I entered the control center, I caught a glimpse of myself in the stainless-steel plating. My pale skin was grimy, nothing like those made up-actors in the vidmovies. My brown hair was dirty and hung limply over my shoulders. Gris had hacked it a few months ago, even so it was still shoulder length. Bulging embarrassingly from underneath the plating were my breasts. I tried to ease them back. I wasn't quite used to them yet. A great hole in my stocking over my midriff matched the one I'd just acquired on my right thigh. My elbows, too, poked through the sleeves of both arms, and I had various burn holes dotted down my forearms. Those were from dismantling sections of the outpost with a blowtorch. I wasn't very good at it. Maybe next trade we could manage a real ship suit, fit for a sixteen year old. For now, I had to live with what I had.

Gris bounced in. He hadn't been brought up on the asteroid like me so he still had trouble with the light gravity. His bare chest was laced with scars and his lopsided trousers were cut above the knees.

He wore a metal apron secured with wire around his waist and buttocks. It saved a few embarrassing moments for both of us. Since his head injury, he tended to undress at odd times. The ties slowed down those impulses and gave me time to exit.

Stretching carefully, I got up to open the beans and placed the hard tack on our plates.

'Tea?' I asked Gris.

'Umm, yes please,' he replied with a thick tongue.

'You did well today, Gris. I think we'll live a little bit longer. Though if you ask me,' I said, plonking down in the command chair. My serving of beans swam in thin, tasteless sauce. I pushed them around the plate without much interest. 'Not much point is there. I mean, we're stuck here unless we want to join the pirates or illegal traders.'

'Captain Stroder,' said Gris, dropping beans from his mouth.

'Yes, I know Dad said we had a duty to man the outpost, but he is gone now isn't he? Let me see,' I said, reaching down and drawing out my routine checklist from under my chair. 'Keep the landing bays powered and functional; maintain client facilities; relay messages and astronomical data; maintain...'

I threw the checklist down and it clattered to the floor. Running that checklist was the only thing I knew. That and vidmovies and dealing with the rogue traders and the occasional pirate. I don't ever remember going to school but I must have once because I could read...a bit.

Everything seemed so pointless. 'What the hell.' I ranted to the ceiling. 'No one's coming. Haven't seen a supply ship since I was 14.'

'Captain Stroder said...' repeated Gris.

I glanced over to him as I swiveled around in the chair. He looked unhappy, so I got up and patted him on the head. He was hunched down, eating his beans on the floor so I could reach him easily.

'Don't worry, Gris. We've got nothing better to do. I'll think I'll take a nap after I re-watch my favorite vidmovie. Do the rounds will you?'

'Yep,' replied Gris, snaffling the rest of my uneaten beans as he left.

I pulled the seat cushion off the command chair and shoved it beneath the console. I crawled in after it and lay my head down. After I stretched out under the console and folded a few bits of circuitry out of the way, I angled down the viewer.

I selected *A Slave's Lament*, my favorite vidmovie, featuring Del Divlan in the lead as a slave girl, slotted it in and hunkered down to watch. The opening sequence flashed up. How I admired Del's clothes and the way she spoke. Would I ever be that grown up? I wondered. I mouthed a few of her lines, practicing her accent. Eventually my eyes closed and I drifted off to sleep to the sound of Del telling her master how much she loved him.

2

THE LOLLYDROP

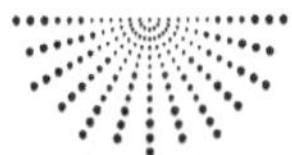

The crackling of the communication console woke me up. Still dazed from sleep, I didn't quite recognize the sound. An indistinct voice sounded over the interference. I shook my head, dislodging my confusion and disbelief. I hadn't heard external comms for quite a while. The voice grew louder and more distinct.

'Outpost 311…in…read me. Outpost…'

I scrambled up and threw the seat cushion back on the chair. While rubbing sleep from my eyes, I straightened my chest plating and eased the back of my metal skirt away from my chafe marks. I should've undone the ties before I slept, but I had been too lazy and too tired to even think about it.

'Outpost 311…please respond…'

I jumped. 'Huh?' Startled into action, I plopped into the command chair and spun around to activate the automated response and telemetry readouts.

'This is outpost 311 receiving,' I said in my best vidmovie tone. I'm sure Dad would've been proud of me.

'Captain Stroder?' came the surprised, posh-sounding voice.

I had to think quickly. It wasn't a good idea to give things away too easily (especially when you didn't know who it was). 'Um, I'm the only Stroder here. Who are you and what do you want?'

I called up the telemetry and stared at it for a while. I traced the blip with my finger and tried to make sense of the readouts. From what I could tell the small cruise ship was still a way out but it was heading directly for the outpost. Turning the communication console off for a moment, I keyed the commlink.

'Gris,' I hissed urgently. 'Gris.' No answer. 'Wake up, Gris. This is an emergency. We have a ship coming in. Wait.' My eyes danced over the readouts looking for the ship's ID. 'Here's the signature. It's from AllEarth Corp. Who in hell is that I wonder?'

I reactivated the communications console. The impatient male voice was berating the outpost. '...are you reading me? This is Alwin Anton, representative of AllEarth Corp. Please activate landing beacon and ready the landing bay. I repeat...'

'Shit, shit, shit,' I began to fidget then pounced on the landing protocol checklist from where it hung on the wall. 'Gris. What do I do? They're looking for Dad. It's official, not some scummy pirate. Gris?'

A crackle of static and I could hear him. 'Ummph,' groaned Gris into his commlink. The sound of him waking up flooded through the center. He must have bedded down in one of the service conduits, probably on the other side of the air filters where it was warm. 'Gris here. What...is...it Rae?'

'Gris, thank god,' I said, grateful to hear his mumbling. I scanned the checklist. 'Ah, power up landing bay Alpha, quickly. We have official visitors. Then get up here and help me find the protocol sheets for official visitors—or was it for emergencies?—that Dad stashed away'

'Visitors?' he said, slowly enunciating the word. I could picture him, standing slack faced, mouth agape as he said it.

'Yes, god dammit. Real visitors. Maybe they'll have real food.' I snapped off the commlink. I hoped that Gris understood what I was saying and would go and ready the landing bay.

I leant over the console and tried to get my bearings. Lights were flashing all over the place and displays were projecting three-dimensional images of the ship approaching in front of my face. I was shaking so hard I nearly tipped out of my chair. I had to get a grip. Clearing my throat, I opened a channel to the incoming ship.

'Welcome to outpost 311, Mr, er, Anton. Landing bay Alpha is at your disposal. The *Lollydrop* will find all services available,' I said in the same vidmovie accent I'd used before, though with a bit more polish. I flicked off the switch and mumbled to myself. 'Except fuel, supplies, amenities and every other goddamn thing it'll want.'

Gris entered while I was rummaging through Dad's records. He'd been an old-fashioned man, keeping paper books as well as storage wafers.

'Pirate,' Gris grunted. I knocked my head on the cupboard I was leaning into and groaned.

'Ow,' I said as I rubbed my wounded noggin. I pulled myself out and bounded to my feet. 'Really, Gris, you think he's a pirate? His ship signature is genuine, matches the auto update we had two years ago. Look,' I added with a smile. 'I've never heard of a pirate that would call himself 'Alwin Anton' have you?'

Gris scratched his groin and thought for a moment. 'Ah, no,' he said slowly.

'It's not Rusty Claw or Cleaver the Curry Eater this time. This AllEarth Corp guy talks like his ship suit shrank a while back.'

Gris held up a hand and frowned. 'Captain say you nice little girl. Speak nice.'

'Sure. I can speak nice, when you're my main company and the only other freaks that come here are criminals with weird names. If it wasn't for you, Gris, I'm sure they would have sold me on the Centauri slave market ages ago.'

I reached up, standing on tippy-toes, and scratched behind his ear. His sagging face split with a grin. I really did love him and it brought tears to my eyes just to think of how much. 'Now, enough of that. Do you remember where Dad put those notes? The emergency ones?'

Gris' face went blank, his grey eyes glazed. 'Notes?' he replied.

I pouted and stared into space. The sounds of the monitors tracking the *Lollydrop's* berthing were like little daggers digging into my flesh. I thought I was going to stress out completely until I suddenly remembered my little-girl stash.

Edging under the main console, I pulled aside the cabinet door. This was where I used to keep my mementos, broken doll bits, a piece of my mother's uniform and a pile of papers. I drew out the papers and shook dust off them. A vidmovie disc dropped down. I bent down to pick it up and gave the title a quick glance. I scrunched my face up. It read *Second Class Humans-Clone Revolt*. 'What's this some kind of documentary? I turfed it back into the cabinet and rifled through the rest of the stuff. A couple of papers were infantile drawings that I flicked in the direction of the cabinet. Then on the next page were Dad's hand-written words, 'Rae, in case of emergency, follow these steps.'

'Here it is. Gris, you'd better head down to the landing bay and switch on the lights and air. Make sure all of the side passages are sealed so that he can only come here. I'll join you shortly.'

Gris nodded and headed out the door. I climbed up to the main console and checked the displays. The *Lollydrop* looked cute and sleek, unlike a hobbled-together pirate ship. It would be another fifteen minutes before our visitor docked, enough time to get a few things done. I quickly read through my father's instructions. I read them again just to make sure, then stuffed them under the seat cushion and sat on them. All the while, I was trying to understand how I was supposed to follow them.

The tracking beep of the ship's approach made my heart twitch. I stopped staring into space and turned to watch the display of the ship. The *Lollydrop* had started docking maneuvers by matching its speed to the asteroid's spin. Then as the tongue of the landing bay crossed the horizon it would line up and descend down to attach itself to the outpost. Just then, I had a horrible thought.

'Oh no,' I said and bolted for the door.

3

ALWIN ANTON

'Lord, what a stink,' I yelled into my commlink. 'Gris, we have a problem. The primary reclamation unit. We forgot to fix it and it's overflowed into the main corridor.'

I pulled my hair in frustration when he didn't reply. 'Gris? Gris. I don't know what to do. Dad's notes didn't cover situations like this.'

Waves of slushy sewerage were oozing over the deck planking. I'd smelt bad things in my time but this definitively topped the list. Hands on hips, I stared at the muck while waiting for Gris to answer.

'Re…re…route,' came Gris' voice through the commlink.

'Sure, no problem.' I thought fast as I tried to calm down. I felt the fabric of my body-stocking give, as I darted backwards and forwards, trying to decide which way to go. We only had five minutes. I would have to stall the visitor at the airlock.

I loped down the main corridor, hoping my clothing would stay on my back. I pulled up at the atmospheric control unit.

'Gris. I'm cycling the air through corridors AB3 to AB5. That should take him around it. But I'm going to have to drain the atmosphere from the main corridors near the docking bay. It's still going to stink. I don't think the filters can do much about it.

'Darn,' I said as I punched the panel. The remotes weren't working

15

I'd have to go down myself. I ran, holding on to my metal chest plate and skirt because they had the annoying habit of thwacking against me and leaving me bruised.

Then when I made the hatch, I unsealed it and put on my respirator mask. After stepping through, I rerouted the air and sealed off the passages. As the corridor filled up with better air, I slipped off my mask and screwed up my face. 'Phew. That still smells strong.' I sniffed and looked down. The smeared remains of an aging turd were hanging off my boot.

'Crap. What next?' I angled my foot and scrapped what I could off onto the verge grating. Time was running out. So I gave up trying to clean my boot and headed for the airlock to meet Alwin Anton, representative of AllEarth Corp, before he stumbled into something he shouldn't, all the while repeating my father's first item on the checklist, 'Act Stupid'. I was doing a good job so far and I wasn't even trying.

The hatch began to open and then halted with a grating crunch. Surprised, I looked up. The darn thing was frozen. With Mr Anton trapped on the other side, I rummaged through a service bin looking for the WD2040. After tossing bits of equipment casually over my shoulder, I put my hand on the aerosol can. I aimed and squeezed it into the frozen seal. I was greeted by the shush of air when the two atmospheres interacted. My ears felt heavy for a moment while they adjusted to the change in pressure.

I looked up from examining my boot, nose still hitched in a sniff when Mr Anton hove into view. He was a head taller than me, with lightly-tanned skin. Athletic looking, his dark eyes glittered as they looked me up and down. With his short black hair, straight nose and white teeth, he'd pass for a movie star. If the expression on his face was anything to go by, he was surprised. He stared for a moment and then his face creased and he staggered backwards. 'Good god. What is that stink?' he blurted out in what the vids would call a private-school accent.

'Sorry, slight malfunction,' I replied with a nervous shrug. 'We're having it fixed right away. Now if you'll follow me I'll take you round to the control room.'

'Who are you?' He crossed the threshold.

I swung round and felt my face heat and my underarms itch with sweat. I didn't have to act stupid in the way my Dad instructed, since it obviously came naturally. 'Oh? Yes, sorry. I'm Rae Stroder. Captain Stroder's daughter.'

'And where is your…Captain?' His dark eyes were narrowed under trim dark eyebrows. He seemed to be looking everywhere at once. 'Avoiding me I suppose. They always do.'

'If you'll follow me, we can discuss your business. And mine.' His eyes settled on me, the dark irises bored into my surprised eyes. I had to look away. I couldn't stand the way he looked at me. Then it got worse. He stepped around me and looked me up and down in my shabby clothes. If there had been a garbage chute nearby, I would have flushed myself. But Daddy's checklist had to be followed so I swallowed what was left of my pride and slunk back down the corridor with Mr Anton grinding his teeth as he passed through the deserted corridors.

Arriving at the control center, I stepped over the remains of five nights' worth of dirty dinner plates and dusted off the command chair and righted the cushion.

'Here have a seat,' I said as calmly as I could.

Mr Anton's eyes seemed to bug out as he surveyed the chair and the control room and then rested his almost black eyes on me again. He stared at me, letting his eyes drop to my clothes.

Everything was silent. The visitor, Mr Anton, seemed lost for words until Gris elbowed his way into the room, grunting and smelling like a pig fresh from his wallow. Mr Anton's jaw dropped so I thought an introduction was in order.

'Oh, um, Gris. Meet Mr Anton. He's here to—why are you here?'

Those dark eyes narrowed. Mr Anton smiled, a fake smile, and didn't bother to shake Gris' extended hand. It did look very suspicious. I wouldn't have shaken it either.

'Gris.' Mr Anton spoke again with that polished voice. Perhaps he was an actor. My mind began to drift in that direction. 'I don't know the name,' he said as he continued rubbing his clean-shaved chin and examining Gris in the same way he had examined me. 'That name is not on the crew list.' His gaze darted chillingly back to mine.

'Crew list?' I blurted. I had never seen one.

'Yes, the crew list. Who are you people?'

I blinked with the force of his words. He seemed to hurl them like accusations. I drew myself up to my full five foot two inches and faced him squarely with my shoulders set. 'We are crew,' I said indignantly. 'What else would we be, holiday makers?'

Gris gawped at me dumbly. I noticed that his breathing was rapid. Having visitors didn't seem to suit him. I frowned at him and willed him to behave.

'There is no need to be impertinent, Ms Stroder. Where is Captain Stroder? There is no point in him hiding from me. I may look young, fresh out of university, but I assure you and him that I am very experienced.'

'No one is hiding from you,' I replied, puzzled. What kind of person was he that people hid when he came a calling?

A sneer appeared on his face. 'I am here on official business. I have a right to ask these questions.'

'Really? What is your official business? You didn't bring supplies by any chance?' I assessed him with my eyes as he had me. He was immaculately clean. His ship suit was bright blue and tapered to his lithe body. He could pass for an actor, but I wasn't sure who. Perhaps Nel Wingham, who often appeared with Del. But when his mouth shrunk to a pout, I thought not.

'Supplies? No, not much. I was expecting to restock and refuel here. This is a refueling post.'

'Yes, it is.' I mentally ran down the emergency checklist Dad had left me. Second point was 'deny everything'. Great.

'I'll need an office or quarters. But,' he gestured to the control room, 'if this is the state of the executive area, I will lodge on my ship. But first I want you to give me access to the data core'.

'What?' I yelped. I didn't even know we had one. I didn't think admitting that would impress Mr Anton so I hid my ignorance.

'You heard me.'

'Yes, I heard you but you haven't given me a reason to give you that access. Even if I…never mind. You didn't say what your official business was.'

'Ah yes, I should have stated that earlier.' He produced, from inside the lapel of his super-clean ship suit, an official storage wafer with a flashy AllEarth Corp logo. He handed it to me with the words. 'You are being audited.'

I suppressed the urge to scream. I had no idea what an audit was, and I didn't know that the outpost had anything to do with this AllEarth Corp. I turned the wafer over. It was self-powered so I didn't need to plug it in to read it. When I pressed the execute button the message scrolled down. Lots of paragraphs about the outpost's specifications, when it was built and inaugurated and the details of AllEarth Corp's ownership. Then right at the end came the bit about Mr Alwin Anton, official of said company, who had been designated to carry out a full inspection and audit. All access was to be given freely and all questions answered. It ended with a cute bit that said thank you for your cooperation. I was a bit numbed after reading it, well most of it, some words I didn't understand at all. They had never appeared on any checklist I had ever read.

Gris looked on from where he hovered by the door but I didn't bother giving the wafer to him. He could only read corridor signs since the injury. I stared at the message as it began to re-scroll, stalling for time. But Mr Anton's smooth manicured fingers reached out and grasped it, tugging it from my grip. When I glared at him rudely, he said, 'I will be examining all of the facilities and transaction records. Though, I must say my first impressions are not good.'

He headed to the door, gingerly edging around Gris to avoid touching him.

'By the way, it would behoove you to dress more appropriately. Your clothing is very distracting.'

I glanced down. I didn't notice anything different about what I was wearing so I shrugged. He was shaking his head.

Drooling over his sleek and clean ship suit, I said, 'If you have a spare one of those I'll wear it.'

His face skin turned pink and he coughed. 'I, er...you are most impertinent.'

'I am?'

'You should just requisition one, though I have the suspicion that you are not entitled to one. You are definitely not crew.'

Now that made me angry. 'Not crew? My father left me in charge here. That makes me crew. I work hard to keep this place running.'

'Hah,' he said and squeezed out the partly opened door. He kicked it before he headed back to his ship.

Gris let out a wet-sounding sigh and asked, 'What is audit?'

'Trouble, I think.' I leaned down to retrieve the emergency checklist. So far I had acted stupid and denied everything. My eyes read the next point.

'Heavens. Dad had to be drunk when he wrote this.'

'Why?' asked Gris as he scraped dirt and muck off his skin with a sharp piece of plating, the outpost's most efficient means of washing.

'He says "lie through your teeth",' I quoted. 'That's all well and good. But what do I lie about?'

4

SPACE AUDIT

'Come in, Ms Stroder…Ms Stroder?' Mr Anton's voice grew louder. I wiped sleep from my eyes and flexed my stiff leg, tingling with pins and needles. I'd slept with the metal plate on again and this time it had cut off the circulation. I could hardly breathe as I rubbed some feeling back into my calf muscles.

'Ms Stroder. I assume you are at your post. It is oh-nine-hundred.'

'Oh asteroid dust,' I cursed as I hopped up from underneath the console and hit the acknowledge button. 'Rae here, Mr Anton. What can I do for you?' I said a tad breathlessly. I was suppressing a moan after all.

'Plenty. I'm sending you a copy of the letter of authority for AllEarth Corp for your records. You can read, can't you?'

I sniffed. Hadn't he seen me read? 'Yes, I can, though I don't have much need for it on the outpost. We don't have a library.'

'If you are attempting humor, then you are wasting your time on me. I don't have a sense of humor. It's not in my job description.'

'Sorry, my mistake,' I replied, through a yawn. I dragged my fingers through my clumped, dirty hair and, as I did, I thought of how clean the auditor's was. How did he manage it?

'I want you to rendezvous with me on level 3. I will undertake a random inspection.'

'Level 3?' I had to think fast. 'Um, that's not a good idea.' I angled my head, trying to see if Gris was around. He wasn't. Bother. I had to think of something else. 'We had to close that down three days ago. There was a radiation leak.' 'Really? A radiation leak? What kind of radiation, Ms Stroder?'

'Can't recall. Gris was looking after it. Please call me Rae. I don't think I've ever been called Ms Stroder before and it makes my skin crawl.'

'I see. Then I will check the Beta landing bay. I assume that's functioning.'

'Yes, it is, but Gris is working on it right now. When your ship docked, it caused a power flux, or surge or something.' I prayed Gris stayed out of sight.

'Are there any areas of the outpost that are fit to be seen, Ms Stroder?'

'Rae,' I prompted.

'Excuse me, Rae.'

'Yes, of course. I'll take you on a tour of the hydroponics bay.'

'Hydroponics? Ms Stroder, I mean, Rae, there is no hydroponics bay listed in the outpost's schematics.'

'Well, I don't know about the schem...the schematics but there's been a hydroponics bay ever since I can remember.'

There was a pause. The line was still open. I could hear it. 'This is most unusual, Ms Stroder.'

'Yes, we've never had an audit before.'

'That is not what I meant,' he replied with a sigh.

'Oh, but I meant what I said,' I added and smiled.

'Meet me at my ship. Right away,' he barked into the comms. My smile faded and I felt quite faint suddenly. I said the first thing that came into my mind.

'Yeah, okay. Be there in a jiffy.' I punched the commlink. 'Shit, shit, shit.'

'Don't talk bad. Gris don't like,' said Gris from the doorway.

I turned on him, fists clenched. 'Gris. Where were you? He's tying me up in knots. What am I to do? Dad's list is a joke and I don't like that guy. He's so, so…stiff. He doesn't cuss—he's clean and he's doing honest work.'

'Gris fixing things.' He fumbled with his lap plate.

My eyes followed his hands. I gulped. It was time to leave. 'Gris, now is not the time to start fixing that thing, okay. Tie yourself up and fix something that's broken or I'm not sure what will happen. Gotta go and meet Mr Anton Audit.'

I ran from the command center before Gris' urges got the better of him. It was probably Mr Anton's visit that had set him off. Usually only the pirates stressed him out that much.

Confused, I took a wrong turn and had to double back. Some corridors were still closed due to the broken reclamation unit. I was huffing by the time I made it to *Lollydrop's* hatch. I hailed Mr Anton and the hatch slid open.

The ship was really clean and new looking. I ran my hand along the walls and when I noticed how dirty my fingernails were, I pulled them back. My scruffy handmade boots clanked on the metal floor as I headed towards what I thought was the bridge. Highlighted arrows flickered and lit the way so I followed them.

He was standing with his back to me, scrolling through data on a screen. In front of the bridge console stood three chairs in a line. I waited for him to notice me. He must have heard my footsteps. Even I could hear them echoing around me still.

He swung round. 'Thank you, Ms Stroder. Take a seat.' He swiveled a chair around for me to sit in.

I looked at it warily and then eased myself down. It was comfortable and didn't appear ready to fall apart.

'So, Ms Stroder. I would like an accounting of where your father is?' Mr Anton spoke as he paced around my chair, stopping occasionally to hold his chin in his hand. My eyes flicked around the bridge, noting its cleanliness and its functionality. The air filters even looked clean and I could smell Mr Anton from where I sat. And he smelt clean too.

I sniffed myself and wrinkled my nose. I smelt bad in these spotless surroundings and I no longer blended in.

'Ms Stroder, please pay attention. Your father is where?' His hand now rested on his hip and he softly tapped his shoe on the floor.

'Dad was taken by pirates a few years ago.' I watched his face. It seemed to freeze.

'What did you say?' he said and began to pace five steps to the right and five back again and again. I watched, fascinated by his precise moves.

'I said he was taken by pirates. A few years back pirates began to attack the outpost. That's when the crew began disappearing or were found dead after the raids.'

He slowed his pacing. One eyebrow tilted ready to slide off his smooth-skinned forehead. 'They were taken,' he repeated. 'When was that?'

'I don't know. I was younger. Dad went…about three years ago, I think.'

'How is that possible?'

I blinked. 'What do you mean how is it possible? We are very isolated. Our comms are weak. The distress beacon was blasted out of space. We've had no ships stop for refueling for years, even before the attacks. Dad said it was the new space station around Saturn that took away our business.'

I shut my eyes, trying to block out the memory of that attack and the loss of my father. I heard a noise and my eyes flew open. Mr Anton had plonked himself into his seat and was running his hands through his short, dark hair.

'Let me get this straight, Ms Stroder. You and Gris are the only ones here.'

'Yes.'

'And the outpost is barely functional?'

Avoiding his eye, I shrugged. 'I wouldn't say that exactly It's…it's almost functional,' I said.

'You have no supplies or fuel to offer ships accessing this station?'

'Ah, not much of that, no.'

He launched out of his seat. 'You are lying to me,' he yelled.

I flinched and covered my ears. 'Not lying. I'll show you.'

'Oh, there is no need for that. I scouted around last night and did a sensor sweep. You are in serious trouble, Ms Stroder.'

'I am? Why? What have I done?' I hated the way my face heated.

He drew closer, almost nose to nose. 'Embezzled funds, stolen supplies, destroyed AllEarth Corp property. Need I continue?' He retreated backwards, nodding his head knowingly.

I stared open mouthed for a bit. 'What does embezzled mean?'

'Theft, Ms Stroder.'

'We haven't stolen anything. We've had no supplies for years I tell you. I don't even have clothes.' I plucked at my body stocking. Unfortunately, a piece tore off in my hand. 'See,' I said waving it at him. He peered at it, revulsion etched on his face.

My outburst stalled him. Then after a few moments, his brow furrowed and he added, 'Embezzled means you took money, the Corp's money, and took it for yourself.'

My eyebrows shot up. 'You're kidding me. Aren't you?'

'No. Here, look at these transactions.' He turned a storage wafer in his hand and passed it to me. I stared at it uncomprehendingly at first and then I saw it. Money transfers to Captain Stroder, salary, supply purchases, crew bonuses and more. Then there was even a list of supply deliveries. I scrolled through the list, shaking my head. There were hundreds of them over the years.

A tear of fear escaped. 'None of these supplies ever came here, Mr Anton.' I handed the list back and gulped. 'But I'm worried about what happens now.'

'You will be taken back to Earth for trial.'

'But I haven't done anything. I don't know about these supplies. Surely your link to the datacore told you that? Haven't you scanned the supply holds...what's left of them?'

'Yes.'

'And were there signs? Even a drop of grain or a smattering of fuel or a crumb of bread?' My hands had near ripped the padding off the seat. I don't think I'd ever been so scared before. I had thought Mr Anton would make a handsome vidmovie actor. At that moment, I decided that I didn't like him at all. He wasn't nearly good looking enough for the job.

5

IDENTITY CRISIS

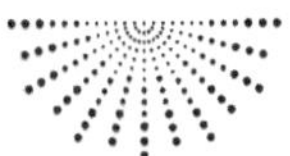

Mr Anton looked down at his wafer, appearing to scroll through it and then he looked me in the eye. 'No. There were no signs. But perhaps you sold them on to these pirates. I mean your story doesn't ring true, Ms Stroder. If that is who you really are.' His voice became a knife, making me flinch.

Right, I was sick of his accusations and his tone.

'Who else would I be?' I was interested to hear, as being Rae Stroder hadn't been too much fun so far. I had no memory of my mother or my life before I came to the outpost.

'Captain Stroder was never married and had no children according to our records.'

I blinked. 'Really? So what if they never married. A lot of people don't bother.' He was glaring at me, so I drew my eyebrows down into a frown. But I couldn't keep it up and I began to twist my grimy hands.

'Yes. You are a liar and a thief. The condition of this station is a disgrace to AllEarth Corp. Thank god I implemented this series of random audits or the company would… Never mind, I can see you are not interested.'

I was shaking my head. Out of the corner of my eye, I saw a light flashing on the command console. At first, I ignored it, as I was lost in my own misery. This wasn't how I dreamed of leaving this place. This wasn't how it was supposed to be.

Remorse got the better of me. 'Yes,' I admitted, hanging my head in shame. 'The outpost is a disgrace. Dad would be very angry if he saw it.' I looked at Mr Anton then, into his dark fathomless eyes. 'But what choice did we have? We had to trade scrap for a bit of food now and then. There is nothing of value here so the pirates leave us alone mostly. Like I said there have been no supplies, for years.'

'But the records show these transactions. More transactions than are reasonable. Why do you think I'm here? I had to investigate. A lot of money has passed through your father's account.'

'But I tell you he's dead, taken by the pirates, really mean pirates. Someone else must be behind these.'

'Ms… Rae. Do you consent to a gen scan?' Already he was readying his equipment.

'What's a gen scan? Does it hurt?' I began to scratch. I'd probably developed a nervous rash.

'It won't hurt, though it will identify you, if your parents are in the database, that is.'

'Sure, but I already know who my father is and my mother died when I was little.'

Mr Anton fired up the scan and he held the scan gun over my hair, hands and eyes. It didn't hurt but I felt weird. This situation wasn't on my checklist and his ship's on-board gravity was making me feel ill. It wasn't what I was used to as it was lighter than the outpost.

He had his back to me as he read the results. 'There, I knew it.'

'What?' I edged out of my seat.

'You are not Stroder's daughter.'

I fell back into the chair as my heart did a flip-flop. 'I'm not? Are you saying my mother was unfaithful?' My heart sank. My life was just like a vidmovie.

'No. Your parents are both alive and living on Earth. Wait a minute, I will correlate the results with the news codex.' The light still flashed on the console almost in time with my heartbeat.

'Interesting. Now this does put a different slant on things.' He looked up, his black eyes comparing my face to his readout. I felt uneasy as he studied me quite closely.

'Why are you looking at me like that? It doesn't say my parents are aliens or something does it?' I didn't know much, but being associated with aliens or being part alien was pretty bad. Or so the vidmovies said.

'No. I don't know how to break this to you. According to the newscast archives, you were kidnapped years ago on Earth. It doesn't say much here but your parents must have been important or rich.' He stilled as he began to mull things over. I could tell because he was rubbing his chin again. He turned slightly and noticed the light flashing on the console. He went over to it. 'That's strange,' he said as he fired up his scanners.

'What?' I asked, still stunned by what he had told me. I only remembered Captain Stroder. I only knew him. He was my only parent.

'Another ship,' he said but his tone was different, curious. Not the hard and concise auditor I'd come to know.

He fired up the view screen and zoomed in. The ship looked very similar to his. He frowned, and I became nervous. Two ships in such a short space of time, that was more than a coincidence, it was downright suspicious. Mr Anton must have thought the same because he threw himself away from the command console while I stood mesmerized.

'Move,' the auditor shouted. He grabbed me by the elbow, dragged me down the corridor and shunted me out of the hatch.

There was a flash of red and *Lollydrop's* hatch snapped in place, severing me from the ship and Mr Anton, who knew so much and told so little.

The planking under my feet shuddered. The outpost was under attack. I ran, dodging falling pieces of ceiling and severed cables. There was a hiss as *Lollydrop's* maneuvering thrusters fired and the tie lines disconnected. The ship lurched once then steadied.

The ship was on emergency launch, and I had to find Gris.

I ducked through to the main corridor and hit the internal comms. 'Gris. Gris.' Static bubbled out of the speakers. 'Come in.'

There was more crackling and Anton's voice came over the comms. He was swearing like a pirate. 'Rae take cover—I'll try and lead them away. Rae?' The comms died.

I was left to guess where Gris was. I ducked into shadows and crept towards the control room, using my mask to help me breathe. The smell of ozone was strong and the air, not good at the best of times, was heavy with smoke. Three corridors short of my target I saw shadows and heard boots scraping on metal planking. My breath caught in my throat. Gris' familiar face loomed out of the shadows.

I ripped off my face mask. 'Gris,' I cried, launching myself at him to hug him close. His huge arms came around me and squeezed. 'Oh Gris, I thought you were hurt.'

The squeezing didn't stop. 'Gris,' I said through clenched teeth. 'You're hurting me.' I looked up and saw the blood leaking from his scalp. His face was blanker than usual and there was no sign of recognition. 'No, Gris it's me.' His hold didn't let up. Darkness grew on the edge of my vision and swallowed up my consciousness.

6

PIRATES' PLEASURE

Cold, hard planking under my chin brought me to wakefulness. A headache thumped in my temples, the after effect of oxygen deprivation. My ribs didn't feel too good either. I felt my head. It was whole and wasn't leaking blood but that was the extent of my good fortune.

As the haze cleared, I noticed there was someone sitting on a chair in front of me. Whoever they were, they were hard to distinguish from the grey fuzz I could see all around me. I tried to focus, but that just made my head spin.

'Hello, Rae,' said my father's voice.

I sat up, wincing. I had to hold my ribs with my arm to ease the pain. 'Dad?' I said, throatily. Fire and screaming had worn my voice thin.

My vision cleared as I blinked rapidly. My Dad was tied up. He had a slight cut on his forehead and his hair was messy, although his uniform looked fresh and clean. He was almost like I remembered him. Although there was something in his eyes, a rheumy redness, that wasn't there before and his hair was almost white.

I crawled over to him, though I felt like retching. Using his lap to climb up, I nudged around looking for his bindings. 'Let me free you. I thought…you were dead. I don't understand.' My eyes misted over and I sniffed. So much pleasure and pain mixed together on seeing him.

'I thought I was dead, too, sweet. But they kept me alive. I was so worried about you,' he said in that familiar voice. It was too much to take in. It was like talking to a ghost. I had a hard time believing that this was really happening. I undid the bindings, but he still sat there with me up close. His tired old eyes looked me over and he said, 'Did the AllEarth Corp guy send any transmissions, Rae?'

Puzzled, I eased myself up to stand and looked around. 'Where is Mr Anton?'

'Dead I think,' said my father, though he didn't sound confident.

'Dead?' I stared at him in disbelief and backed away. This had to be some kind of nightmare. 'Oh, no this can't be happening.'

'I asked if he sent any transmissions.' My father's voice hardened, and he sprung out of the chair to tower over me.

'How would I know?' I gaped at him, looking at his familiar and much mourned face. I felt so guilty about the outpost but I was confused, too. If he wasn't dead why hadn't my Dad come for me? And what about what Alwin Anton had said. Was he lying? What was the truth?

My father leaned in closer his words sharp and demanding. 'Rae, it is standard procedure to monitor transmissions of docked ships.'

I was riveted to the spot. 'Really? But no ships ever docked while I've been in charge. It wasn't on your emergency checklist.' My fists curled up, tight with tension. Something wasn't right. I found a focus for my anger. 'That was a stupid list by the way. How come you never let me know you were alive? Gris said he saw your body. Where is Gris? He…'

The door slid open and Captain Stroder turned round at a leisurely pace. Another man walked in, a pirate by the look of him, his dark greasy eyes looked me up and down. No one had ever looked at me that way before and I instinctively didn't like it.

'Well, Captain, what have you found out?'

'Nothing of importance,' said my father. 'I told you she was useless and as thick as solid, titanium-plate shielding. What about the AllEarth Corp investigator?'

He turned away from me and started to walk out with the pirate. They didn't even spare me a glance. A knot of boiling anger rose, dampening my fear. The realization that the auditor had been telling the truth hit me. Stroder wasn't my father. My whole life was a lie.

'We haven't got him yet. Managed to slip behind the asteroid and blind our sensors,' said the pirate half in and half out of the room.

'We have to make sure he doesn't get away.'

'Excuse me,' I said, my voice choked with emotion. My fake father swung around, his eyes, once kindly, were now hard. I squirmed as he looked me up and down, sneering at me like I was scum. If he had punched me in the gut, he couldn't have hurt my feelings more.

'Mmmm I guess we will have to do something with you. You're old enough for the slave market. I can recoup my costs and get some compensation for the years of boredom of being with you.'

'She'll get a good price once we clean her up.' The pirate leered at me. I cringed away. Captain Stroder's eyes lingered on my breasts and my legs. The look on his face made me want to puke.

'Mmm, yes never noticed the potential before.'

I found a wall inside me that wouldn't let me back away. I straightened up and ignored the way they ogled me. 'Mr Anton said I was kidnapped. But you're the only Dad I remember.'

The slap on my cheek made my face burn. 'Shut up.' Stroder grabbed my arm and dragged me along. Still dazed I heard him say to the pirate, 'Jackal, find the auditor and kill him and while you're at it set up a rendezvous with the slavers. I'll be wanting top price.'

7

PIRATE WOMEN

I resisted the attempts to beautify me as long as I could. Mostly I did it on principle. I felt so bad, so depressed, that most of the time I didn't care what happened. I was still dealing with the fact that my life was a lie. I wasn't Rae Stroder. The man I had loved as a father was not dead, or my father, and was making very firm plans to sell me on an illegal slave market.

At least a few of the female pirates gained bruises in their attempts to bathe me. Warty, a particularly nasty pirate woman, bound me to a hook on the wall and ripped my clothes off my back. She brought pliers to cut the metal reinforced ties that held the metal plating.

'You're disgusting,' she said, as she let scraps of my body-stocking drop from her hand. She was shorter than me, much older and had three warts on her face. That didn't really make her ugly, but I guess that's where she got her name. Her ship suit was red and her breasts bulged out of the split at the front that went all the way down to her navel. She didn't have much to hide, I thought, when I saw almost all of her white breasts float around, barely constrained by her suit. I could even see a small trace work of blue veins.

I wouldn't be caught dead exposing myself that way. Lush, a tall thin woman with a purple scar from the tip of her chin to the top of

35

her collar bone came over to stare at me, strung up and naked. Her lips were large and glossed. I didn't like the way she looked at me. 'Better wash her real good. I'll help you.'

'Get off,' I yelled. Both Warty and Lush thought that was hilarious, if their laughing and slapping of thighs was anything to go by. I hated being hung up, naked and dirty with them looking at me and making comments. More pirate women came in.

'Hi, I'm Case,' said a girl only a few years older than me. Her eyes were clear blue and hard and her lips were thin. Her head was shaved and she was flat-chested. But it was the way her face twitched that unnerved me.

She was shoved aside by Venus, a huge dark-skinned woman, with hands bigger than Gris'. Next to her was a swarthy girl, pretty and slim. She didn't smile, and the others called her Nipper.

Warty walked up to me again. 'I'm going to unhook you and then you bathe.'

'No way,' I shouted, cursing them, and brought my foot up to kick her in the gut. Venus grabbed me from behind and lifted me off the hook. They all grabbed bits of me and stretched me out so I couldn't kick, scratch and bite. They managed to hold me in the san cubicle to wash me in real water for a whole ten minutes. Afterwards, my voice was hoarse. I must have screamed the place down.

I watched the water sink into the hole in the san unit. I'd never used so much water in my whole life and had never washed in it as far as I could remember. Even on Earth, it was a luxury only the rich could afford, or so I'd heard.

I did feel better afterwards. I didn't even cry when they trashed my clothes in the garbage chute. I had hated those for a long time, though I did balk at the ones they wanted me to wear. 'I'm not wearing those,' I said, shaking my head. I was huddled naked near the san unit. 'Give me a ship suit and I'll wear it, but not those.'

All that time I had been craving a real ship suit, just like the ones in the vidmovies and what they gave me to wear was something else altogether.

Lush grabbed me by the hair and shook me. 'Put them on sweet, or you'll tempt me to beat the defiance out of you.'

I turned, clutching my hair to ease the pull, and saw her lips close to my neck, tongue ready to lick my skin. Eww, I thought. That woman was disgusting. They all were.

'Okay,' I said, turning to the others. I didn't like Lush at all or the way she looked at me. I seem to remember a character like her in one of the vids I had watched. The character did bad things and I expected Lush would too. 'Give them to me.'

Lush let me go, and I escaped into the hands of the others. They draped me in pieces of translucent cloth, a mixture soft blues, whites and mauves. The sheer fabric was tied together and hung in layers. It felt kind of strange, like I was still naked and yet not. When I took a step, the clothing floated and moved around me, caressing my skin.

Then they sat me down and brushed my hair. While the last strokes drew down my back, I studied myself in the mirror. My hair shone like starlight. I never knew my straggly locks had auburn lights in them. 'What about her face?' asked Case. 'She needs more.'

Nipper spoke. 'I'll do it. The rest of you don't know what you are doing.' Nipper had been quiet, always Venus' shadow. I was wary as she brought a small case and sat down next to me. 'Lie back,' she said.

When I hesitated, Venus' large hand urged me back onto the sofa. Nipper brought out a tool, like a pen. 'This won't hurt, much,' she said and smiled.

With a clip attached to my eyelids to hold them open, she tattooed the rim. Eyeliner she said. My tears welled in the corner of my eyes, but I didn't cry. I wasn't prepared to give them the satisfaction. The same instrument served to laser my eyebrows into a fine arch. That hurt like fire on my skin. Next, she tattooed color into my lips. Her clip immobilized my mouth but didn't deaden the pain. I moaned in my throat while tears leaked down my cheek to pool in my ears.

My cheeks were blushed up. I wasn't sure if it was permanent or not. To finish it all off, they pierced my ears with five jewels along each lobe. I stopped screaming by the time they finished the second lot. I felt sick to the stomach and hot and cold at the same time. By the time they let me up, my face was one throbbing ache. I couldn't lie down because my ears hurt. I couldn't lie on my face because all of it hurt. In the end I propped myself up in the corner with pillows and leaned my head back, breathing through the pain.

Although being angry and physically hurt served to distract me from my real fear, I was left to wonder. What was going to happen to me? What was going on? Why were they dressing me like Del Divlan in a slave movie? What kind of slave market was my father...Stroder going to sell me at? I began to shake and shiver at the thought of being sold. Life wasn't meant to get worse than it was. I always thought that the future would be rosy and wonderful to make up for the crap I had already endured. Right then Outpost 311 seemed like paradise. It was all that auditor's fault. He came along and stirred up trouble.

God, what had happened to Alwin Anton? Was he really dead?

8

POOR LITTLE SLAVE GIRL

After few days, when the pain had lessened, I took a look at myself in the mirror when all the pirate women were out. I was amazed at my transformation. I looked like an actress, like Del Divlan. I was almost beautiful. I pivoted and watched my reflection as I felt the fabric swish around me. It felt divine. The door swooshed open. Too late the pirate women caught me at it and laughed and jeered so much that I withdrew to the corner and sulked.

Luckily they grew tired of hassling me or had work to do. After they left I surged out of the corner to try the doors but they were locked. Case came in, face twitching. I backed up into my corner, keeping my eyes on her as I slid to the floor. She kept pace with me and lowered herself to a crouch next to me. Her face contorted momentarily, then she said, 'Come with me. Someone wants to see you.'

'Who?'

'Never mind, just be quick. We have to get there and back before Warty returns.' I scrambled up and followed her out. I wondered where she was taking me. I hadn't seen my so-called father since he put me in these quarters to be readied for sale.

We climbed down three levels and headed down a narrow corri-

39

dor. A familiar shape was bent over a worktable pulling apart some circuitry.

'Gris?' With a quick glance at Case, I edged over to him. I think he heard me but he hunched himself up and turned away. I wanted to hug him. I missed him so much. 'Gris? Please talk to me,' I said softly. I touched his shoulder and he shied away. I heard him weep.

'I thought you wanted to see me, Gris. I'm okay really.'

His head popped up, and he sniffled and wiped his face with his sleeve. He was listening at least. 'Love Gris?' he said to the wall.

'Yeah, sure I do.' My heart was breaking. This wasn't the Gris I knew. Something had snapped inside of him. He angled his head in my direction. I did my best to hide my surprise. Gris' eyes stared in different directions and one side of his face sagged much more than the other one. They'd hurt him, hurt him bad.

Gulping back the lump in my throat, I touched his face, 'Glad to see you're okay'. A tear slid down his cheek and he turned away again, repressing sobs. I glanced back at Case but she was looking at the ceiling. I didn't know what to do.

'Gris?' I ventured.

His shoulders tensed and I saw his hand clench the tool he was holding. I was stressing him more than he could bear. Suddenly he yelled at me, still facing away from me. 'Go now.'

I flinched at his words and drew my hand back, which had instinctively reached for him. He let out a breath. 'Must work for Captain. You Captain's Stroder's not Gris''. He spun round, dribble dangling from his slack lips but his eyes flashed with anger. I jumped back and gazed at him warily. Part of my life was gone. Gris' condition opened up a gaping hole inside of me.

'Sure, I'll go,' I whispered and swallowed the sob that threatened to choke me. I pivoted on my heel and strode to the door, trying to keep my dignity and averting my face from Case.

Gris rasped out as I stepped in the corridor, 'Ssssorry,' then cried to himself. The echoes of his sobs lessened the further we walked.

I paused, ignoring Case's neutral expression, and looked back at him. I didn't know who I was more angry with, me or Stroder? Case grabbed my elbow and led me back to the women's quarters. She said nothing while we walked. Her twitching got worse though. When we reached the quarters, she punched in the code and shoved me through the door and secured it.

Left alone to ponder my predicament, I went and huddled in my corner. If the auditor was dead, there wasn't much that could be done to get me out of this. Gris was Stroder's man and not himself anyway. I felt betrayed by him and stupid because I had loved Gris more than I had loved anyone. How could I do that? Love someone who can't control himself? Because he was all you had kid, I told myself and blinked back tears. I had never felt so desolate before. I didn't want to be a slave. Even if the vid slave movies had happy endings, I wanted to be free. I didn't want to be owned by someone and I didn't want to be vulnerable.

That night, I paced around the quarters, ignoring the women's mess and the snores of the huge woman, Venus. I started thinking. I was alone. I had no one to help me. What choices were left? My mind raced with dead-end options. Stroder was right. I was useless. I couldn't think of a way to get out of this.

There was a sound at the door. I swung round as it opened. Reflexively I stepped back. It was Warty. I'd learnt that not only was she the meanest of the pirate women, she ruled them and no one crossed her. Apparently, she was the head pirate's woman, and she flaunted it, just as she did her breasts. I gulped as she stepped into the quarters. She had a smile on her face.

'It's time,' she said. 'Time to meet your fate as a slave girl.'

I tried to stall, by pretending I had to go to the san unit. She leant forward and nearly wrenched my arm out of its socket. I managed to pull my arm free and followed her out.

'Have fun sweetie,' called Lush. The door closing behind me cut off the sound of the women's laughter.

Warty sneered at me but continued to talk. 'He's chosen the Centauri market, you know. All kinds of weirdos there. You should last a few years before you're used up and finally expire.'

I didn't have to think too hard about what she was talking about.

She had to mean Stroder and the name of the market didn't leave too much to the imagination. Vidmovies had been good for one thing, at least.

We went to the next level. Here there was less traffic from pirates moving through the corridors. Her metal-heeled boots echoed in the passageway. They must have been magnetized to supplement the gravity.

We turned a corner. It was deserted. Next thing I knew I was against the wall with Warty's hands on my throat. She leaned in close and breathed into my face. 'So you're the little girl he kept in that outpost.'

My eyes bulged. 'Stroder?'

She nodded and her lips drew back over her teeth. 'Yes, Stroder. Stupid cow.'

'I thought he was my father,' I rasped. The pressure eased.

'So you weren't his lover?' Warty seemed skeptical. She stepped back and eyed my slave-cloth draped body.

My fear turned to revulsion. 'What are you saying? That's disgusting. He never laid a hand on me. He's been gone for years.'

Another slap sent me reeling and my cheek smarting. Warty then grabbed a fistful of my hair. 'I saw the way he looked at you through the monitor. I won't have him buying you himself or holding you back from market.'

Just then a familiar shadow blocked out the light. Gris. He grabbed Warty with a meaty arm across the chest. The pirate woman writhed and spat curses.

'Go free,' said Gris.

'Fool,' yelled Warty. 'What do you think I was doing you great clod.'

'Don't listen to Stroder's woman. If you go in there without going into stasis they shoot you. Stasis, Rae. Go stasis.'

I hesitated and looked left and right. Warty was making a terrible racket and Gris would have to clobber her to keep her quiet. His eyes looked everywhere but at me.

'Come with me, Gris.'

A great heave of his chest let me know he was fighting back tears.

'No. Can't. Must stay with Stroder.' Warty got a hand free and thumped Gris in the head. 'Quick, can't hold long.'

I nodded and turned to the hatch release. I broke the seal and it ripped open. Warty managed to kick me and I tumbled down in a heap of arms and cloth.

Warty leaned in, clinging to the hatchway. 'You won't get far,' screamed Warty after me. 'But at least you'll be out of my life.'

There was a dull thud and I could see Warty's boots on the floor. Gris leaned in, holding a bleeding ear. 'Remember the stasis or they… blow you up.'

The hatch closed and I was tossed against the bulkhead as the life buoy jettisoned. Dazed, I ran through my options. Stasis. Oh God. There were 10 nodes. I clawed my way into one and triggered it. Cold seeped into my limbs as the freezing agent speed through my veins. The ship stayed whole around me while my awareness faded.

It had worked. I'd be safe in cold sleep. Now all I had to ponder was how I was supposed to be rescued. I did wonder, as my mind numbed, that a life buoy was very small in the cold blackness of space and that no one would be looking for me. But the thought that Gris had helped me made me smile.

9

HIGHEST BIDDER

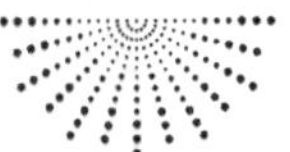

There was a strange scent. I sniffed, breathing it in, and wondered where I was. My sense of smell seemed heightened. I struggled to move my hands since every part of my body felt stiff. I tried to shake my head to dislodge cold sleep from my mind, but it wasn't obeying my directions. I'd never been in stasis before, not that I could remember at least. In fact, I'd never even thought about what it was like.

There were noises, which were distinct, yet at the same time jumbled together. A mumble of voices, sounds of oozing, of globules swelling up and plopping onto a hard surfaces, and of footsteps. The clatter of metal and the buzzing of power relays merged.

My finger flexed next to my ear. I was no longer in cold sleep. A hard surface was under my bare feet. That meant I was standing. It seemed to be a funny position to wake up in.

Hesitantly, I squinted out of my half-raised eyelid. I shut it quickly. Expectations of rescue had skewed slightly. I opened both my eyes and took in the surroundings. After a minute, I remembered to breathe. It was like a scene from the vidmovie, *Slave Traders Meet the Turai* to be precise, but it was so much more. Where the vidmovie had

45

only humanoids as sellers and buyers, this place had aliens. Lots of aliens.

My instinctive reaction was to bolt. The hum of the restraining field sizzled when I tried to move. I eased back, attempting to feel around the edges. Panic was a good option but I was too awestruck to let it take hold. I was at once horrified and fascinated by the slave market.

The smells were the scents of unwashed aliens and humans, who mingled in rows between stands where beings like me stood suspended. Scales, goo, cold-looking flesh, arms, claws, nobs of gooey ooze, flexed and moved through the throng. My jaw flopped open. Strange noises gurgled in my throat.

After I calmed down, I felt someone's eyes on me. My gaze slid sideways. I could see there was a woman in the next stand. She looked humanoid but old and dried up. 'What are you looking at?' I asked, curious and annoyed. Her violet-colored eyes were unnaturally bright and they unnerved me. I lowered my gaze, suddenly self-conscious.

'You, of course,' she said in a voice like scrunching paper. 'You don't know what you are about do you? First time?'

I swallowed. It looked like I wasn't even any good as a slave. 'Uh yes. Is there any way out of this?'

The woman smiled though her eyes were dark pools. Obviously, she had a way to alter her eye color in line with her mood. Within the bounds of her restraining field, the woman managed to convey shock and horror using body language. 'Out? Why would you want out? If you have a first-rate owner life can be good for a slave.'

'Good?'

'You have to be careful, though, to pick the right buyer.'

I was more than stunned by her words. 'Pick my buyer? But I'm standing here in full view being eyed off by...'

The woman dripped excitement. 'Exactly,' she said as her eyes darted here and there, not randomly, but pointing out particular beings. 'Like him,' she whispered. 'And her and it there.'

'Really?' I was awed by how she could work those eyes, be so precise and by how much she knew about these races and beings that I'd never heard of before.

'But you need to choose and then you *will* them to buy you. Doing this helps.' She chose that moment to stare at a tall humanoid, draped in a hooded, multicolored robe with his face covered in a bronze mask. It could have been a breathing apparatus. With the stink I could smell, I could understand the need.

Despite the restraining field, the woman managed to move her body, a dance of seduction that was surely more real than any actress' attempt I had ever seen.

The humanoid stared at the woman, and she repeated her move. 'Now you do it,' she said to me once she had her buyer mesmerized by her bodily contortions. I glanced at her sideways and wondered if either of us was sane.

'Me?' I said, suddenly realizing what a pity it was I'd ever been born.

"Yes. He's a Ridallian by the looks of him. They have a good reputation. But if you don't mind the smell, green ooze and scales, that Nuvral standing near him wouldn't be a bad owner. My last owner was Nuvral and it was an interesting placement—if you don't mind tentacles.'

'But you're here. Can't have been that good.' I managed to smirk. I needed to prove the woman wrong. Her eyebrow came down. Clearly, it was a gesture of disdain. But I was sure my comment had hit home.

'It was good,' she said, and her eyes seemed to cloud with memories. 'But there was a military coup and he was killed. None of the opposition wanted me permanently, even though they found me interesting. I was sold to buy arms, when they had satisfied their curiosity.' She sighed and a faint smile crept onto her face. Her eyes darted among the crowd of buyers again.

'Their culture was so unstable,' she added forlornly. 'Now I have to break in a new owner all over again.'

'I'm sorry then.' Either my situation was depressing me or that sick feeling in my gut was the after-effects of being in stasis. 'I can't do what you just did.'

'Shut up and listen. See he's passing by again. Throw out your chest, breathe deeply and imagine your lover's hands caressing you.'

'What? I don't have a lover. I'm just a...' What was I? I was sixteen and that meant I was no longer a kid. I shrugged. The other aliens didn't look appealing. If I was going to end up as a slave, I guessed I'd have to take the advice. Better to choose than be chosen.

Still, I doubted whether the slave woman's tactics would actually work. Mysterious, alien eyes behind the mask slid down my body, and I had to meet them. I thought of Del Divlan and replayed her slave girl seduction scene. Doing an approximation of it, I self-consciously jutted out my breasts, draped in pale blue, mauve and white translucent material. So much for hiding them behind metal plating, I thought. Simultaneously, I arched my back, causing the drapery to flutter ever so slightly along the back of my legs. I knew I was playing with fire and began to worry about what would happen if the Ridallian did buy me. Did slaves have a checklist to work off?

The Ridallian's robe fluttered. Did that mean it worked? I looked at him and smiled. He lifted a dark, gloved hand and signaled. My smile turned to puzzlement as he turned his back on me and walked away. Two hairy bovine types took his place. I glared at them belligerently.

'What happened?' I whispered to my slave woman companion. There was no response. I shifted my head so I could slide my gaze in her direction. The stand was empty. Obviously, she'd been purchased already. I felt alone. The sinking feeling nearly toppled me.

If it wasn't for the restraining field I would have collapsed. That woman had kept my mind off things, a bit. A tear slid down my cheek. It tickled but I couldn't wipe it way.

The crowd of aliens and humans swirled around me. More eager faces stared at me from different angles. I could hear them discussing me. A human came up and started a sales pitch. Apparently I had all my faculties. I could be trained to do menial tasks. I could sit on an Ovariates' nest and care for the young while the wife worked. I could learn to cook and clean in any ship's galley. Some of my potential buyers asked questions about the legalities of owning me. There seemed to be some concern about my age and status in relation to some unsavory duties. When I heard what they were, I felt my face heat.

The guide led the crowd of buyers off to another stand. In the distance, I could hear him begin again. The other slave had nearly the same abilities that I had. The smells, the ooze, the colors bubbling like a cauldron of soup surrounded me. A tentacle wrapped around my ankle, having edged in under the restraining field. I think I screamed.

'Get off me,' I said through clenched teeth. I'm not sure what the alien was called. It was squat, looked like a plant and had twelve tentacles sticking out of its head, flopping around to look for things to touch. It was dark purple at the base and sickly yellow at the top.

I twisted my foot and tried to flick off its appendage. It groped my ankle some more. A bit of the yellow tentacle slid under the sole of my foot. I put pressure on, placing my weight on it. The string of yellow flesh quivered once and then slid away at lightning speed. When I looked up the little plant thingy was gone.

There weren't any more reasonable-looking buyers in my aisle. More and more of the stands became empty. I felt vulnerable, standing there by myself. I thought I looked okay but evidently, I wasn't very interesting to buyers of slaves.

I lowered my eyes, not wanting to see more and more of the others being led away. I wondered what would happen to me if I wasn't purchased. What did they do with unwanted slaves? I had visions of myself floating in space, bloated, exploded, rotating in a slow circle as I drifted with the other space garbage. Didn't that happen to Nel Wingham in the vidmovie, *In Space There Is No Refuse*?

My restraining field snapped off with a ping. Doing my best not to fall on my face, I looked around. I was about to flex my arms when armlets clicked into place and a tar-skinned humanoid dragged me off the stand. He tugged me along. My numb feet thumped the floor as he angled me through the crowd.

My repeated questions gained no answer. He was almost naked. I wondered whether he worked there or was a buyer? The shifting light played on his skin, showing a tracework of scars on his black, shiny skin all the way up to the top of his shaved head. He wore a short metal skirt and matching armlets high up on his biceps and that was it. His muscles wobbled and bulged as he walked. He spun round abruptly and I caught sight of his eyes. These were inorganic and glowed a sickly green. I couldn't repress my start of surprise. He grabbed me by the armlets, spun me and pushed me roughly through a hatchway. I tumbled and fell backwards, cracking my head on the bulkhead. It didn't knock me out, but it left me feeling very woozy.

10

DARK DESTINY

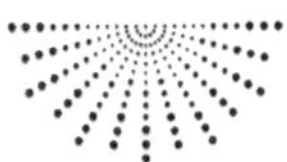

Four grey metal walls surrounded me, interrupted with an ugly hatchway. I had no idea what was going on. It looked like I was in a storeroom. Somehow, I was expecting something grander than this. Del had a much better welcome into slavery in the vidmovie.

The thrum underneath my bare feet made me believe I was on a ship. That thought was confirmed when the gravity hiccupped as the ship fell away from its moorings. I tensed as I felt the ship fire its thrusters. After about five minutes, the drives engaged. I clung to the floor planking with my toes and clutched the bulkhead with my hands and nails. The dizzy feeling in my stomach took most of my energy to control. A slave covered in puke would not please my new master, whatever or whoever he or she was. I pictured the tentacled plant creature and felt queasy again. Please not that, I prayed to myself.

I struggled to my feet only to slide sideways and land on the floor in a heap. The gravity was not what I was used to. Perhaps the owner or the Captain didn't stabilize the gravity until it cleared the surrounds of the docking bay. Gradually, I felt the spin engage, supplemented by an attraction field. My stomach adjusted.

51

I sat up but didn't bother trying to stand. My head was spinning. Last time I'd been on a ship, I'd missed this part as I'd been out cold. Now, though, I got to experience the wonders of space travel. I slouched against the bulkhead, studying the ceiling tiles. There weren't too many air filters in the storeroom but I was used to bad air.

I had almost grown used to the feel of the ship and the comfy storeroom, when the door slid open. My eyes snapped to attention and met the masked face of the Ridallian, who stood very tall, cloaked in his multicolored robes.

'Come,' he said with a grating voice, turning his back to me.

My mouth hung open as a few astounding things crossed my mind. The slave woman's trick had worked and oh god did that mean he expected me to know how to be a good slave? I had a great desire to fall to pieces, but I had to think of something else. How would Del cope with this situation? She always seemed to know what she was doing. I remember a few choice scenes that had always fascinated me. I shuddered. I couldn't do that, could I?

Another thought crossed my mind, Dad's, I mean, Captain Stroder's checklist. It was an emergency checklist after all and should be applicable in this situation. I thought hard, trying to remember what it said. I started to get to my feet and lurched to the door as I ran through the list. Mmm act stupid, it had said, then deny everything, and what was the last one? Yeah, lie through your teeth.

The Ridallian turned back in a swirl of robes. I shook myself and followed him as fast as I could with bare feet in that gravity. He kept walking, his robes spread out like wings with each step. I'd never been this close to an alien before, except for the yellow tentacle incident.

My feet were sweaty and my grip slipped on the planking, making me look like a monkey. I noticed something, the ship was new, smelled clean.

The Ridallian entered a cabin, sleeping quarters by the looks of it. I glanced around trying to ignore the quaking in my stomach. It must be the gravity, I thought to myself. He pointed to the bed. I looked at where he was pointing and started to shake. Oh lord. This is worse than Gris, worse than the way Captain Stroder looked at me. This was real.

I began to sweat all over and tugged on my hair, twisting it into tight twirls. All of a sudden I couldn't stand still and I started to squirm, foot over foot. I felt his eyes looking at me, dressed in my flimsy cloths tied together, and I stilled.

Thoughts of punching him in the head and making a run for it came to mind. Unfortunately, I recalled that the ship was already moving, and I couldn't pilot it. I could possibly crash it into something but I'd probably stuff that up too. Right then I wished I had learnt more than reading checklists and watching vidmovies. But I knew enough that he would take exception to me stuffing around with his head and not giving him ownership rights. He did pay good credit for me after all.

'Well,' he said, his voice thick as it emitted from the mouthpiece of his mask. I edged over to the low bed, crawled over the top of it and lay back like a stiff rod amongst the pale colored cushions piled up against the wall.

It felt kind of strange, the way his eyes seemed to burn into mine. I hoped I looked confident because I didn't feel it. Goosebumps came out everywhere, I had to stop myself from trembling so much, and my breathing was all wrong. I think I was hyperventilating.

Spots began to dance in front of my eyes so I closed them. What would he say if he knew I didn't know how to cook or clean?

'You do look very appealing, Rae,' he said.

My eyes flew open. My tension released as I heaved out a *whoosh* of surprise.

'You,' I growled. 'How did you get here?'

The robes slid off his shoulders and landed in a heap on the edge of the bed. The facemask dropped next to it with a clunk. 'It wasn't easy, I assure you,' replied Alwin Anton.

'But, you, he…' He sat on the bed next to me and edged closer. I was so dammed mad I slapped his face and got ready to launch myself at him. 'Of all the low down tricks.' I struggled with him as he held my clawed fingers away from his face. I would've kicked him too, but my clothes felt like they would fall off.

'Hey, hey, take it easy, Rae.' He was panting himself in his effort to keep me at bay and nurse his stinging cheek. 'It was no trick. I had to improvise and get you out of the market before Stroder caught up with me.'

'But, you…I thought you were dead.' I lowered my hands, but I was still itching to slap him again. I think attacking him helped me stop wanting to cry.

'Yes, so did I. Sorry, I left you behind. But I had to act quickly. The least I could do was rescue you, after the way I treated you.'

'You bought me at an illegal slave market,' I pointed out indignantly.

He blushed and ran his hand through his short-cropped dark hair. 'Yes, I did.'

'That doesn't sound very correct,' I added, sensing a crack in his wall of bureaucratic procedure.

His blush deepened and spread down his neck. I enjoyed seeing him uncomfortable. I'd felt nothing but embarrassed and stupid since I had met him.

'You're right. I'm afraid the rules were hard to apply in this situation. You cost a lot believe me, and if your parents don't foot the bill, I may be up for embezzlement myself. I used company money to secure your purchase.'

I stared at him open-mouthed, not quite getting it all. 'You broke the company's rules? For me?'

'Well yes. And more than that. Trafficking in slaves is illegal. Possession of one is not, technically.' He seemed to be looking at me strangely. 'Right now you're my property.'

'I sort of know that part, Alwin.' My eyes rolled up.

'You chose me didn't you?' He seemed to be closer. I could hear his breathing, smell his soft-minted breath.

Now it was my turn to blush. I was distracted by my toes winking pinkly at me. How could I tell him what had happened? 'Ah, yes.' I had to explain quickly. 'Um, the woman next to me recommended you as a possible purchaser of my services.'

His face was so serious, as I spoke. I could feel the heat radiating from mine. Silence ticked on. Without warning, he barked out a laugh that nearly made me leap to my feet. He kept on laughing, and his eyes brightened, showing reflected light. I gaped at him, couldn't help it really. When he settled down, his face relaxed.

'I'm glad you thought I was suitable slave master material,' he said when he was able to talk again. His eyes grew serious and slid down my body, glittering with speculation. 'I thought you were distracting in your ripped up body-stocking and salvage, but now...'

I felt my face heat up all over again. I put my hands up to cover my cheeks. His words made me ache in places that hadn't before and I didn't like that feeling. The clothing was very unsuitable. It made me look older and the way the pirate woman had enhanced my face with permanent make up didn't help matters either. I wasn't comfortable with how I looked at the best of times. At least when I was dirty and covered in rags, the auditor didn't look at me in quite the same way. In my dreams, I might have wanted a handsome actor to look at me like that but in reality it scared me.

'What about my...Captain Stroder? He's in with the pirates.' I decided to change the subject, so my breathing would ease.

'I haven't forgotten about him, and I had already put two and two together about the pirate connection. Now that I have you safe, AllEarth Corp enforcers would have moved in on him already. He stuck around to supervise your sale and to be sure he received top price. Luckily, my bid was well over his ridiculous reserve. He had the nerve to haggle even then. Well he'll get his due now.'

'Are you sure? He wanted to kill you. I heard him give the order.'

Mr Anton shrugged. 'Yeah, well, it goes with the job, sort of an occupational hazard.'

'I can see why,' I said, smiling when his eyes grew round with shock. 'Well you aren't very pleasant.'

His left eyebrow rose. 'It's my job to be thorough, skeptical and objective. Being nice isn't part of the job description.'

'But you scared me half to death.'

'Sorry,' he said, brows drawn together. 'I guess I bit off more than I could chew. I suspected that something was going on. Not the extent of it. And you were in charge of the station and you're not exactly a typical AllEarth Corp employee are you?'

I shrugged. His explanation was getting way too complicated for me. 'Okay, I guess not,' I said.

'Okay?' He blinked rapidly. 'Those payments and shipments did happen. But there has to be someone in the company that's corrupt, some sort of collusion. Those pirates didn't attack by accident.'

I drew back slightly at the tone of his voice. 'I thought it was unusual at the time. Two ships so close together.'

'I'm glad you're safe,' he said, and it felt like the truth.

'Me, too. I mean, glad you're safe. I'm happy to see you, too.'

He smiled, a genuine smile, and I laughed softly.

'Believe me,' he began, looking into my eyes, 'no one is ever pleased to see an auditor.'

I moved closer, all of a sudden bold. Without fear, I lightly touched his hair and smooth-skinned face. Brushing my lips to his cheek, I said, in true vidmovie style, 'I'm pleased to see this auditor.'

He backed away, his face heating up all over again. 'Ah, well, I'm not sure there is a protocol to cover this situation.' He stood up and ran his hands through his hair. He even leaned away from me as if I was contagious.

Obviously, I hadn't got that down right. My first kiss and the boy practically runs away screaming. Life isn't like the vidmovies after all. I had been watching them for so long I thought that they represented life elsewhere. Living on that outpost meant I never considered how normal people lived, really lived. Too busy trying to survive, I think. With all that I'd been through since being dragged off the asteroid, I couldn't say this was my first lesson about real life. But it hurt like hell to be rejected, especially after what my supposed father had just done to me. I really didn't understand my own feelings.

'Never mind,' I said breathily, blinking my eyelashes to hide my tears. I needed something familiar, an old friend. 'Do you have any vidmovies on your ship?'

Alwin's eyes narrowed. He seemed wary all of a sudden. 'Ah no, some documentaries and sports.'

I pouted. I was feeling very out of sorts. 'This will be boring.'

'No, not at all. I have some news for you that should cheer you up.'

'Really? Like what?'

'Your name is Rayessa, not Rae and your parents are—'

11

FRIEND OR FOE?

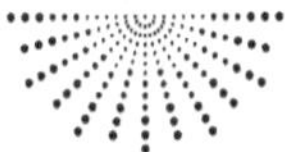

Kaboom! The ship shuddered around us. I was thrown into Alwin's lap and he toppled backwards off the bed.

'We're under attack,' he hollered, as he dragged his feet under him to race out the door.

'What?' I choked out as I scrambled off the bed after him. The *thwack, thwack, thwack* of laser bolts resounded on the hull.

'Hurry.' He grabbed my hand and urged me out the door. 'I've left the ship on autopilot. It has an evasive routine but not a very effective one.'

We tossed and bumped down the corridor to the bridge. The door opened as we approached. I was a bit winded. Being in a space ship that's under attack will do that to you.

Now this part of the ship seemed familiar to me. This was where Alwin had questioned me. I glanced at him. His face was pinched with worry. I didn't know what to expect next. We ducked through the door quickly. An alarm blared. Alwin hit a switch to silence it. I stood there dumbly. The command console was an array of blinking lights. Three empty chairs lined up in front of the shuttered view screen.

Alwin threw himself in a chair and started flicking switches and buttons. A three dimensional tactical display sprung up and he studied it.

A larger ship and two others loomed closer. I stared at Alwin's face. He looked surprised and then his eyes met mine through the display.

'Who is it?' I asked, although I could guess.

'The two enforcers who were meant to come to our aid and your pirate friends.'

'But…' My eyebrow lowered in puzzlement.

Alwin frowned. 'I know.'

He began steering his ship as if I wasn't there, sending it careening this way and that with his evasive maneuvers.

Another volley of fire hit the ship. Alwin accelerated. I was amazed at how his fingers danced over the command controls. It was like a ballet. 'How do you do that without a checklist?'

He spared me a quick look, half puzzlement and half amusement. 'I learnt it Rayessa.'

'Oh,' I said and sat myself down. 'How silly of me not to know.' The lights winking mauve, green, red and blue were quite fascinating.

'Rayessa?'

'Huh?' I dragged my eyes away from the blinking lights and met his.

'We need to eject the aft fuel pods. Get ready on my mark.'

I sat up and frowned at the controls. It was a maze of light and labels.

'Now,' he said.

My hand hesitated. Without a checklist, I couldn't do it.

'Rayessa, what are you doing? I said now.'

I looked over my shoulder nervously. 'I don't know which button to press,' I said. His dark eyes glowed and he frowned at me.

'Sorry.' I shrugged.

He hit a switch and veered starboard. 'I'll come round again. It's the switch marked "Eject Aft Fuel Cells".'

'Oh.' My hand hovered on the console. With all the lights and switches, I just couldn't see it.

'Rayessa, there. Just above your right hand. No, back a bit and to the left.'

Just then I saw it. My hand hovered above it waiting for his command. 'Now,' he yelled. The switched depressed with a clunk. We did an inverted spin and he fired at the fuel cell. We were past it and away when it detonated. Not only did he take out the two enforcers but he blinded the pirates as well.

Unfortunately, their ship was well matched to his in speed. 'They're hot on our tail,' Alwin said as the tactical display cleared. 'I'll have to try something else. Oh, wait, they're transmitting.'

He leaned over and flicked the switch on his left. Stroder's voice filled the cockpit. 'Hand her over, Anton, and I'll go easy on you.'

Alwin spoke. 'I paid good credit for her, Stroder. She's mine and you know it. We both know you won't let either of us live.'

The voice crackled through the speaker. 'Oh, she'll live. But you won't.'

Stroder's assurances were not comforting and the look Alwin's face gave me made my stomach turn all icy. 'Hold on,' Alwin said to me. 'I think he's going to… Yes, he did.'

I was half out of the chair. 'What?'

'A displacement missile. If it explodes near us it will shake us pretty badly.' Alwin spoke calmly.

I felt myself relax a little. 'And if it hits us?'

'You don't want to know. Hang on, I'm going to try a spurt.'

'A what?' I had a feeling that I needed to hold on. The edge of my seat was as good a place as any. My fingers turned white, I gripped the chair so hard.

'A spurt. I've been building power slowly. I'm almost ready. I can shoot ahead on thrusters and get out of range and hide for a bit.'

'I see. And that will do what? Delay the end?' My jaw ached from clenching my teeth. I was amazed that he understood what I was saying.

Alwin cast one quick look at me and smiled lightly, confidently. 'I hope so.'

There was a roar of power as the ship shimmied then bucked. I felt a slur of reality and then stillness. 'Are we there yet?'

Alwin spun towards me, the excitement of his success making his eyes gleam.

'Yes, now we wait.' The view screen unshuttered when Alwin hit the release. A space mist, small particles of dust suspended in gas, surrounded us. I saw little lasers firing into the mist guided by Alwin's manipulation of the controls.

With no idea what he was doing, I stared at him, not able to hide my puzzlement. He smiled at my look. 'I'm charging the mist. There are a lot of iron particles here. The charge I'm sending should blind the pirate.'

'But it will blind us too won't it?' Here I was showing that I understood, even though the way Alwin's mind worked daunted me. I wasn't used to feeling so stupid all the time, only some of the time. Now I wish I had done more than read checklists.

'Normally, yes.'

His smarts were really frustrating. I looked at the particles outside the ship and back at him. 'We're not normal now?'

He shook his head. 'Just wait and see. You'll like it. I have to fire some more shots so all of the mist will charge.'

As things were quiet, I thought it was a good time to ask. 'Do you have a spare ship suit?' I fingered my slave clothes, looking down in despair.

'Hmmm,' he said without looking up. 'Ship suit?'

I ran my gaze along his one. 'Yes, like yours. Do you have a spare?'

'Not one that will fit you. Don't worry. You'll have all the clothes you want soon.'

I was beginning to give up hope of ever getting one of those nifty suits. The top-of-the-line ones were self-cleaning and never creased. I shrugged and huffed out a puff of air.

'You're tired. Why don't you bunk down for a bit while I finish this? I'll wake you if anything happens.'

I yawned at the mention of sleep. My hand barely covered my mouth. 'Okay,' I mumbled around another yawn. Who would have thought with all the excitement that I would feel tired. Nothing was happening at that moment. Even a short nap could work wonders.

'Do you remember how to get back to my quarters?'

Nodding, I said around another yawn. 'I think so.'

I headed for the doorway and, when it opened, stepped into the corridor. I passed by the clean white walls, and trod over the grey floor panels. I was becoming accustomed to the gravity so my path back to Alwin's sleeping quarters was easier this time.

Alwin's sleeping quarters, when I took a better look, were neat and comfortable, nothing much to see though. I took a pee in the san unit and flopped down on the bed. Even though it was clean there was a slight scent of him on the bed. It was pleasant. Suddenly, warm air flowed over me, which gave me a bit of a fright.

When I sat up, it stopped. I inched back towards the bed and when I was fully flat, the warm air flowed again. I played with it for a while bobbing up and down until I felt less fearful and could sleep. I wondered how Alwin could stand to sleep in a bed that was active all the time. Very soon though the tiredness got the better of me, my eyelids floated down and I was submerged in sleep.

Immersed in pleasant dreams and caressed by the warm air blanket, I wasn't too happy to hear Alwin's voice over the comms.

'Rayessa. Wake up. They're here.'

Darn. I wished he'd stop calling me that. Then it hit me that Alwin knew more about my real parents than I did. It hadn't sunk in yet, Stroder's betrayal, and the fact that he wasn't my Dad at all. From a stable, subsistence existence, I'd been swept up in a solar flare storm. I still hadn't found my feet.

I squeezed back into the san unit and eyed my puffy, painted face. One of my ear studs was red and I hoped it wasn't infected. I washed and dried my face and fell sideways when the ship shuddered. Bolting out of the san unit like a piece of ejected effluent, I bounded, literally, to the door and out into the corridor. I hadn't done this since I was fourteen but felt like doing it now. I pushed off the floor and touched the ceiling with my fingertips and landed lightly six feet sway. I did it again and had to stop. The gravity was fluctuating.

I spilled into the bridge. Alwin was busy reading displays and readouts. The console was alive with winking color. The view screen was unshuttered. Nothing but mist showed, swirling extremely slowly.

'What is it?' I asked, sitting in the chair next to him.

'They're here, I told you, trying to scan the mist.'

'How do you know?'

'I dropped a miniature Scantran. It's so small they can't see it but it can transmit to me on tight beam. I can see them but they can't see me.'

I was nodding my head but I couldn't understand why that was so important.

'So do we wait then?'

'A bit, but not for long.' He hunched over the controls.

'Can you tell me about my parents now and what happened to me?'

Alwin's head shot up and he peered at me queerly. 'Rayessa. We are just about to be attacked. We'll discuss it later.'

That got me riled. 'Well stop calling me that. I'm Rae okay. Not bloody Rayessa. If you haven't got the time to tell me what's going on and who I really am then don't call me strange names.'

His expression looked pained. 'Sure, Rae. Charge up the guns for me, second button, third row from the top, center section.'

My hands hovered over the controls. They were shaking. This really wasn't my thing. He'd have to write me a list if he wanted my help. All the controls seemed the same to me. The harder I stared the more similar they seemed. I was about to say I couldn't find it when I saw it. I pressed it and waited tensely.

'Now,' said Alwin, and I jumped. 'This is what I want you to do.' My eyes widened and I listened carefully. 'Hold on,' he said.

We surged out of the mist, firing our guns on the pirate ship. As soon as they saw us, Stroder started yelling through comms. 'Get you...tards...'

He might have said more but the guns were carefully targeted.

Alwin had been studying the ship through his little Scantran and worked out exactly where each strike would do the most damage.

It was quite frightening really, his quiet precision. This auditing sounded like an interesting profession.

Then I realized what such precision could do. 'Gris. You mustn't hurt Gris.' I tried to push Alwin away from the controls. He held firm, poised to strike.

'Gris isn't on that ship, Rae,' he said firmly. Still I struggled with him. 'Stop. He was sold at the slave markets. Do you hear me? Sold.'

My eyes met his and saw the truth in there. Gris had betrayed Stroder by helping me. Of course he was sold along with me. I nodded. Alwin sent his missiles away. I saw the explosions, saw the debris explode outwards.

I sat there silently. 'Promise me you will help me save him?'

He held up a data stick. 'I will. I have his real name, Jakob Bear. I guess that is why you called him Gris.'

A MESSAGE DELIVERED

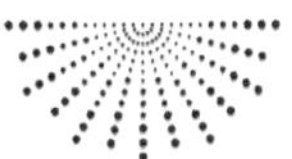

We sat in silence as the debris continued to roll away. The pirate ship was dead in space.

'What do you think?' asked Alwin, after he turned his chair toward me.

'About what?' I was still a bit dumbfounded about the pirate ship, about almost losing Gris. I also felt a bit raw about Stroder. Alwin hadn't blown them up completely, just disabled the ship and blown up the bridge where Stroder was likely to have been. I had to blink back my tears. Despite everything, I had loved Stroder. At least Gris wasn't on that ship. I hoped that whoever had bought him would be good to him until I could find some way of buying him back or rescuing him.

As we maneuvered around the wreck, Alwin dropped a distress beacon so the survivors could be rescued quickly. That was humane I guess. Maybe Stroder had a chance. Then I thought about what had happened and how badly Stroder had behaved. Maybe Alwin had given him a better chance than he would have given us.

'Rae, how do you think it went? Lucky escape for us,' he said as he powered down his weapons and entered stuff into his logs.

'It went fine. Your precision with destruction is quite frightening.'

'Thank you.' He stopped and smiled at me. The edge of my mouth lifted in response. He had saved me. I was grateful.

'Now we have time, will you tell me what's going on? Why was I with Stroder, who are my real parents and where the hell are we going?'

Alwin sat back and put his hands behind his head. He stared at the ceiling for a few minutes while I swung my feet back and forward. 'I don't know why Stroder had you, Rae, but your real parents are Opeia and Carl Gayens. I've done a little research. Opeia has stacks of money and comes from a long line of corporate top heavies, and Carl Gayens was heavily into genetic research. I believe he ran Future Gen, a company that grew clones, until the riots closed them down.'

'Riots? Clones?'

'Oh you were probably a bit young at the time, but surely you studied it in school?'

I frowned at him. 'What school?'

He looked away and then returned his gaze to the ceiling. 'No school, huh? That explains a few things. Well clones were freely manufactured for a few years. Future Gen almost had a monopoly. They made top-of-the-line clones, special order ones, or de-identified ones for general labor. The human rights people were making big noises about the definition of a human being and about abuse of life. Of course, Future Gen put a lot of money into gagging them.'

'So my family makes clones, copies of people, and sells them?'

'No, only your father made clones, but he used Opeia's money to do it. She put a stop to it in the end by withholding the funds. It might have been the riots or maybe something else.'

'Who rioted? The human rights people?'

'No, Future Gen's clones did. It was hushed up but I found some early reports in the news codex's archive. There was only one or two references before they gagged it.'

'I don't understand you. Gagged?'

He looked at me sadly and sighed. 'Rae, you've got a lot to learn about the world. People in power can do a lot of things and people with money can do more. And right now, or very soon, you're going to be reunited with your money. I mean your family.'

I gaped and then shut my mouth. 'Truly? How? Where?'

'I have to check my mailbox first but I think we are going to rendezvous with your family. I just hope they still check their email.'

When I stared at him blankly, he smiled. 'There was an address, private, discreet, but it said "any information on the whereabouts of Rayessa Gayens please email". So I did.'

It was suddenly cold, and I couldn't stop shivering. Alwin got up and held out his hand. 'Come on, let's see if we can find you something warm to put on.'

'Thanks.' I got up and followed him out.

'Pity though, you look nice in those clothes, very feminine.'

The sound of my teeth chattering was the only answer to his comments. He went through his gear and held a ship suit up to me, a dull grey job, but it would have swum on me. Then he fished out a cloak, a smaller and more colorful version of his Ridallian disguise. I settled for the cloak. I could wear it over the slave robes. I think he enjoyed withholding a ship suit from me.

Hunger pains soon became audible groans. His eyebrow shot up.

'Food? I do apologize. You haven't eaten. Come down to the mess. It's only small but I've a reasonable selection.'

I was out the door before he could finish his sentence, elbowing him neatly in the gut as I did so. I was absolutely starved.

The mess was like a second heaven. There were roast dinners, and casseroles, vegetables and reconstituted fruit. And there was coffee. I picked up the container. I had only seen it in the vidmovies. Del always enjoyed a cup.

'You want coffee? Are you sure?' asked Alwin as he heated three types of meal for me. 'It will keep you awake. This isn't the synth kind, it's real.'

He popped the lid and a wonderful aroma full of promise filled the small mess. I inhaled deeply. I was going to drink coffee and it smelled wonderful. Now, I knew why Del had that look on her face, so content, so confident.

'Yes, of course I want to try it. I've never tasted any kind of coffee, synth of otherwise. It smells divine.'

He tossed mugs up into the air. They spun slowly and took a little while to fall back down. In the meantime, he'd pulled out milk and sugar. He caught the mugs, sized me up with one eye and placed three sugars into one of the mugs. After that, he poured hot brown coffee into the mug and stirred it.

I couldn't wait to try it. I sniffed the aroma and licked my lips. Then I took a gulp, swished it around my mouth experimentally and swallowed cautiously. I had a hard time reconciling the smell to the taste. One was rich and aromatic the other was bitter and thin. I was disappointed.

Alwin was watching me. 'More sugar?' he suggested, holding up the spoon. I struggled with myself for half a second and held my mug out. We reached five sugars before I could drink my first mug of coffee.

Those instant meals were the best food I had ever tasted. I ate too much. I wrapped the cloak around me, suddenly feeling cold and sleepy.

Alwin took a look at me. He'd been keeping an eye on the monitors from a small screen in the mess. 'I best show you how to use the san unit and then a nap I think. It may be a while before we hear anything.'

'You mean you want me to bathe?' I asked not used to being required to wash. I sniffed and I smelt good, in fact.

'Yes.'

'Again?' I said, my voice rising. I'd been bathed by the pirate women. I wasn't keen on that happening again.

'Why are you so stressed? It's easy.' He showed me the little cubicle and explained how to use it.

'Okay.'

He eyed me. 'You take your clothes off first. Put the dirty clothes there to clean and change into something else.' He picked up the grey ship suit and shoved it into my hands. 'This will do.'

He left his quarters. I stared at the cubicle and shook my head. No way was I getting in there. I'd sleep on it and consider it later.

13

TO BE AND NOT TO BE

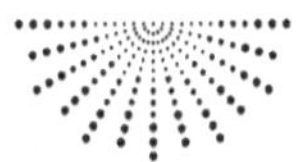

I woke up from a long nap. I was in Alwin's bed. I had no idea where he had bunked down. I decided to give the san unit a try. He always smelt so clean. It made me conscious of my own scent, which was stronger now. I guess I had no choice but to wash regularly myself.

I slipped off my clothes and stood in the tiny rectangular contraption. I put my arms up in the air and stood with my legs apart and my eyes shut.

'Engage,' I said to the unit.

Fine spray shot all over me, a hard mist that sluiced me down. Then some sort of light, flickered over me and then jets of hot air. I stepped out feeling and smelling clean. There wasn't a drop of water anywhere to be seen. I wrapped the cloak around me, while deciding what to wear. It was a choice between the dirty slave clothes or the large, ugly ship suit that Alwin had offered me.

I settled on the ship suit, rolling up the arms and legs and tying it around the waist with a belt. I put the slave clothes in the sanitizer as Alwin had instructed me and went to join him on the bridge. He should have had a response to his message by now. He had sent an email Opeia and Carl Gayens saying he had their daughter in his custody.

When I got to the bridge I stopped short. Alwin had his head in his hands and was groaning. 'What is it?' I asked, coming up behind him.

'Oh, there you are. Mmm, you look clean.'

'Yes I'm clean, what's the matter? You sounded upset. Is there something I should know? Have you heard? Are they coming?'

'No, I haven't heard. But I found something in the database.'

'What? About me?'

'Yes. It's a story about your kidnap. It was linked to the clone riots. Two weeks after the riot it says you, Rayessa, were returned to your parents.'

'But you said I am Rayessa.'

'I know, the gen scan said you are. I'm sure you are. I just don't know what this article means. It could be a scam. It could be a hoax to scare off a ransom, anything. It could mean that they won't answer the email.'

'Well, forget the email. Let's go find them.'

'Calm down, Rae. I'll do some more research.'

'Why? Can't we just go to Earth?'

'It's not that simple. I'm following a few leads. It's not easy to track company ownership. AllEarth Corp is owned by a series of holding companies and trusts. The Gayens' money is all over the place and so are they. I can't find where they live or where they are now or even where they will be. They like their privacy it seems.'

'Umm, I have no idea what you just said. What does AllEarth Corp have to do with my parents?'

He shrugged. 'I don't know, just a hunch. I can't prove anything, but I have an inkling that the Gayens' family fortune is spread far and wide. Your mother is very rich and powerful. It would take me a year to sort through who owned what and trace it back to the Gayens' family.'

'Are you saying they aren't nice?' I had a feeling that they weren't. All that money to buy whatever they wanted. That had to warp them in some way. Part of me couldn't believe my luck and the other felt squeamish about it. After eking out an existence for so long, I don't think I could cope with ease. It would be like a vidmovie. I tried to remember the title of the one where Del was adopted by a rich uncle and ended up with everything she wanted. Then she left it all behind for love. Alwin speaking again brought me out of my daydream.

'No, not at all, just difficult to find.' He turned away from me and I sensed he wasn't telling me everything. I didn't know if it was because he thought I was too stupid to understand or because he didn't trust me. I went back to the mess to watch a documentary on Jupiter. It was the most interesting thing in Alwin's vidmovie collection. The narrator was a famous actor and that was all the entertainment I was going to get on this trip.

The smell of coffee woke me. I must have fallen asleep in the chair. Bleary eyed I mumbled to Alwin as he dropped a plate of breakfast in front of me.

'Scrambled eggs,' he said. 'Straight from the rehydrator.'

'Thanks.' I dug in with a fork and looked at him from under my eyelids. He'd showered and slept. He looked happier than he had the previous night. My eyebrow rose in query.

'I got a response,' he replied, reaching for some sauce.

'And?'

'We have to go to the Saturn Space Station and meet them in their private suite at the Regency Grande Hotel.'

'Is that good?' A Class-Five Space Station. I never thought I'd see one of those.

'It's excellent. I've never been to the Regency Grande myself, but I've heard it's a top-of-the-range hotel. Last time I was at the Saturn Space Station I had to stay at the Hyatt. That was good but nowhere in the Regency's class.'

A puzzled frown met his eager face. 'You like hotels?'

'Not particularly. But I travel a bit. I like to compare them. Anyway we're not staying there, only having a meeting.'

'What if they don't like me, Alwin? What will happen to me then? Will you still want to own me?'

He swallowed his eggs, his face still. 'I don't know what will happen, Rae. I can't think of any reason why they wouldn't like you.'

'What about the money to pay back the company for buying me? Will you ask them for it?'

'Well, I'm hoping the reward will cover it. Or I may have to rely on you to bail me out of jail or send me food packages when I become an escapee or a pirate.'

I laughed. 'A pirate? You?'

'Why do you laugh? I'd make a very good pirate.'

I shook my head, still convulsed with laughter. 'Not with that accent, that name and those looks.'

He looked downright upset with me as he tossed his empty plate into the waste disposal with a flick of his wrist. The skin on his face darkened. He swung back towards me and said, 'What's wrong with my accent, my name and my looks?'

I laughed some more, nearly falling off my seat. He grabbed my plate and tossed it into the waste disposal with twice the amount of force he'd used for his. Little particles of scrambled eggs spattered around the flap. He must've been upset. Making a mess wasn't like him. I wasn't going to clean it either. I calmed down a bit.

'Well?' he asked with a bit of anger in his voice.

'Nothing,' I said. His eyebrow rose in a silent command. 'You don't know many pirates do you?' I asked.

'I've met a few.'

'Hardly real ones.'

He scoffed and waved his hand dismissively.

I leaned in close and said in a steady low voice. 'They're mean, Alwin. Smelly, nasty, foul-mouthed and ugly.'

'Oh,' he said, his anger draining away. He leaned forward, interested. 'And?'

I tried to hide my smile. He was listening to me, to something I knew and he didn't. That wasn't something that had happened before. 'You're sweet, clean, speak like a posh, private-school boy and very handsome. No one would believe you're a pirate.'

His eyes glittered in a strange way. I began to squirm. 'Anything else?'

I looked away, avoiding those deep, dark eyes of his. 'Yes, you're way too clever. You'd never end up a pirate by making a mistake.'

'What about the money I paid for you? That could leave me in a lot of trouble. Any suggestions?'

He seemed a little nearer. I could feel his body heat seeping into my clothes. 'Oh if my parents don't pay, you'll just have to sell me to someone else to get the money back.'

Both of his eyebrows shot up. 'What a great idea! I'd never have thought of that on my own.'

His shoulder was in reach so I punched him lightly. 'I don't believe you,' I said. I got up to step around him. I didn't like the look on his face, a smug, knowing cleverness. 'You're smarter than me.' As soon as I said it I regretted it. I sounded like a spoilt child and ruined the mood. I tried to save myself the embarrassment. 'You've probably thought of selling me a hundred times and planned to take me to five different slave markets.'

I stood there and he stood too, not quite towering over me. 'Now, Rae, how could you say that? I haven't thought of it a hundred times and it was seven slave markets.

Quite suddenly I felt the sting of tears. I knew he was joking but everything seemed to well up and wash over me. My life stank. A sob fought its way up my throat. I couldn't hold it back. Then I was shaking with my hand jammed in my mouth.

'Rae?' He stepped closer to me. 'I'm sorry, Rae. I wouldn't sell you. Of course I wouldn't. We'll work something out.'

He touched my hair. I wanted to pull away. I was ashamed of my tears, and I hated feeling this way, so alone, so cast off. He pulled me toward him gently and held me close. That undid me. I clung to him, cried all over his immaculate ship suit and mumbled into his lapels.

I felt his hand stroking my hair down my back and patting me softly. It felt soothing, nice. He handed me some paper tissues, and I wiped my face and blew my nose.

It was hard to talk and hard to look at him. 'I, I'm sorry. I don't cry, well not normally. I feel so…lost.' The tears started again, and Alwin wiped them with his thumbs.

'It's okay to cry. I forget sometimes you're just a kid. Not as grown up as you look.'

'What?' I half cried, half laughed. 'I'm not a kid.'

'Oh but you are. Naive and young. Nothing to be ashamed of, though.'

A whole lot of feelings washed over me then. I knew I was uneducated compared to him, and he was definitely older than me but how dare he say that to my face. A fresh wash of tears trailed down my cheeks. He brushed them away again.

'You have such lovely grey eyes, and you're spoiling them with those tears.'

I hugged him. He didn't back off as I thought he would. He rested his chin on my head, since I only came up to his shoulder. I felt his body through his ship suit, trim, muscled and strong. I stepped back slightly so I could look at him. His face was so alluring. I had to touch it. His gaze seemed to darken when I did. I stroked his hair, felt the dark bristles tickle my fingers. Next thing I knew I was pulling him down to kiss me. Oh what magic. He kissed me back, softly and gently.

And then it was over. 'Rae,' he said. He was shaking his head. 'Don't do this to me. I have a job to do. You have no idea what you are playing at.'

His serious tone annoyed me. Obviously, he had no sense of mood. 'I know what I'm doing,' I said bravely, chin edging up.

'Really? I bet you don't. I'm at least three years older than you. That's not so bad but I'm better educated and more experienced.'

'I'll catch up,' I countered.

'In some ways you will, but not now, not on my time. I am on the job right now and there is no rule book that covers this.'

I tried to kiss him again.

'Don't,' he said, pushing me away lightly. 'It's not right. You are putting me in an awkward position.'

'Alwin, I want to.'

His eyes burned into mine. Before I knew what was happening he enveloped me in his arms, his mouth closing over mine. Oh god, I thought. He kissed me deeply, like they did in the vidmovies. It felt nice and out of control at first, and then when he wouldn't let me go it became frightening. It wasn't just a kiss, it was passion. It was him smothering me, it was him frightening me and it was him over-whelming my senses. What he did stirred me and scared the hell out of me.

After pushing him in the stomach, I struggled out of his grip and broke off the kiss. Wiping his saliva from my mouth, I glared at him, breath heaving in my chest.

'Sorry, Rae, but you needed to know. Life isn't a game or a vidmovie script. It is real and dangerous.'

'Jerk!' I spat at him and whirled round, heading back to his quarters. I was still sobbing when I reached them. I locked the door and threw myself down on the bed. I was in misery, truly sunk. I really didn't know why he did that. Why did he make something so simple so complicated? Why did he reject me? Why did he try to scare me by acting all out of control? I truly didn't understand what he was doing or why.

I stayed in those quarters for the better part of two weeks sneaking out occasionally to grab a meal from the mess when Alwin wasn't about. I felt so angry, embarrassed and stupid, that I couldn't bear to face him.

His voice hailing me on the comms roused me from another tear-drained sleep.

'Rae, we're coming up to the space station. I thought you'd like to get ready and see the approach. It's really a big place.'

I didn't answer him but scampered off the bed. I showered and dressed and raced down the passageway. It was a Class Five Space Station and I was going to meet my parents.

14

SPACE STATION ALPHA

I stepped onto the bridge, dressed in my slave clothes and multicolored cloak. I looked halfway decent and certainly better than in an oversized, grey ship suit. Alwin looked up as I entered. 'Rae.'

I turned away without acknowledging him and sat in the other seat. He keyed the view screen shutter and it opened.

I sucked in a breath. The Saturn Space Station was huge. It must have had two hundred levels, with protrusions and spires up and down its skin. Small pinpricks of light emitted from it and it glowed silver in the sunlight. So this was a Class Five Space Station. This is what drew people away from Outpost 311. This was the place I'd dreamt about. Although in my dreams my arrival was always grand, like Del Divlan's promotional tour. With the press taking images and broadcasting them live. No, I was arriving like a fugitive without even decent clothes to wear. I began to fear that this family Alwin had found wouldn't want me or perhaps it was a mistake and I wasn't related to them at all. A nervous clenching worried my stomach.

As my gaze tracked along the skin of the space station, all of the hubs, ports and gantries merged into one. My heartbeat upped a notch, leaving me short of breath.

Our ship headed to the lowest level of the space station, or was it the top? I couldn't tell because as we drew closer we could only see what was in front of us. Other ships were circling in, following the assigned holding pattern. We were inserted in the queue and when operations cleared us we headed for our allotted landing bay.

Alwin groaned loudly when the landing fee notice flashed up on his screen. Then I saw him wince as he authorized the transaction. His gaze slid in my direction but I looked away and stared at the console, trying to count the number of green lights. Perhaps being an auditor wasn't so interesting after all if the pay was so low that a mere landing fee hurt.

I forgot my angry, nasty thoughts about Alwin because the approach to the landing bays was even more breath-stealing than the approach to the station. As I watched, things that were miniature grew larger, vagueness turned to detail. Some of the rivets in the outer skin looked as big as I was.

'Rae,' began Alwin, 'can you power down the main drives for me. Centre panel, bottom row.'

'Sure,' I said, thawing a little. I'd just realized that I was going on a big adventure. There were more people on this space station that I'd ever seen in my whole life. I was going to see them all at the same time, not drawn out over the years of my life.

Alwin used the thrusters to nudge himself into the landing bay's buffer field. There was a slight bump when it engaged and slid us into place.

He powered down the ship and launched out of his chair. 'Give me five minutes, Rae. I need to clean up and I think a change of clothes is in order.'

I shrugged, feigning disinterest. Guiltily, I realized that I'd locked him out of his quarters and that he was probably itching to shower. There was a san unit off the bridge, he'd been able to use that at least.

Looking over my shoulder I saw him bouncing down the passageway. I tapped my fingers on the console while I waited to step into my dream world. My mind started weaving different futures for myself but they all came to nightmarish conclusions because of my failings.

My parents were going to be disappointed in me, I just knew it. Hey, I was disappointed in me and Alwin… No need to even dwell on what he thought. I sighed to distract my tears. I had to think positively. I looked out toward the other landing bays. I could see small ships whizzing around a large freighter and also other ships that came to dock and gantries that were sliding along deep grooves in the skin of the station. That helped to pass the time and help me forget about my self-doubt.

When Alwin returned I tried not to stare. He wore a suit, not quite a ship suit, but something tailored. It was dark, with a white insert like a 'V' down the front. My eyes travelled down to take in the narrow leg of the suit and the fitted boots. He looked, well, great. Even better than Nel Wingham. And that was saying something. My mouth hung open for a bit and then I snapped it shut, deciding it was better to ignore him. There was no point in torturing myself over him after all.

'Come on, let's see some sights on the way to the Regency Grande. We're a bit early so we have time.'

He keyed the hatch and stepped out. The gravity was very odd at first. It seemed to fluctuate. I already felt seedy so the uncertain footing didn't help. I scrambled after him with a handful of robes clutched in my hand and found the gravity steadily increasing as we entered the corridor. I felt self-conscious but he didn't comment about my outfit or my bad footing.

An official in a pale, blue uniform greeted us as we passed out of our landing bay. I stared at him until Alwin tugged my hand and drew me forward.

'Don't stare like that, Rae,' he whispered to me.

'Sorry. He's the second-cleanest person I've ever met in my life.'

Alwin's brows drew together and then he shrugged. 'Let's take the lift to the main promenade. We have time for a quick look at all the beautiful people before we meet with your parents.'

'Sure, why not?' My mind was everywhere at once. I didn't think it was possible to contain such excitement. I was taking a stroll towards the rest of my life. What happened in the next few hours would change my life or destroy it. Alwin had made it clear that I couldn't be part of his world. I'd never forgive him for what he had done to me. Him and his stupid audit and that kiss, of course. I flushed with embarrassment at the thought of it.

There were only a few people in the large corridor as we waited for the lift. The ceiling was rounded and easily three times my height. It was so clean too. Obviously there was no need to cut it down for scrap.

'It's so big,' I said as I gaped again, unable to hide my wonder.

'Yes,' replied Alwin, a smile quirking his lips. 'They drive huge conveyors along here.'

I blinked. I'd seen a conveyor on one of the documentaries on *Lollydrop*. I didn't want to be standing in the corridor when one lumbered through.

The lift doors hissed open. It was already half full of humans and aliens. They didn't even glance at us when we stepped in. Alwin stared at the lift door after telling the lift where we wanted to go. I did the same, if only to stop myself from gawping at everything and everyone. I couldn't help letting my gaze wander. Everyone stared at the lift doors, like they didn't care to notice anyone else. As each stop passed by, Alwin drew me out of the way, as people got out on their particular floors. More people flowed in and soon we were pressed up against the back wall of the lift. I noticed how everyone adjusted themselves so that there was an equal distance between the next person. The resulting spacing had an odd sort of symmetry to it.

I was very aware of Alwin, standing next to him. His hand flew around my waist as the wall behind us slid open. He prevented me from sprawling onto the floor of the main promenade. My gasp of surprise petered out when I took in the people, the shops, stalls, and glittering bits of hanging decorations. The noise of the people as they walked and talked washed over me and hurt my ears.

'Oh god, I can't do this!' I began to shake, my stomach looped over itself. I turned to run.

'Rae, what is it? Come back.'

15

THE SERVICE ENTRANCE

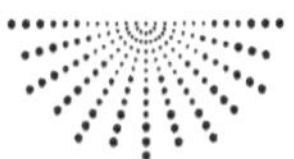

Before I had gone too far, Alwin grabbed my hand, squeezed it once and stepped forward. I clung to him, overwhelmed by the colors, people, smells and sounds. Then as I grew accustomed to my surroundings, I noticed things. The people wore all types of clothing, sleek ship suits in all colors, uniforms in the same pale blue as the officer that greeted us and others in a muted green and pale mauve. There were rich robes like the ones I wore and people dressed in gems and gold and nothing else. Elaborate hair or none at all. I hadn't seen anyone dressed as well as Alwin.

He turned and drew me back against a shop window. 'How about we get out of this crowd and grab a coffee?'

I shrugged. Coffee didn't really thrill me. 'I guess.' I was slightly dazed.

'Not coffee then. Something else.'

I never knew what it would be like being in amongst so many people. I felt like I was sleep walking. He tugged me along, weaving through the crowd and led me to the back of a reasonably dark café. He spoke to the table. 'One fresh-brewed, organic, water-decaffeinated, espresso with hot fluffy milk on the side and a cold, original Coke with five cubes of Plutonian ice.'

The table hummed. Alwin looked at me. 'It's not really Plutonian ice but it makes your drink fizz and it's very cold. Believe me it will take your breath away.'

I wasn't quite gaping at him, just stunned really. I didn't know what a Coke was. A chute opened and a steaming cup of coffee floated out, along with a tall glass with dark liquid in it. Little bubbles spat liquid onto the tabletop. I eyed it warily. It looked like coffee to me.

'Go on,' he said. 'It won't bite. Trust me.'

'I don't trust you,' I said and meant it. I could tell I hurt him. He looked down and sipped his coffee and didn't try to make conversation or look at me. I hoped he felt as bad as he had made me feel but I doubted it. Nothing could shake him. He was Mr Know It All, Mr Perfect, Mr Handsome and Mr I'm So Experienced and You're Such a Child.

I picked up the glass and touched my lips to the rim, hesitating. The glass was cold and the effervescence tickled my nose. With a mental shrug, I took a huge sip and nearly gagged. It burnt the back of my throat as the taste exploded on my tongue. Gasping, I put it down and flicked my gaze to Alwin. He was ignoring me. I casually looked around the café, hiding my distress. No one seemed to be looking at us so I tried some more of the Coke, not to be outdone by him. The second taste was better. It was sweet and refreshing. By the time, I finished it, I had really enjoyed it.

'Thanks,' I said to Alwin. His eyes met mine but his face was clenched with worry.

'No problems. Time to meet the parents.'

I bounded off my seat and followed him out. We had to walk a ways, impeded by the crowd, to take the hotel wing lift. At this end of the main promenade the clothes became less varied and the people more hurried. Simple ship suits in dull shades matched the worn expressions of the people here.

When I asked Alwin about it, he said, 'Meet the workers.'

'Oh.' We must have missed a lift because we entered a service lift full of the workers we'd seen in the promenade. These people did stare at us. Our clothing made us stick out.

Alwin smiled at their scrutiny and said, 'Audition.' They turned away and ignored us. I was yanking on his arm but he ignored me. I had no idea what he was playing at.

When the lift spilled its contents, Alwin dragged me behind a dormant auto-luggage trolley. 'Rae, listen. We don't have much time.'

'What are you doing? What audition?' I demanded, hands on hips, exposing my slave garments. 'Why are we coming in this way?'

A burly security guard came round the corner, before I even had time to register it, Alwin grabbed me and smothered my mouth with his, snaking his arms around me and crushing me against him. I tried to struggle and gave up as his kiss began to affect me. The guard's step slowed. I could almost feel his gaze burn through my back. Then he sped up and kept walking. When he was gone Alwin released me. My cheeks were burning and Alwin looked flushed too.

'Sorry.' He smiled at me.

I couldn't stop myself from smiling back. 'Is that what you wanted to say?'

'No, just escaping notice. If anyone asks you are auditioning for the show. Now, I want you to stay here while I go to the main desk and pick up the security key for the Gayens' private suite. Then we are going up using the service elevator again. We will get out on the floor below and float up through the emergency chute.'

'Why? I thought these people were my parents. Should I be afraid of them?'

'No, I don't think so. I want to be careful. You never know.'

A bad feeling crept up my spine. 'You're not telling me everything, Alwin.'

'Let's just say I'm overly cautious. It comes with the job. Now I'm off. If the security guard comes back tell him I'm taking a leak. Don't move from this spot.'

'Sure.' I folded my arms and glared at his back. He strode smoothly down the corridor and headed for the reception desk. A maid shuffled past. She looked through me. I stared at the ceiling and counted the air filters. I nearly stumbled when the auto-luggage trolley I was leaning on powered up and sped away.

I was left standing in the corridor with no camouflage, counting of the seconds until Alwin's return. I was going mad with waiting. I started to edge down the corridor. When I checked over my shoulder the security guard was heading back my way. I was almost to the corner when a hand latched onto mine. I was tugged forward and crashed into Alwin. He held up a gold security keycard. 'We're all set.'

Alwin pushed and shoved me into every doorway and storeroom as we made our way back to the service lift. We were in sight of it when he dragged me into a large rack full of freshly laundered clothing. He squeezed in next to me.

'What are you doing? Have you gone nuts?' I hissed to him.

'I don't want to be noticed,' he said peering out through the legs of a fluoro orange jumpsuit.

'Well you're doing a good job of being noticed. Nothing attracts the attention more than skulking about.'

He smiled at me, pushing the sleeve of someone's gown out of his face. 'What would you know?' he whispered tightly.

'I saw it on a vid once—more than once. Anyway, it only takes common sense.'

'Really? You have that ship loads, I imagine.'

'Well it beats you kissing me every time someone comes by. It's becoming tedious.'

He looked shocked, then his eyebrow drew down. 'You're not being nice. We have to be careful. You have no idea what type of security big money buys. Do you want to actually see your parents or not.'

'Well, of course, I do.'

'Come on then.' He stuck his head out of the rack and did a quick sweep of the corridor. The lift chimed. He bolted out of the clothing rack and drew me at a sprint into the lift.

He played with the controls and keyed an express ride to level 154. I leaned back against the lift, tapping my feet nervously on the floor. Alwin paced, though this time it was three paces left and three paces right. When the door chimed and slid open, four maids stepped in, paused in their chatting as we exited, and stared at us.

He took my elbow, looked down his nose at them and strode

purposely out as if he was a guest caught in the wrong lift. The doors slid shut over the cackle of the maids' laughter.

He let go of me and prowled through the corridor. I hurried along after him, thinking his behavior was attracting more attention than it was avoiding. But he wasn't going to listen to me.

He found the emergency chute. It wouldn't open. 'Now what?' I said as he leaned back against it to wipe sweat from his brow.

'It won't open.'

'Really. Never would have guessed it. Why don't we take the lift like normal people? I'm sure someone's seen us and called security already.'

His eyes met mine. 'You don't have much faith in me do you?'

'I do, a lot of faith, I just think your methods are a bit over the top.' I sighed. He wasn't paying attention to me. He was looking all the walls up and down. Next he was running his hands over them. I leaned back against the wall and stared at the ceiling. I thought it would be nice to count the air filters.

'Alwin.'

'Rae, I'm busy.'

'Yeah I know but look at this.'

Out of the corner of my eye, I saw him look up. Above us, there was an access hatch.

'Great work.' He jumped up and went up, not so slowly, to push against the panel. Of course he rebounded back to land and roll on the floor. I walked over and peered up into the chute.

'Yep looks like it would join up with your emergency shaft system.'

'Yes,' he said, adjusting his suit. 'It's for rescuing people, spying on them and other covert operations. I don't think I'll be staying at this hotel.'

'Sure you wouldn't. Hey what are you doing?' He'd grabbed me, face pressed to my abdomen and lifted me off the floor.

'I'm giving you a shove.'

'Put me down, Mr Anton.' He let me slide down the length of him and frowned at me.

Hands on hips, I glared at him. 'If I can do one thing it's leap in this gravity. Stand back.' I pushed against the floor and arrowed upwards. My fingertips felt the edge of the hatch and I levered myself in.

Dusting off my hands, I peered down at him with a lifted eyebrow. 'Well, what are you waiting for?' I reached down to help him up.

He shook his head, muttered to himself and was beside me in a jiff. He slid the hatch cover back and edged along the narrow tube. My hair started floating up and crawling became a little awkward. The attraction field had minimal effect up in the ceiling.

We reached a junction of the emergency tunnel system and Alwin grabbed the rails and somersaulted out and up. 'Smart ass,' I mumbled under my breath.

I crawled out, hands firmly on the rails. 'Come on, don't be shy.' Alwin was doing slow body spins. It was okay for him he had a suit on with leggings that clung tight to his legs. I was wearing floaty bits that I was having a hard time controlling at present. My cloak billowed out behind me.

'No, after you.' I was sure he was having fun at my expense. I had to stop every few rungs and tug the slave clothes down. I caught him eyeing my legs and thighs a few times. 'If you don't mind, I'd like some consideration.'

'Nice legs,' he said.

I bounced off the wall and shot straight for him. 'Not that kind of consideration.' He grabbed me and we tumbled together. I didn't like the free gravity. The Coke was threatening to reappear. I must have looked green because he slowed the spin and grabbed the rail. His other hand held me tightly, more than was necessary.

'Sorry.'

I felt very warm, floating there with him holding me like that. It was as if time stood still.

With a few more tugs of his arm we were at level 155. Funnily enough the emergency chute was easy to open from this side. Alwin added this to his list of the hotel's defects. 'I definitely prefer the Hyatt,' he said, as we stepped onto the gold-burnished hallway.

16

GAYENS' PRIVATE SUITE

The door to the Gayens' private suite slid open with a luxurious *swoosh*. Alwin ducked in, eyes darting to every corner and then dragged me in after him.

I couldn't stop shaking as I took in the huge main room. It looked bigger than the whole of Alwin's ship. Pale, soft floor coverings went right up to the huge floor-to-ceiling view port. Large sofas, a piano, a whole wall-sized entertainment unit with screen dominated the far wall. We stepped down in the sunken lounge and faced the row of doors on one side. Alwin dropped my hand and tried each one, three on one side and two on the other side of the entertainment unit.

'Locked,' he said, running his hand over his head. With a glance at me, he stared out the view port.

'What do we do now?' I asked, moving up behind him. He was nervous. I could tell. I wished he would confide in me.

'Wait and hope for the best. It's the best I can do. Sorry.'

'I don't believe that. You're way too smart. You're planning something.'

'I wish I was, Rae. But I really don't know what will happen next. I'm completely stumped. I've tried to figure it out but I just can't make sense of it.'

'And a good thing, too,' said a familiar male voice.

We both swung round to face Stroder pointing a gun at us. I stared at him, astounded, at first, then puzzled. He looked identical to Stroder but he was in much better shape. His hair was clean and trim and dark. His face looked fairly young compared to Stroder, but it was the same man.

'Dad? Stroder?' Those eyes stared at me without warmth. Alwin stepped in front of me, so I peered around him.

'No, Rae, be careful.' He tried to push me back. To the man with the gun, he said, 'Mr Gayens, I presume.' There was something akin to triumph in his voice.

Those cold eyes shifted to Alwin. Gayens sneered. 'I'll deal with you later, meddler. But first I have to get rid of her.' The gun lifted higher, straight for Alwin. I stepped back and into my father's line of sight.

'You're my Dad? But you look like Stroder. Please tell me what's going on.' My brain was seriously overloaded.

'Oh, I think I get it now,' Alwin said, squaring his shoulders, seemingly unperturbed by Gayens' gun.

'Shut up twerp or you'll get it before she does.'

'One of you is a clone. I'm thinking Captain Stroder was your clone.'

'So what. There wasn't a law against it at the time. Stupid moron he was, traitorous, stinking pirate. Who'd have thought my clone would turn out like that blackmailing brigand.'

The gun moved to me again. I couldn't speak. Alwin edged closer to me, keeping his eye on Gayens at the same time. I could tell he was ready to jump Gayens at any moment. His muscles were tensed and his jaws clenched so tight I could hear his teeth grinding.

'How did he blackmail you, Gayens? Was it with Rae?' Alwin looked at me, concern evident in his dark eyes.

'Rae? Her? Idiot was supposed to kill her for me. But he chose to keep her and blackmailed me instead.'

'So you're the one,' Alwin said, the company auditor again. He seemed happy to solve that riddle. 'The payments to Stroder. It won't look good you know—financing pirates.'

Alwin was very close to me. I could feel the heat radiating from his body. He was going to shield me. That made me feel so uneasy. Why did he have to do that? I wanted to be angry at him for rejecting me but now he had to be noble and make me feel guilty for being angry.

'Don't worry "wonder" brat,' Gayens said to Alwin. 'I've got the money to cover it up, to buy my way out.'

'I get it now,' Alwin replied, nodding his head. 'The *Clone's Rights Act* of 2044 meant Stroder got a new identity and a substitute gen record. That's why he didn't match up as Rae biological father.'

'Shut up. I know you, recognize you. Your family is washed up aren't they? Used to be up there with the rest of us elite, but not anymore. There will be no help for you when you're charged with her murder.'

'No,' I shouted and darted in front of Alwin. 'You can't do it to him. If you want me dead you have to kill me.'

Alwin sighed audibly. 'Rae.'

Gayens laughed. 'I intend to,' he said. 'But I won't take the rap. You should have been dealt with a long time ago. You've outlived your usefulness. You're nothing but a pathetic scrap of genetic material.'

Gayens was sweating and his fingers moved nervously on the gun. He wasn't used to this, I thought. I'd seen cold-blooded pirates before, seen how they acted. They weren't like Gayens. He was an amateur.

'You're saying she's a clone?' Alwin's bellow nearly parted my hair.

Gayens hacked out a laugh. 'Oh, yes, just that. She's is evidence I want destroyed, nothing more.'

That jarred me. 'I'm a...clone?' I was flabbergasted. I couldn't speak for spluttering. What did that mean for me? Was I less than a person? A thing, property? How I wished I'd paid attention to what Alwin had said about the riot. I don't know what the outcome was. Oh yes, he said something about an Act.

'No.' Alwin shouted back, standing up to Gayens. 'You're a liar and a cheat. I know she's not a clone. I did the gen scan. She had no flag on her DNA.'

Gayens frowned, then laughed again. His eyes began to water. 'I didn't put a flag on her. You can't tell if she's the original or not. No one can.'

'Why would you do that? You made a clone of yourself and your daughter. Is your wife an original or a copy?'

That made Gayens step forward and jerk his gun at Alwin again. 'Damn straight the bitch is herself. She found her clone and destroyed it before I animated it. But I'd already made Rae's replacement by then. She never knew.'

'Replacement?' I choked. My head was swimming. I was having a real identity crisis.

'Yes, he made a replacement after the kidnap, hence, the news codex reporting you had returned. He did it for the money.'

'Oh you know so much whiz kid,' Gayens snarled, baring his teeth. 'But I know all about you, Alwin Anton. How sure are you that your own parents didn't have you manipulated in vitro? Clever kid, sporty, almost perfect. No way you're a pure breed.'

'But it's not about me, Gayens. It's about the money. Your wife has all the money. Clones rioted and kidnapped your daughter. You hid the fact and replaced her. Only Stroder's a dirty, betraying slime wad just like you. He didn't get rid of her to save your skin. He milked you for all he could get. I'm not surprised your clone turned out that way.'

Gayens struck Alwin across the face with the gun. My scream was cut off when Alwin fell sideways leaving me exposed. He lay on the floor dazed.

I looked around for a way out. My eyes flew forward as Gayens' gun pressed against my forehead.

'I just have to squeeze,' he said, though his hand was shaking.

'Why Dad?' My tears started to fall. 'Please, don't kill me…Daddy,' I said brokenly.

'You're in the way, honey. Sorry.' His finger squeezed.

17

REAL CLONE

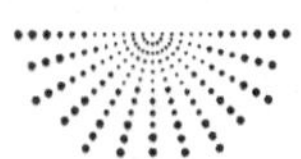

'I'd back off if I were you, Carl,' said a firm, feminine voice, from behind Gayens.

He stilled. Casting a look of hatred at me, he stepped back and lowered the gun. He didn't surrender it, but he turned slowly to face the woman.

'Opeia, darling,' he said, smoothly. His whole mannerism changed. My eyes flicked from Alwin, who was struggling to stand, to Gayens, who was still close enough to snuff me, to the woman, a very familiar woman.

'Don't darling me, Carl. You really think I'm that stupid. I've been monitoring this room since they came in. You didn't know I was watching that mail account did you? I know everything. Have known everything from the beginning, except where you had hidden her. I come from a long line of business sharks and you have finally played into my hands. It's takeover time.'

'Opeia, I can explain. She's a clone. I know I shouldn't have made her. I wanted to get rid of her so you wouldn't find out. I know how much you hate the idea of clones. Why do you hate my research so much?'

The woman stepped forward and my breath caught. Somewhere inside me, I recognized the auburn hair and creamy skin. Her eyes were grey like mine but larger.

'Opi?' I said. A faint image of a room with toys and a laughing face, overlaid with a sense of happiness loomed out of my mind. I was mesmerized by my mother. Her eyes bored into mine as she walked over. They were kindly and sparkled with tiny dots of light.

'In a minute, honey. I have to deal with Carl first.' She glared at him, those kind eyes now hard. 'Let's get a few things straight, Carl. I'm not stupid, and you're an ass. You think I didn't know Essa wasn't mine? Do you think I couldn't tell my own daughter? Do you think I let you hang around because I desired you, liked your company? I cut your funds and closed down your research because I was getting ready to jettison you.'

Alwin butted in. 'But when Rae went missing you couldn't do it.' She assessed Alwin. I think I saw a flash of recognition in her eyes.

'Bright boy. Exactly.' She took another step towards Gayens. 'So I've kept you near me, waiting for this moment.' Gayens' gun came up again, though he didn't know where to point it.

'Bitch. You undid me. Ruined me. I lost everything in that riot.' Spittle was flying out of Gayens' mouth. His hands were shaking. I didn't like it. Desperate people did unpredictable things. I knew that much.

'I know,' she said, smiling in a predatory way, 'that's why I started it. It was what I needed to get the law changed.'

Gayens' gun wavered. All three of us were on a knife-edge. Opeia's aim never wavered. She was waiting for the opportunity to puncture him, I was sure. I could almost see her desire for him to play into her hands. I shook my head. She was a brave woman. I don't think I could've done the same in her place.

I took a risk. I bent my knees and pushed up. Lightly suspended by gravity I took aim. Alwin, seeing my move, ducked and toppled Opeia. My foot connected with Gayens' gun. It spun in apparent slow motion up and away.

Opeia yelled frantically into her communicator. 'Now, now, now.' Three security guards burst in, one from the main door, one from a side door and one from the ceiling. Carl Gayens was buried under three muscled bodies, his screams of outrage muffled by the security guards' bulk.

I stepped back, eyes searching for Alwin. He stood behind Opeia, watching everything at once. I supposed his mind was thinking, calculating as was his usual way.

They dragged Gayens to his feet. He flopped between the guards and the beginnings of a huge bruise puffed his eye.

'Thanks,' Opeia said, dusting off her hands. 'Did you get all that, Lieutenant?'

Another man sauntered in, young looking, but not young, with beady eyes and thick eyebrows. He had a dark goatee on his rather wide chin. He reminded me of a pirate I once met. 'Yes, thank you Ms Gayens.' His voice grated like a rusty conveyor belt with misaligned spokes and cogs. 'Mr Gayens won't be troubling you for some time. Perhaps never.'

'Great.'

The guards dragged the sagging Gayens out. He glared at her. 'By the way, Carl, you'll have to represent yourself in court. You have no assets remember.' He groaned and began cursing her loudly. The door shut with a snap, cutting him off.

I stood there open mouthed. Opeia stepped towards me, touched my cheek with her forefinger and smiled.

'So you remember me, Rae?' she said softly.

I examined her face. It stirred a ghost of a memory. 'Not much. I associate the word "Opi" with you. I don't know why.'

Alwin looked embarrassed, not knowing whether to go or stay. I reached for his hand and squeezed it.

'Because that's what you used to call me.' A tear slid down her cheek. I was feeling pretty choked up myself. Just then, the main door opened and a girl with a long plait, deep in the embrace of a young man with long blonde hair and dressed in leather and studs, fell through the door. At first I thought they were wrestling but then I realized they were kissing.

Alwin gaped at me and I shrugged. 'What next?' I said to myself.

Opeia's eyebrow rose and she angled herself in their direction. 'Honey, Essa come and meet your sister.

18

FAMILY FOUND

The girl extracted herself from her boyfriend's embrace. She adjusted her exquisite beige pants suit and tossed her braid over her shoulder. 'Oh Mummy,' she said in a posh voice. 'Didn't see you.'

My mouth opened and shut. It was me, but not me. She walked elegantly and sounded like a female Alwin Anton. I sneaked a look at him. He was staring open mouthed at Essa, my clone, the other me.

'Dirk,' Opeia said to her clone daughter's male companion. 'Wait for Essa in her room dear. We've got some family things to discuss.'

Dirk turned and headed for the middle door. Opeia aimed her security pass and it slid open, revealing a large elegant room with a huge bed on the other side. I couldn't help staring at Dirk. Now that I looked at him I realized he wasn't wearing much but a few strips of leather and studs. His well-tanned backside was suspended in a strappy affair and his back was painted with shimmer gloss.

Opeia spoke, 'Really Essa. I've told you before, associating with him is bad form.'

Essa sniffed and walked over. 'But I like him and I'm on holidays. You know it's nothing serious, just a bit of fun.' The girl's grey eyes met mine and she stood stock still. 'Who is that? She looks like me.'

97

I was dripping with envy. My clone was evidently educated, classy, sophisticated and well dressed. Everything I wasn't. I'd been eating beans and hardtack while she had lived the life I was meant to have. I was being rejected by Alwin for being young and naïve, while she was romping it around with all types of people. Life sucked, really sucked.

'This is your twin, honey,' said Opeia, keeping her eyes on me. 'Rae's been lost for a while. Rae, meet Essa, your twin sister.'

Essa was fascinated with me. She stepped slowly around me, head angling up and down as she took in every detail of my identical form. 'A twin? You're kidding me aren't you? You've had a clone made. Oh Daddy is so funny sometimes.'

'I'm not a clone. You're...'

'Now dears let's be nice about this,' Opeia said neatly. 'Rae was stolen away quite some time ago. I've been searching for her ever since. I never told you, Essa, because I didn't want to distress you. But Rae is my child as you are. She hasn't had all your advantages but she'll catch up.'

Essa took her gaze off me and stared at our mother, confusion evident on her smooth creamy features. 'Mummy, this is all very strange. Is she going to live with us?' My mother didn't answer, yet Essa saw the response in Opeia's face. Her hand went to tug on her braid. 'I can't take this in right now. I need to...to, um, see to something. Catch you later, um, Rae.'

Essa backed away then catching sight of Alwin, paused. 'Oh, you're nice. Want to play later? I'm sort of distracted right now.'

'That tears it,' I said. 'Listen here you brat. Keep your hands off the company auditor. If I can't touch him, neither can you.'

'Brat. Me?' Her fists bunched up. Swinging round the words toppled out of her mouth, 'You smelly, slimy, little cow, waltzing in here saying anything that pops into your ignorant mouth. How dare you speak to me like that?' Essa looked past me. 'Mummy, tell her not to speak to me like that.'

I glanced over my shoulder at my mother. Her eyes rolled up and she sighed.

'Essa dear, go to your room. Relax honey. I need to speak with Mr Anton and your sister, okay.'

Essa pouted, then tearing her gaze from my mother to me, then flounced off to her bedroom. Staring at her closed door, I was very tense. How did I deal with another me? Someone who had everything I had ever wanted. My emotions were climbing over each other. I did not know what to do or say or think.

Alwin's hand found mine, and he drew me to the couch. 'Come on relax now. The worst is over,' he said gently.

Opeia sat down too. 'How I pined for you dear,' she said, from my other side. She picked up my hand and stroked it with her finger. 'I wondered if you were alive or dead for so long. I loved Essa in your place, knowing she wasn't you but a part of you. Sort of a twin. I hope you can get along. She doesn't know she's your clone. It would destroy her. Promise me you will never tell her.'

'But she's lived my life. She is everything I've ever dreamed of being. I can't help feeling resentment.'

'It wasn't her fault you know. She had no choice.'

'But...'

'Rae, please, promise me.'

'Okay. I promise. But it hurts. It really hurts.'

She lightly stroked my hair. It felt wonderful and strange. Only Gris had been affectionate with me. 'Clones have equal rights to humans now. That's the law. She has the same rights as you do. I have a duty to her as a parent. That's why people don't make them anymore. There's no value in it. If a clone is a human then they can't be used for labor, or body parts or to replace people.

'Your Dad wasn't always bad you know. He loved his research. But it got too much for him, science versus ethics. He couldn't deal with both. Being God and creating people was all that mattered to him.'

'How did you know Essa was a clone, Ms Gayens?' Alwin asked. I looked at his handsome face, watching his mouth as he spoke. He was always so clever, asking the best questions and looking good doing it.

'Carl was right, she didn't have a flag on her cells. It was hard to differentiate her that way. He'd tried to transfer Rae's memories to

Essa and he succeeded in implanting some, but not all. There were small differences. She never called me Opi, for instance.'

'So that's why I couldn't remember my life before I went to the outpost.'

'Probably.' Her soft grey eyes studied my face and her lips tensed. 'Can you give your mother a hug? I've missed you so much. If I didn't have to go to jail for doing it, I would have killed that slime bag husband of mine.'

I uncoiled myself and edged closer. My mother smelt like a garden of sweet-smelling flowers. It teased another memory within me. Her perfume was the same as it had been when I was a child. I clung to her. I was finally home. I had found where I belonged.

I felt Alwin get up. As I hugged my mother close I said, 'Please stay, Alwin. Just a little while.'

Opeia nodded. 'Yes, you must stay,' she agreed. 'You can have Gayens' room. Order whatever you need.'

'Sure,' I heard him say. He sat back down next to me and I smiled on the inside. I'd been through so much, loved and lost two fathers, gained a mother, a sister and a home. But beside me there had been Alwin, smart, brave and there to help me. I couldn't let him go. Not then, not ever.

19

SISTERS & LOVERS

Sisters are very interesting creatures, especially when they seem to have everything you don't. Like a good eye for fashion, for example, or an annoying desire to have the man you want for yourself. Essa was articulate, or so she told me. She talked with Alwin about galactic events, Earth history and the latest techno gadgets. To really show me up, she talked business with my mother.

I felt like wiping the smile off her face when she strode confidently around the living room, posed in front of the view port and named the model, make and manufacture of all the ships she could see and could pretty well guess which home planet they were from.

I sat on the sofa and glared at the ceiling, trying to unclench my fists. She ate delicately, with more utensils than I knew existed. I was putting on weight and had to watch what I ate. Even Opi had told me to stop wolfing down my food. I couldn't help it. I'd never had so much food before—real, delicious food.

Essa sat down opposite me and smiled. I grimaced back. I was dressed in my very own top-of-the-line ship suit. I had twenty of them in all colors. This particular one was violet, like the shade of the slave woman's eyes. Alwin was watching the news broadcasts, on about ten channels at the same time.

Essa swapped seats to sit next to me, leaned over and whispered in my ear. 'I really like him. If he's not taken, do you mind if I, you know, try my hand.'

Alwin had been so polite. We'd never spoken about that kiss on the ship and about what he'd said, about my youth, our age difference or feelings. He stayed with us because every day at breakfast when he said he had to leave I asked him to stay. Opeia would chime in on queue and give him some silly business-related task to do and he'd agree. He'd paid the company back and got a huge reward. He'd invested it wisely, so my mother said. Typical, I thought to myself.

Then the penny dropped. I turned to Essa with my face screwed up. 'I don't know how you do it. Just leave him alone. Believe me, if he's interested he'll let you know.'

'Oh, I don't know,' she said. It sounded like my own voice, richly cultured. 'I'm used to taking the initiative. It's part of the price of being so rich. No one is game to ask you out or seduce you, unless of course they're slimy, money-grabbing bed crawlers. In that case you get rid of them quickly.'

'I see. Doesn't sound like much fun.'

'And what would you know. It's bleeding obvious you've never even kissed a man, let alone anything else.'

'I have kissed a man,' I said, head held high. 'Several times.' I'd just counted them up.

'Bet you've never been to a highflyer's party or Jack's anti-grav disco, or drunk Martian champagne.'

'Don't worry, I will.' Not content to leave it there. I thought of a comeback. 'Look here dear, sis. Have you ever lived on an asteroid with hardly any food, been attacked by pirates, kidnapped, sold on a slave market and…'

'Enough, Rae. I think Essa's heard enough to be grateful she's had such a good life.' Opeia said before they started arguing again.

I glanced at Essa's face. She looked shocked. I guess my experience beat hers hands down. I stuck out my tongue.

She sniffed the air and then oozed off the sofa. She headed for Alwin. I watched out of the corner of my eye, feigning indifference.

I was pleased that he didn't take his eyes off the news casts when she came over. Not to be outdone by his lack of interest, she ran her hands lightly across his shoulders. Still he took no notice, so she deepened the touch to a massage. He pivoted in his chair, thus stopping her ministrations, but ended up giving her his full attention.

I was looking now. He was wearing a ship suit, indigo-colored and tight. It hugged his body like nothing else I'd seen. It left nothing to the imagination. Given Essa's tendencies I could understand why she found him hard to resist. I found him hard to resist. I was fascinated with him, dreamed about him, lived and breathed him. But I never said anything, never let on. I couldn't bear the rejection.

My eyes tracked her as she whispered to him. He shut off the news broadcasts with a snap. 'Rae,' he said, leaping to his feet. 'Come here.'

My ears rang. Was he ordering me? I nearly bounded off the sofa to race over to him. But at the last second I changed my mind. My mother glanced up from her desk in the corner, a smile about her lips.

I eased out of my seat and sauntered over, doing a very good imitation of Essa or Del Divlan. I kept my eyes on Alwin as I approached. He didn't fail to notice. His eyes were practically glued to me. My ship suit didn't leave much to the imagination either. Two can play at that game.

'Yes, Alwin, you called.' I looked at Essa, she was backing away slowly. My eyes were drawn back to his.

'Did you tell Essa you had no interest in me?'

'I don't recall…saying that.' I said, all the time wondering what Essa had said. I was playing it cool.

'Did you say that I was all hers?' he asked, his voice suddenly deep.

My eyes bugged out. 'Hell no. That rotten cow.' I turned around and eventually spotted her hiding behind our mother.

His hands were on my shoulders. He dragged me round to look at him. Stunned, I stared into his deep, dark eyes with my mouth hanging open stupidly.

'Good,' he said. Then he grabbed me to him and kissed the life out of me. It didn't scare me this time, so I kissed him back.

After a while, when the world became real again, and I was safely enfolded in Alwin's firm embrace, I heard Essa and Opeia laughing.

'Took her long enough,' said Essa.

'Yes, but it was fun watching them,' Opi said.

Families, I thought, I could grow used to this.

Alwin pushed me back by the shoulders. 'Now we have Gris to find. Ready?'

'Yes. Let's go.'

EPILOGUE

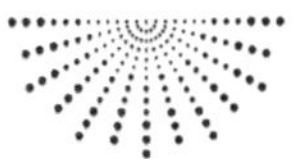

The clean, white corridor smelt strange. Thick antiseptic scents covered the metallic taste of blood. I scanned each door, looking for number 97. I reached out a hand, feeling nervous. What if Gris didn't want to see me? I knocked twice, *rap, rap*. There was no answer.

Hesitating, I wondered whether I should go in when I heard my name called.

'Rae.'

I looked down the corridor and there he was. I knew Gris, even though he had his head shaved and it was covered in scars from surgery. There was something in his eyes, too, they were brighter and more intelligent.

'Gris,' I gasped as I ran toward him. Up close, I could see his face looked better. It did not sag as much as it had the last time I'd seen him on the ship. The facility had repaired some of the damage, releasing the pressure on the brain. Dressed in plain, grey overalls, his body was thinner. The weight loss was from his time as a slave. Alwin and I had got to him just in time before he was too far gone.

'Are you okay?' I asked him as I touched his cleanly shaved chin.

He grabbed me to him and squeezed so hard. I could hardly breathe and I loved it.

'I am much better now for seeing you, Rae. I thought I would never see you again.'

After he placed me back on my feet, I smiled through my tears. 'Nah. You can't get rid of me that easy. You're family.'

'Family. I like the sound of that. Your friend Mr Anton filled me in on the details. I'm sorry about Stroder and that business with your father.'

'Well it is all sorted now, though it was rather a strange story. I'm glad we found you, at least. Sorry you got sold because of me.'

Gris frowned. 'Mmm. My memory is a bit patchy and I don't remember the slavery bit at all. I was pretty beat up by then. Good thing I suppose.'

I stared at Gris in amazement. I hadn't heard him talk normally before. He had a laid-back way of speaking and there was no slurring or the thick-tongue talking I was used to. My memory of him before the pirate attack was vague. I remember he was nice to me and that's all. Now he was his old self. I felt good about that. Good that the Gayens' foundation could put some things right.

He hugged me again. With my cheek resting on his chest, I said, 'Time to come home now, Gris.'

'A real home?'

'Yes. And if you behave nicely I'll give you hardtack and beans. As much as you want.'

We walked down the corridor, laughing at our shared joke.

BONUS MATERIALS

Emergency
Checklist
Rae use this in an
emergency
1. Look stupid
2. Deny everything
3. Lie through your
teeth
4. Cause a malfunction
5. Hide
6. If all else fails use the
escape hatch
Dad

RAE'S FAVORITE VIDMOVIES

In Space There is No Refuse
Starring Nel Wingham, Nicola Del Star
A Slave's Lament
Starring Del Divlan, Nel Wingham
Heart's Torture
Starring Del Divlan, Jake Rockham, Nel Wingham
Breaking the Barrier
Starring Prin Newly, Rick Banham
Within Saturn's Rings
Starring Del Divlan, Nel Wingham
A long long journey
Starring Red Tang, Macy Riverland
Another star
Starring Nel Wingham, Prin Newly
Once was of Earth
Starring Del Divlan, Nel Wingham and introducing Xtek Grn

HARDTACK RECIPE

Rayessa and Gris live on an isolated and practically forgotten space outpost. Their main source of food is hard tack and beans, usually canned baked beans. Hard tack is a kind of hard cracker, which is made from flour, water and a little salt and it can keep for years. It's very hard to chew, almost jaw breaking, but it is fairly nutritious and with a few vegetables grown in their makeshift hydroponics bay and vitamin pills, Rayessa and Gris survive.

Hard tack has a long history in human diet, particularly for long voyagers and during war time. It is known as sea biscuit, sea bread, ANZAC wafer, ship biscuit and cabin bread.

At http://www.wikihow.com/Make-Hardtack

The recipe is

3 cups of flour

1 cup of water

And 2 teaspoons of salt.

These are mixed together to form a dough and then rolled out, then holes a pricked in them, cooking for 30 minutes on one side and then 30 minutes on the other. This simple recipe is based on the civil war recipe.

Arnott's Recipe used in World War 1 is here at the Australian War Memorial.

https://www.awm.gov.au/education/resources/hard_tack/

This has more ingredients in it, such as powdered milk.

Cabin Bread, which is a commercial brand of hard tack is available in the Pacific Islands and is widely sold in New Zealand. You can also buy it in Australia. It looks like a large SAO biscuit but with a crunch factor of steel. Watch those teeth.

Here is a site that sells Cabin Bread in Australia.

http://www.justkiwi.com.au/Lees_Cabin_Bread_400gm-details.aspx

And there are other sites if you search on Cabin Bread.

This site says hard tack goes back as far as the Tudor period. See below.

http://cookit.e2bn.org/historycookbook/904-hardtack-ships-biscuits.html

However, I read that as soon as you add things like butter, spices or even more salt, it affects the hard tack's shelf life and they don't last for years. Look out for weevils and grubs! Yuk!

ACKNOWLEDGMENTS

Acknowledgements 2013 Edition

I've been at this writing gig for a long time now so I've stacked up a lot of people to say thank you to. Thank you to my children, Taamati, Shireen, Erana and James for putting up with me being attached to my computer almost constantly. I'd like to acknowledge the support of the Canberra Speculative Fiction Guild; the ACT Writers Centre; the Australian speculative fiction tribe for always being supportive; and Romance Writers of Australia and their great conference (August 2012), where I heard about Harlequin Escape. Thank you to Nicole R Murphy for encouraging me to go along. I'd like to thank Stephanie Smith, former publisher at HarperVoyager for her encouragement over the years and to Matthew Farrer who is one of a handful of people who has read Rayessa. He said he liked it. Finally, to Kate Cuthbert and Haylee Kerans, thank you for saying yes and the rest of the Harlequin Australia team for all the author love.

AUTHOR NOTE 2019

Here I am again. This time I am publishing *Rayessa and the Space Pirates* after the rights were returned to me. Rae is still fun for me. My first published longer work that led to two more in the series. Of course, there are more ideas, more ideas than time.

Over the years, I have had some lovely feedback on the story, particularly because it contains a portrayal of a character with a disability.

I hope you enjoy the story. This version has some bonus material in the back. I've also opted for US spelling this time, just to be different. And I believe this is my most pirated book. Enjoy *Rayessa and the Space Pirates*!

Donna Maree Hanson
    November 2019.

RAE AND ESSA'S SPACE ADVENTURES

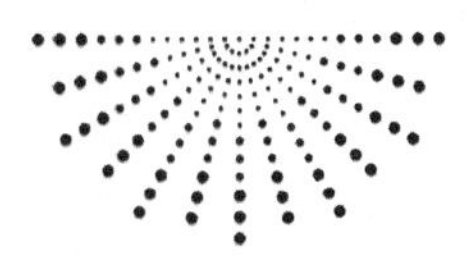

To my children Taamati, Shireen, Erana and James. Thank you for the inspiration.

1

EXTRA-CURRICULAR ACTIVITIES

My sister, Rae, bowed low to Kazusensei, the school's karate instructor.

'Do better,' he growled out. 'Try harder. Stop wasting my time, Rae.'

Rae stood there, face impassive, only the flicker of an eyelid giving any indication that he was getting to her.

My fingernails bit into my palms. I wanted to storm over and slap him across the face for talking to her like that. She was a Gayens. But it wasn't my fight. I had to stay out of it. Rae and I had boundaries — I might have been the one to erect them, but they weren't so easy to take down.

Rae nodded and Kazusensei stepped back, his hands on hips. 'Again, *hajime*.'

Rae performed her *kata* with the sensei looking on. If only he'd lose the sneer and the attitude, I'd be calmer. Most of the time he showed no emotion to the private school girls he tutored, but my sister brought out the best in him. I couldn't figure out whether it was her spirit that annoyed him or that there was another me ready to give him grief. But Rae took what he gave out without complaint. Something I never did.

I shook my head as I watched on. I may not have an abundance of sisterly love, but I'd give credit where it is due. Rae rocked at karate and that annoyed the sensei. Perhaps money and talent weren't combinations he was happy with.

Ending with a bow, Rae stood waiting.

'No, pathetic.' The sensei's hand chopped through the air. 'Again.'

I ground my teeth as I watched. He would never have dared to speak to me like that. I would have had his ass kicked from here to the city limits and used all Mother's connections to make sure he never worked again. But he was speaking to Rae and that was not my business. We did have an agreement, after all.

From scratch, Rae restarted her *kata*, her concentration almost tangible. She kicked, punched and blocked according to the well-rehearsed form. Her movements looked precise and snappy. My gaze flicked to Kaz. Yes, I got away with calling him that. Rae was good. He had no right to be so hard on her, getting on her case. He gave a slight nod and Rae went to the sidelines to pull on her gloves. Rae let the world heap crap on her and asked for more.

I checked my handheld for messages. A thumping sound drew my attention and there was Rae, kicking the living daylights out of the kicking shield Kaz held. He gritted his teeth as he braced himself and I smiled. She was going for it. *Thump, thump, whump.*

Go, Rae. Kick a little higher. Wipe that smug expression off his face. My breath caught as I waited for her move, only to let it out again when Rae moved on to punches. I would not have missed that opportunity. I pictured Kaz with a fat lip and blood in his teeth and nodded. Yeah! We had a history, he and I. He'd never put his hand there again.

At the end of her lesson, Rae staggered to the bench, wiping sweat from the back of her neck and tossing the towel onto her carryall. Kaz walked out of the gym, slamming the door behind him.

Rae stripped her *gi* pants off and adjusted the gravity straps on her legs. She had serious bone weakness from years in space and no therapy. Muscle and calcium loss. It was lucky she'd had some therapy as a child, and that it had lasted her a number of years in captivity. Mother said it could have been worse.

Rae connected the electrode to the metal strip attached to her tibia. It forced the bone to strengthen. I shuddered. It was so ugly. How could she bear it?

On Earth, with its full-strength gravity, Rae needed assistance to walk. She hated it. That's why she took this class, to beat it. She'd come a long way, too. Her academic grades were average but improving. I'd been loath to tutor her, so Mother had arranged an array of special tutors within a week of Rae being back in the bosom of her family. Alwin Anton helped her too. Boy genius was pretty easy on the eye, even if he was a smart ass.

Coming up beside her, I asked, 'Why do you let him treat you like that? It's demeaning to the Gayens' name.'

Rae glanced at me and sniffed. 'It's not personal. I want him to push me. I'm so behind on everything else, at least I can beat this physical disability.'

My nail polish glimmered and I examined it for chips, spreading my hands to catch a shaft of light. 'So? You received treatment. You'll beat it eventually.'

Rae drew on a wrap, slipped on some shoes and picked up her carryall and stalked away. 'And I still need to work on my fitness. My body is the only thing I can control.'

We'd had this discussion before. I liked needling her, liked seeing her crack. 'Mother is happy with your grades.'

Rae grunted as she pushed through to the cleaning block. I followed, sensing victory.

The mini cubicles contained nozzles attached to the walls that flash-cleaned skin. A minute later Rae was punching her legs into a onesie. They were so past tense, but she loved them and called them ship suits. I shook my head.

'My grades are mediocre. Nowhere near as good as yours. I can do better.'

With a flip of my hand, I quipped, 'Maybe.'

Technically, we should have nearly the same grades, as we were genetically identical. It went back to the nature versus nurture argument. I thought the case was closed — I'd been nurtured, she'd been neglected.

A light glinted in her eye. 'What do you want anyway?'

'Ohh grouchy. Missing the boyfriend are we?'

Rae let out a grunt of disgust as she pushed past me.

After stumbling back, I kicked out my hip so I had somewhere to place my hand for my pose. 'We were going out, remember? I was going to show you how to kick the trust account dependency.'

Rae paused before the door, her head tilting to the side. 'Now I remember. I didn't think you'd come all this way just for fun. I'll meet you out front in ten minutes. I've got to stow my gear.'

'And check if Alwin Anton has sent you a transmission.' I smiled smugly.

Rae shook her head. 'Whatever.'

'I'll be waiting.'

'**W**hy are we breaking into this building?' Rae hissed in my ear. She'd been jittery since she'd pieced together that her lesson did not involve law-abiding activity.

'Shut up, there are sound sensors.' I slid the conductor strip into the circuit, allowing the monitoring to think it was receiving feed. The steady blue pulse let me know it worked. My handheld synced with the security system and I calibrated my patented break-in app. My eyebrow lifted. The building had countermeasures, so I unleashed a designer micro-virus, which flooded the system with echoes and ghosts so it didn't know where to focus. Sufficiently diverted, my app completed its sequence, overrode the security system and the door slid open.

Rae gasped behind me. 'We'll get busted.'

'No, we won't. I'm good.'

Rae tugged my hair and I turned to glare at her. 'What?'

'Essa, you're a criminal.' Her face was flat against mine.

I inhaled her breath and shoved her back gently. 'I'm not a criminal. I'm a consultant.'

Lifting my handheld, I concentrated on the information scrolling along the screen, keeping Rae in my line of sight.

Rae's hands squeezed into fists. 'If you get me into trouble I'm so going to thump you.'

I rolled my eyes. 'I can't guarantee you won't get into trouble. Grow up.'

Rae stood up. 'Sorry, I'm out a here. See you back at the dorm.'

I sighed. What a waste of time educating her. Concentrating on my job, I grinned as the door slid open.

Rae was waiting for me when I got back.

'How do you know how to thwart security?' Rae launched at me as soon as I came in.

I put my stuff away. 'I'm smart,' I said, feeling smug.

Rae plonked down on her bed and pressed the release on her boots. She looked up from rubbing her feet. 'I think I understand that bit. I was wondering why.'

'I get paid.'

'You never!' Rae's dark eyes goggled.

'Not for a syndicate or any criminal element. By a security firm. They design and install security systems, and they pay me to crack them so they can refine their product.'

Rae sat there half-dressed. 'And what's that, like pocket money?'

'No. Not pocket money. Big money. I don't need Mother's handouts, but I take them and spend them so she doesn't get suspicious. You could do the same.'

'The same what?'

'Earn your own money.'

Rae's sleep wrap engaged and she snuggled into her bed. 'I don't need much money. I have stacks in my account.'

'You do?'

'Yes, Opi has been putting money in my account since I went missing. The same amount she said she spent on you or gave you as an allowance.'

I whistled, impressed, and went to the san unit to wash off the dust.

Rae snored softly while I filed my report on the security system, including recommendations to improve it. I checked my bank account, the bank account that my mother didn't know about, and grinned as the zeros grew. I liked my life.

A message came in from Mother. I pursed my lips when I looked at it. The message was the same as her last and that was plain odd. I put in a call and waited as the relays engaged, as mother was off-planet. After ten minutes, I received a 'no response' message.

Something about it bugged me.

I sent a message to Alwin Anton, who was with her. He didn't respond either, but then, he often ignored my calls — something about not upsetting his girlfriend. I wrinkled my nose as I took in my sister sprawled on the bed and then shook my head in wonder.

I reread the message from my mother and tried to put it down to a glitch in her system that sent the message twice. I'd have to check with Rae in the morning to see if she had heard anything or had any new messages.

Because I worried, I slept badly, dreaming of all sorts of scary things, like kidnapping and ransom demands. That was always a specter for the family — being rich and powerful made you a target. Except for Rae, we'd been lucky so far. And Rae's disappearance had been an inside job.

When I woke, groggy from lack of sleep, Rae was dressed. After yawning and blinking away sleep, I noticed her. 'You look nice. Date?'

Rae had make-up on. Mine, most likely. Her hair was shiny and straight, reaching past her shoulders and she'd chosen a cream onesie with a leather tunic, which ended just under her butt and accentuated her waist. I shook my head. I might have to rethink my views on the onesie — Rae looked grown up and attractive. We were 17 now, nearly adults. I reminded myself that we were identical, so if Rae looked that good then so would I.

'Yes, Al is due back today and we're meeting up at the Centra Hotel.' She posed sideways in the mirror, checking if her hair was straight. To check her lip gloss, she leaned in close with a pout. 'Gris is meeting me downstairs to fly me over.'

I don't know what she saw in Gris. Big men made me uncomfortable. But they shared some unshakable bond and he volunteered to be her security. My security team was good at carrying my shopping. 'Is Mother back too?'

Rae opened her pouch and dropped in her handheld, credit card, ID, more lip gloss, and sealed it. It flattened for easy insertion into her onesie's hidden pocket, high on her chest. 'I'm not sure. Opi was meant to be, but I haven't spoken to Al for three of four days as he's in transit and that plays havoc with comms. He mentioned Opi had another meeting planned. Something unscheduled.'

I leaned back on my bed and stared at the ceiling. I could see the translucent images I'd stuck up there, in spite of the school rules. You could only see them from this position. 'I see. You know she's rooting out the pirates in the company? Dad left a network of corruption behind him. Mother is determined to get rid of them.'

Rae shuddered visibly. Traumatized by Dad's attempt to murder her, she hadn't quite come to terms with it. Frankly, I'd always distrusted him. Our connection was never real. There was always something insincere about him. It was weird to feel that way, because he's my father too. In the end, I was right. Rotten to the core! He'd said that about me on numerous occasions so I took great satisfaction knowing it was proved about him.

Rae smoothed the fabric of her onesie, pressing the auto-clean when she saw a piece of lint.

She made eye contact. 'Al said as much. I don't understand what he does, but he can follow their transaction trail in cyberspace or something like that.'

Rae slid on her boots and activated the seal and colour change. Her boots now matched her onesie and clung to her calves like second skin. Slick. I was impressed that Rae had finally developed a sense of style, even without my advice and despite my teasing.

There was no point entering into the Alwin Anton adoration society so I didn't respond to Rae's blatant invitation to talk about her boyfriend and kept to the topic. 'Did he tell you their coordinates in that last communication?'

Rae activated the bed's refresh sequence and picked up her edupad, sliding it into her study nook. Her bed was sanitized and made up with her favorite bed cover, the one with some old actress on it — Del Divlan or something. Did Rae actually realize that the actress was as old as their parents? I let the thought go. Rae didn't want to hear it. The actress was like her sookie blanket and Rae wasn't letting go any time soon.

'Not directly, but they were on the message receipt. Do you want me to look it up now?' She withdrew the edupad, eyebrow quirked.

'No, no. Have fun.

2

A PUFF OF NOTHING

Tired after a day breaking into Rae's email account to read her love letters (and laughing a lot) and checking if Mother wrote more to her than me (jealousy assuaged), I woke from my nap as Rae bounded in.

As she had weekend leave, I wasn't expecting her back and did a quick mental check that I'd signed out of her account and put the edupad back in the same spot. Fighting with Rae could be a pain, considering Mother thought it was a great idea to have us share a dorm room at school.

'What are you doing here?'

Rae swung around, her hands clasping and unclasping. 'He didn't turn up. His ship didn't land.'

Rolling over, I sighed. 'He'll show eventually.'

'No he won't. He's missing and so is Opi.'

I sat up and tossed off my bed covers. My designer tracks had a crease and I glowered at my legs. I'd be getting my money back.

'What makes you say that?' I asked as I set my flask for a refill of mild stim.

'This,' she tossed me her handheld. 'That's the security feed from AllEarth Corp.'

I lifted an eyebrow and assessed my sister with new respect. Miss goodie-two-shoes she was not. Her eyes were puppy dog sad.

'How did you get access?' I said, tossing my head back.

'I stole Al's password so I could keep an eye on things, you know, control my anxiety. It says there is a Level One alert on Mother. Al was with her.'

Scrolling through the message, I saw that Mother had not checked in for four days. Mother was never out of comms range with the Corp. I flicked the feed. Alwin Anton had also not checked in. My stomach did a flip-flop. I feigned disinterestedness. 'So? The company has the best security ever. They'll be found.'

Rae sat on the bed, burying her face in her hands. Muffled sounds escaped through her fingers.

'Are you crying?' I wasn't sure how to deal with tears. Rae had never cried in front of me. She wouldn't dare. Would she?

'Maybe,' she replied, though her words were faint.

The sight of her crying fed my guilt meter. I knew I should be doing something, like offering comfort, but I didn't know where to start. 'They will be fine. It's Mother. Nothing bad happens to her.'

Rae flung herself down on the bed and rubbed her face into Del Divlan's right breast. It was serious. Rae would never disrespect her idol in such a way.

'Okay. Here is what we'll do. We'll go downtown and break into the comms center and send a private, encoded message to Mother. No going through relay channels.'

Rae sat up and wiped snot with the back of her hand. My stomach knotted at the sight. Eww.

'You'd do that?' Her mouth flopped open like a guppy.

Why did she have to be so incredulous? I cared for our mother too.

'Sure I would and I can. You have the coordinates of that last message and I have mother's ship security key. If she's on her ship, she'll answer.'

'Let's go then.' Rae stood by the door waiting.

There was no way I was leaving wearing creased track pants. 'Give me a minute.'

After pawing through my wardrobe, I decided on a stealth onesie. It had arrived that morning, along with a few others I'd ordered after seeing Rae looking so good in them. The silver-grey fabric deflected light and sensors. It looked pretty hot, too, as the suit hugged me and held me tight.

After opening the door, Rae ran down the corridor.

'You'll have to ditch, Gris,' I said right before we left the dorm building.

'No we won't. I already sent him home. I told him I was staying in.'

Smart girl, I thought to myself.

At the comms center, I opened the doors. Hovering on the threshold, I waited to see if the delayed alarms went off. It wouldn't surprise me if there was a redundancy in the security system.

Rae kept pacing and muttering until I could no longer tune her out. 'Will you keep still, I'm concentrating.'

Rae blew air, setting her bangs askew as the room's hidden sensors came into view. I loved my break-in app. It told me there was an independently operating security system in place and where it was hidden in the wall opposite.

'What's the problem?' Rae squatted beside me, interested despite her reservations about my activities.

'One more minute. There! Alarms silenced.' The comms panel stood on the other side of the room. 'It's clear.'

Rae seemed to forget her nervousness about breaking in. She raced over to the huge comms panel with its whistles and whirs and bright flashing lights, before I'd even shut the door behind us. I watched her and chewed my lip. She just stared at the console until I twigged what the problem was. She was clueless. I nudged her away with my hip.

'For heaven's sake, you key in the coordinates here.' I tapped the numbers in. 'The transmission will be monitored. We won't have much time before they come to investigate.'

Rae shrugged as she initiated contact. 'It's an emergency.'

'I know it is, but it's not through channels.'

I lowered my eyelids as I read the display. The transmission was received by the ship but no one was answering. That wasn't good.

'They're in trouble,' Rae exclaimed as she slowly comprehended the readout. 'I have to find them.'

'They could be too busy to answer.'

Rae faced me and narrowed her eyes. 'You said she'd answer if she was there.'

'I did,' I replied, but my cheeks started to burn. 'But I could be wrong.'

Rae shook her head. 'You aren't wrong. Al would never leave me hanging for so long, not when I was expecting him. He booked the hotel and you know he wouldn't waste money by doing that and not showing.'

Instinctively, I nodded. He was an auditor after all and he was good with money.

Rae backed away from the console, her gaze focused on the machine but her mind clearly elsewhere.

'You can't seriously be thinking of going off-planet to look for Mother and Alwin.'

Her gaze flicked to me. 'I can. How can you think otherwise?'

'Easily. Mother is quite capable of looking after herself and I don't want her grounding me because we did something stupid. You do know she has the best security money can buy. As for Alwin, he's none of my business.'

'Okay then,' she said, half-listening as she headed for the door.

'Rae?'

She swung around. 'Come with me.'

Backing away, I shook my head. 'No. I hate space travel. Besides, you shouldn't go off-planet. It will play havoc with your grades. Come back to the dorm with me and we'll think of something else…'

Rae turned her face to me. 'But I can't think of an alternative.'

I squeezed her hand, doing the caring sister thing. 'Let's get out of here and back to the dorm first.'

She hovered by the door as I began to disengage my software, then we scooted out of the building.

The auto-response was initiated after I removed my jam on the alarms, and sirens blazed. A detective routine had begun as I backed my app out of the security system. I chewed my lip. Silly mistake to make, I should have been faster. I usually made sure I didn't leave evidence of my methods behind. Maybe I was more perturbed by this business than I thought.

Robo Guards came whizzing around the front of the building. Others were flying overhead and there were probably some in the back too, forming a perimeter.

'Problem. Let's move.' Rae held my hand and we bolted.

Robo Guards were pretty easy to confound, being logical and working to a grid. They hadn't even registered us when we zigzagged our way out of it. These were cheaply made Robo Guards, probably imports from New China. I'd bet they were configured to scanning and tracking heavy weapons, of which we had none.

The darkness enveloped us and sirens screamed in our wake. We slipped into Humphrey Mall and sat down to drink a mild stim. Rae had hers with ice-cream. I couldn't get her to talk to me so we sat in silence and kicked our feet as a Robo Guard skimmed through the building, dodging shoppers. It didn't even scan in our direction.

I downed the last of my stim and let out a huge sigh. Luckily the comms center didn't use the new-fangled DNA scanners or we'd be in trouble. Leaving the kiosk, I urged Rae to act calmly and shop with me. When the surveillance cameras were reviewed, they would find it hard to see anything unusual in our activity.

In one of the boutiques, there was an array of pantsuits. After selecting a few, I directed them to be delivered in the morning. Rae paced the whole time, which made me grind my teeth. What was the point of appearing calm, relaxed and going about my business when she was jittery and anxious? Perhaps I should have recommended a nil stim drink.

'Stop that. You will stand out,' I said, while pretending to show her dance boots. 'You're shopping remember.'

She nodded. 'Those are really ugly and clunky.'

'Yes, they are.' I put them back and lifted my nose as we walked out.

Rae ducked into a sweet shop. I tapped my foot while she made her selection. How she got away with eating chocolate and sugar and still remained slim, I don't know. By the time she came out with an over-sized bag of sweets, I was conscious of the late hour.

'Come on, we have enough time to get back before the gates engage.'

'Sure, let's go.'

Rae didn't settle when we returned to the dorm right on curfew. She'd had way too much excitement, and possibly sugar, for one day.

'I'm worried,' Rae said. 'I have to go after them. I can't think of anything else to do.'

'You don't have to go yourself. You can send someone else.'

Rae shook her head. 'Are you so insensible to other people? If it was me, Alwin would come after me. He did it before and now it's my turn.'

'Yes, but this is different. What about a security firm?'

Rae frowned at me. 'You said Opi had the best security money can buy. So finding another firm won't wash either.'

'Well…' I had run out of arguments.

'I've just found Opi. I don't want to lose her. Come with me.'

'I might be able to thwart security when it's a paid assignment. I may be able to get us into the secure comms downtown, but I can't fool the school. If we break out of here, there will be a big security scare. It will affect the school, the other pupils, and it will clang like a gong right up the corporate chain to Mother.'

'But what if she is in trouble?'

'If I thought she was really in trouble I'd be off like a shot. Right now, I don't know if she is or not.'

'Okay, I'll try her again in the morning.'

Satisfied that Rae had seen reason, I decided to download a book. The mind-to-mind zap gave me a bit of a thrill that soon wore off. I could understand why my literature teacher preferred reading old style — the slow unfolding of the story, the play of the words across the page, the *ah ha* moment. Too bad I was too lazy to try old-style reading.

I drifted off to sleep.

The next morning, I jerked awake. I knew something was wrong before I looked across the room and saw Rae's bed was empty.

How did she manage that? She didn't wake me, nor did she set off a security alert. It hit me suddenly that she was on weekend leave. The alert wouldn't activate for her until curfew Sunday night. She had ample time to make a break for it.

'Damn it.' Throwing off the bed covers allowed me to vent. I stomped around the room, all the while knowing I'd have to go after her. She was such a child. The possibility of her securing a charter ship was small. She was probably moping around the spaceport unable to engage a ship, too stubborn to come back.

'I'll show her who the mature one is,' I said as I slid into my stealth onesie and matching boots. In my carryall, I tossed in supplies and clothes in case Rae gave me the slip and I had to go after her. Her wardrobe was emptier than usual. Dirty karate gear was scrunched into a ball and shoved in the bottom of the cupboard. She must have left as soon as I crashed.

Grinding my teeth, I slammed out of the room. I was meant to be the scheming, sneaky one. It really smarted that Rae tricked me.

3

CAPTAIN HUNK

The narrow corridors of the spaceport looked greasy and grey. I felt dirty just being there. It was like a bar that let anyone in. Drunken humans, equally tranquilized aliens and disreputable enforcement officers lurked in dark niches or stumbled over when I walked by.

I lucked out. A hand landed on my forearm. 'Identification, Miss.'

Spaceport security had hold of my elbow. He looked like an old, out-of-date rock star and was wearing a dirty uniform that reeked of stim smoke.

Disguising my revulsion was difficult and I didn't try to smile. 'And you are?'

He flashed his ID, the hologram sharp and accurate. The logo imprint looked legit. Passersby were taking an interest in our little interplay. Not good. I flashed my fake ID at him. He looked me over.

'You expect me to buy this ID? If you're twenty one, I'm a newborn baby. Come along to the holding cell, my lovely. We'll call your folks.'

'Wait.' I drew out my handheld and activated a preset button. 'Maybe you can overlook me being here.'

He glanced at the figures on the screen, licked his lips and let his jaded gaze slide over me. After a few moments, he nodded. He touched his handheld to mine to transfer the bribe and then strolled away, shaking out his shoulders as he turned a corner. Watching him leave made me curse myself. In my clean, expensive clothes, I stood out. I should have at least tried to blend in, particularly in this part of the port, away from the mainstream carriers and luxury liners. With a shrug, I figured it was too late now. Rae was here somewhere and I had to find her before she did something stupid.

The departure hall for regular supply routes was teeming with activity. I was tempted to check it out, but a regular transport ship wouldn't have been what Rae would have gone for. None were flexible enough to get her to a set of coordinates in the Nova sector, far from one of the orbital space stations or major traffic routes. She'd try for a smaller, independent charter. At least, that's what I would do and she was nearly as smart as me.

The pricing lists of the small charter vessels were a bit dodgy. Some were way too cheap, which set off all kinds of alarm bells. You never know where you'd end up on a charter like that — a girl like me or Rae traveling on our own would likely end up in a slave market on Centauri, or worse, on an alien world with no embassy to assist us. Rae had told me of her experience in that slave market. I couldn't believe she was still sane.

Shaking my head, I realized that Rae had to be sensible enough not to have taken one of those. I wasn't prone to praying, but right then I was tempted to call on God and maybe a few of his friends to watch out for Rae. While I gazed down the list of charters, I noticed a tall, broad-shouldered blond guy leaning against the wall. His hair was down to his shoulders, shorter bits curled around his neck and his pecs rippled as he moved. Our eyes met. I stopped in spite of myself because he was gorgeous.

Distracted, I found myself smiling, admiring the view as much as he was. His mouth lifted in an inviting smile, making his sky blue eyes flash. His skin was tanned, which made his white straight teeth stand out when he smiled. Excellent.

I sashayed over, exaggerating my gait so he'd notice the light playing on my stealth suit and how my breasts were high and firm and how my waistline slid gracefully into the curve of my hip. My mother taught me to know my assets. I just had a broader definition of what they were.

'You do charters?' I asked, toning down my smile so I'd appear cool and collected, but interested.

He lowered his eyelids. 'Yes, I do.'

His voice was warm, with a pleasant timbre that made my spine tingle. I held on to my sigh. Looks good and sounds good. No way.

'Thorn Hanover, captain of the *Mighty Star*, at your service. You need a ride to your next picnic, little girl?'

My teeth clicked as I shut my mouth. Little girl? There was nothing little girl about me. How dare he? He couldn't be that much older than me.

My chin rose. 'I'm going deep space, old man. Your crate go that far?'

His eyebrow lifted. 'It's not a crate. She's Zero Class — top of the range and specially configured to work with the new accelgates to reach maximum speed and distance.

This was good news. An accelgate opened a ship to the network of wormholes which sped up access to key sectors of the galaxy. Just what I needed. I smiled and sidled closer. 'I can pay well. I need to get to Nova sector, near the Hornet's Nest and fast. No questions.'

He stood up straight and crossed his arms. 'I don't take minors off-world illegally. Although your slutty routine is a surprise. A bit young for that, I'd say.'

'Slutty routine?' I lost control. My hand came up, aimed at his cheek, but he blocked me gently and narrowed his gaze.

'Don't try it. Or I'll flip you onto my knee and paddle your backside.'

'You wouldn't dare. That's assault.'

He nodded. 'My father never thought so.'

I calmed down a bit, but no way was I backing off.

'Look,' he said, unfolding his arms. 'I don't know why you've come back. I told you to go somewhere else.'

'Me, but I... You've seen Rae?'

His eyebrows arrowed under his furrowed brow. 'You're not her?'

'No, I'm her twin, Essa. I've got to find her.'

'I'm not falling for that.' He shook his head and walked away.

My fists curled. How *dare* he turn his back on me? I followed, then pulled up short when he began talking to a skinny teenager with greasy hair hanging limply to his shoulders.

'Slick. Didn't that young girl we spoke to last night score a charter with Milson?'

The young man detached himself from the comms panel he was sitting at. His legs were too long for his body and his face too thin to be attractive. 'Yeah, Thorn. You asked me to follow her and I did. They left hours ago.'

Thorn turned around and tilted his head when he looked at me. 'Your twin?'

With folded arms, I leaned my shoulder against the wall, flicking my gaze over Slick and then over to Thorn. 'I'm not lying. She's too young to be in outer space on her own.'

Thorn stood taller and squared his shoulders. 'Tell me you aren't playing a sympathy card.'

I saw a crack emerging. 'My mother is missing. That's why Rae took off. I'm chasing her so that I can bring her back safely. Will you take the hire?'

'Can you pay?'

I threw my head back. 'Are you kidding me? I could buy your ship, but I'm no pilot. I don't like space travel unless it's on a luxury cruiser.'

After studying me for a minute or so, he shook his head. 'I don't need the hassle. Try Browns. They're reliable.'

With a nod to Slick, he ambled away. Anger washed over me. I wanted to pound on his retreating back and storm off. I did nothing. I stood there, torn. I don't think anyone had ever treated me with such a lack of respect, except maybe spaceport security twenty minutes earlier.

A rumble under my feet reminded me that this was a spaceport and that I needed to move if I was to get a charter. Independent charters were taken up quickly, I couldn't afford to waste precious time.

Browns were booked out. They were expecting a ship in tomorrow or the next day. Could I wait?

'No. Thank you for your trouble,' I said to the clerk manning the desk.

I checked a few more charters but either the ships weren't up to scratch or the pilots weren't. Two hours later, I was back at the charter hall where I'd seen Thorn. His business and berth number were listed. My boots clicked against the concrete flooring as I headed to where his ship was docked. I'd be lucky if he hadn't already picked up a charter and taken off.

Rounding the corner, I saw his sleek, shiny ship. Slick was working the refueling control panel. My gaze skimmed the Zero Class' sleek lines and when I ducked down I spotted a pair of legs on the other side of the ship's undercarriage. They belonged to its captain.

Standing behind him, I placed my hand on my hip and sighed. He looked over his shoulder and then turned back to the power relays he was cleaning.

'You back already?'

'Yes. I can't find anything suitable. Will you take me?'

He finished cleaning the carbon particulates off his relays and turned around, inserting his ultrasound buzzer into his tool belt. In the light of the landing bay, his eyes were a vivid blue, like a clear sunny sky. His olive skin was unblemished. I stood straighter. He was a hunk. Captain Hunk.

'I really have to find them. Please?'

'Show me your ID.' I passed it over.

'Your real ID.'

I locked gazes with him, tried to bluff.

'No way you're twenty one and a consultant.'

I had to trust him, because he didn't trust me. Shaking my head, I passed him my real ID and his eyebrows rose.

'Rayessa Gayens, student.'

'Actually, I'm called Essa.'

He tapped the card against the palm of his hand. 'I know that name. Let me see, Rayessa Gayens, daughter of Opeia Gayens, President of AllEarth Corp?'

Captain Thorn knew his heiresses.

His gaze flicked up and down. 'It still doesn't change your age.'

'Age is relative. I'm seventeen going on twenty five.' I tapped the side of my head, indicating I had smarts.

His eyebrows rose. 'You think so?'

'Yes, I know so.'

He tilted his head and blinked. 'You're twins and both called Rayessa?'

I sucked in a breath. 'My parents are rich and eccentric.' I didn't want to explain why we had the same name.

'That's really kinky. Your DNA is the same?'

'Yes.'

'Fingerprints?'

'No. Are you finished with your interrogation?' I lifted my chin and my foot was aching to kick him in the shins. My fingerprints were definitely different. I'd had mine removed, even though they weren't identical to Rae's. It was a phase I went through. Periods of self-hatred will do that to you.

He whistled. 'Didn't realize that there were two of you. But you're definitely not the other one.'

'You could hardly mistake me for my sister. She has no style and is so...so—'

'Earnest?'

'Sheesh. Enough already. Are you going to take the hire or not?'

He stood closer and stared down at me. I had to bite my tongue in case I drooled. Captain Hunk was within touching distance and his physical presence caused a fire to burn in my gut. My knees were in danger of unlocking, which would make for an embarrassing crumble. I inhaled to steady myself only to catch his light, spicy scent.

'Here's the deal. You pay up front, the whole amount. You pay premium because you can afford it, and I can't take other passengers with you on board. You'll also have to sign waivers, although being a minor they won't be worth much.'

My luck was changing. Captain Hunk was buckling. A smile crept onto my face and he glimpsed it.

He showed me his handheld. It displayed such an astronomical figure I nearly turned around and walked away. Yet I knew there were no other alternatives and maybe with Captain Hunk I could have some fun during the voyage. Still, it didn't matter how handsome I thought he was, or how tall, I wasn't going to let him rip me off because I was rich.

'Here's the deal. I pay you the going rate, which is about 70 per cent of this figure. I pay you a bonus when we find my family. I pay you another bonus when we arrive home safely. Deal?'

His eyebrows rose but he nodded. 'Fair deal.'

I guess he didn't think I was some dumb rich kid after all.

We touched handhelds and the funds transferred. He turned to walk away and paused. 'One other thing. On my ship, you follow my rules. Got it?'

'Sure,' I agreed, my smile widening.

'Rule number one. None of that.'

I cocked my head, my smile dropped. 'None of what?'

'Flirting, smirking, schmoozing, oozing or whatever you call it.'

My face heated. He'd noticed!

His right eyebrow lifted, questioning me.

'How many rules are there?'

'Lots, so you'd better pay attention.' When I didn't agree right away, he lifted his handheld as if to refund my fare.

'I'll obey your damn rules,' I said in a rush.

He pushed his face close to mine, filling my personal space with his scent and his slightly minty breath. 'You'd better, or I'll have you out the airlock before you can unlock your handheld.'

'You can't make threats like that.'

'My ship. My punishments. You give me cause and I'll have you across my knee for the spanking you should've got from your parents.'

I sniffed loudly. My parents did not believe in spanking. I thought of Rae. Well, Father believed in using weapons as a form of punishment — though murder *was* a bit extreme. If I didn't need this jerk I would have walked, but the next available ship was Monday morning and the school alarm would be wailing for both of us before then. He seemed less handsome to me at that moment.

He walked past me and called out to Slick. 'Prepare for lift-off.'

Without looking back, he boarded the ship.

I had time to retrieve my carryall while he listed the ship in the launch queue. My scanned and sanitized carryall was delivered to the berth chute after I paid a small fee. The cost of stowing bags of any kind was only thing at the port that wasn't a rip-off. It was for security. No one carried luggage, except personal pouches, because of the threat of terrorism. Pouches did not carry explosives or volatile chemicals — the inbuilt sensors set off all kinds of alarms if anyone tried. At the spaceport all luggage was scanned in special rooms built to withstand a range of explosives. Some even had the technology to neutralise a range of non-standard explosive devices. Not that there was a current threat, hadn't been for years, but old habits die hard.

The alarm sounded for lift-off.

'Wait!' I scrambled up the ramp and the door slid shut behind me.

4

A BIT OF FLIRT CAN'T HURT

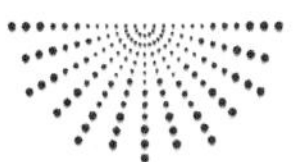

The ship was tiny, but clean. Inside there was four staterooms, a common area, a mess and a medical bay. Two weapons pods extruded from the outer hull, but inside they looked like little offices. I was ordered not to climb the short number of steps to investigate them. The guns were for pirates or less-than-friendly aliens. They were not normally called for on the main shipping routes but we were going off the beaten track on this trip.

Countdown was ten minutes away. I was in the way of the preflight checks. Thorn and Slick shouted back and forth and dashed here and there when something didn't go right. With a nod in Thorn's direction, I went to my assigned stateroom and lay down. Even though that was entirely boring, I was tired from scouring the port for a ship and Rae. I could've done with a mild stim, but a nap was a better option.

The ship's engines purred nicely and slowly rose in crescendo. Thorn's voice over the intercom jerked me out of a doze.

'Secure harnesses. Lift off in ten seconds.'

The bed didn't come with a harness so I shot out of the blanket into a turbulence niche. Damn the man. He could have given more warning; I could have made it to a safety chair.

The mesh of the safety harness wrapped around me as the engines groaned. I was pressed back into the niche as the ship pulled out of port. My teeth vibrated with the sound, and my lungs captured the bass thrum of the engines. With my hands caught in a web of harness, there was no way to block out the high-pitched whine as the ship tore through air. The ship jerked and yawed around me as it fought gravity and the heavy cloak of the atmosphere.

A headache pounded in the back of my head. I hoped the pressure wasn't going to rupture anything important, like a blood vessel in my brain.

I couldn't remember the moment I lost consciousness, but I woke to the sound of Thorn's voice rattling off engine stats — trim and vectors and some such. I had sagged against the harness and, as I pulled back, I instructed it to disengage.

My chin was damp. I must have drooled. No way.

The door chimed and I tried to wipe the saliva away with the back of my hand as I slammed the release.

'You didn't answer,' Thorn said. His gaze travelled over my head and lower. 'I had to check if you were all right.' A smile caused a dimple to appear on his cheek.

'What is it?'

That eyebrow lifted again and he grinned.

I drew my mouth into a line and headed for the small san unit.

'God no!' Half my face had the imprint of the harness on it. I looked feral. My hair was in disarray and I had dark patches across one breast, most likely dribble stains. I switched on the auto-clean on my suit and rubbed at my face.

The door was still open and Thorn stood there. 'Is everything okay?' His voice was laden with a smirk.

'It's fine!' I shouted back.

'Good. Meet in the mess in twenty. We have orientation to go through and then Slick will prepare a meal.'

I snorted. 'Sure. See you then.'

Thorn hit the release button and walked out. The hatch closed behind him. He had to be kidding. I was not going to sit through some boring orientation.

'I did promise to obey rules,' I said to my reflection.

'He didn't say this was a rule, did he?' I answered myself, rubbing at the indents in my cheek.

I didn't want to show my face with its newly acquired criss-cross imprint. I checked the mirror ten minutes later and it was still there, all red and puffy. It wasn't fading any time soon.

Bored out of my brain, I checked the entertainment panel and selected a vid. It thoroughly sucked me in. I vaguely heard a voice over comms, but the action sequence of explosions and gunfire drowned it out. Before I could blink, my room went dark. The entertainment panel rebooted and Thorn was at the door.

He pointed at me. 'You.' Then he pointed outside. 'Mess. Now.'

I blinked.

'Oh, the orientation. I'm fine without it. You go ahead.' I flapped a hand at him and then went looking for the controls for the entertainment unit.

An inarticulate sound emitted from his throat. Turning, I noted that his fingers were white where he gripped the edge of the hatch.

'The orientation is for you,' he ground out.

'As I said, I'm fine without it. What happened to the entertainment unit?' I pressed the controls and frowned.

'Nothing. I switched it off.'

I was ready to rip him up about that when I looked up and saw his face.

'Young lady, you get your butt outside and in a seat before I count to ten, or I'm turning this ship around and taking you back to Earth. You feel me?'

Shocked, I nodded dumbly. His nostrils flared and then he pushed away from the door.

No one had ever talked to me like that before. I shook myself to ease the tension from my body as I digested what had just happened. I had no doubt he would take me back like he threatened. So I had to comply. I didn't like that one bit.

Muttering to myself, I half floated, half stomped to the mess. Slick was there, a checklist in his hand. I parked myself on a chair and folded my arms. Thorn was leaning back against the dining table, wearing a sleeveless vest. His crossed arms were stacked. They looked good. I sat up higher in my chair, forgetting I was peeved with him.

'Miss Gayens, thank you for joining us. Passengers on this craft must understand all safety procedures and respond to directions from the crew immediately,' he said using an affected posh voice. He paused, 'and without question in times of emergency.'

Thorn sounded like a salesman. I reckoned he put on that fake voice just to needle me.

While pretending to listen to him, I ran my eyes down his body and nodded absently. Not bad, I thought. I may not be able to flirt but I could look, couldn't I? He was streets better than James, Slyv and Preston, all previous crushes. Much better than Alistair, my last crush. Alistair was twenty, and he'd been after my money. Luckily, I don't fall easily, and the only thing damaged by that encounter was my ego.

Thorn was older too, but I wasn't sure how much. I'd find out, I always did.

Thorn continued on with the instructions on how to engage the escape pod, how to use the breathers and put on the extra-vehicular activity suit — EVA — and he pointed out which one had been set aside for me. He ran over the emergency comms and the way to launch a navigation buoy and an emergency broadcast beacon. I yawned and then my stomach rumbled.

Behind me, I smelled food. Turning, I saw that Slick was preparing a meal.

'Ooh, no Robo Chef?'

Thorn pushed away from the table. 'Did you listen to anything I said?'

'Yes, of course. Safety first. That's your motto.' I arched my body towards him and gave him my best come-hither smile.

His brow furrowed as he looked at me strangely, like he'd seen a pile of vomit. 'What are you doing?'

I straightened. 'Nothing.'

He nodded and crossed his arms. 'Sure it's nothing. Well, you're wasting it on me. I gave up on spoiled brats ages ago. Eat if you want.'

He bounded into the mess and took a plate of food, guarding it so he didn't lose a portion in the light gravity. 'I'll eat in the bridge. It's my watch anyhow.'

'Okay.'

Captain Hunk left with his dinner. Slick brought over a plate and placed it on the table. With a nod, he said, 'Yours.'

'Mine?' It was some kind of stew. I looked from the plate to him. 'You didn't even ask me what I like to eat. What if I'm a vegetarian? Or have allergies?'

Slick's mouth went slack. 'Are you a vegetarian?'

'No, but that's not the point.'

'Do you have allergies?'

'No. Like I said, not the point.'

Slick shrugged. 'I guess so.'

He straddled his seat and sat down. Without looking up, he shoveled the food into his mouth.

'What happened to your Robo Chef? I thought it was standard with Zero Class.'

'Something went wrong with its programming or circuitry, I think. It's been that way since I've been on board.'

My food steamed and it smelled delicious but I refused to say so. These two were bumpkins or fools or something, taking on passengers without a Robo Chef. It was criminal. Sitting at the table, I played with my fork. I shouldn't eat it. That would show them.

My stomach protested. Maybe I'll not eat dinner another time, I thought, and slipped my fork in. A rich aroma filled my nostrils. I took a bite. Oh my god, it was wonderful. Some sort of spice I hadn't tasted before. I shoveled another mouthful in, munched and swallowed.

'Do you like it?' Slick asked.

I nodded. I couldn't quite bring myself to speak, given my mouth was full.

'Excellent,' he said, nodding as I stuffed more food in.

After that, we ate in silence until my plate was empty. I sat back with a contented sigh and eyed Slick. 'So, how long have you been working for the captain?'

Slick wiped at his nose with the back of his hand. I tried not to notice. I was not in the mood to upchuck my meal — it had been too damned good.

'About two years now. I'm indentured.'

My head jerked up. 'Indentured. Like a slave?'

A chuckle greeted my comment. 'Not a slave. He pays me and I learn. If I wanted out he'd let me.'

I sat back and twirled my fork. 'You can't be older than…nineteen.' I was fishing. I couldn't help it if I was curious.

He nodded and stood up to scoop more stew into his plate. 'I'm eighteen, just last month.'

'So much for not taking minors off-planet.' I sneered, remembering Thorn's excuse for not taking my hire at first.

Slick swallowed a half-chewed morsel. I saw him strain as it slid down. 'You don't know much about the real world, do you? Captain Thorn saved me from dying on the streets. The only way he could take me with him was to indenture me for five years. The authorities on Prima Nova don't want their brats back and don't want more mouths to feed.'

'You were on Prima Nova? The failed colony?' My eyes bugged out.

'Yeah.'

'I've never met someone from there. How was it?'

His eyes grew dark. 'I won't talk to you about it,' he snapped.

I jerked back. 'Why? What did I do?'

'Have you ever known a day's hardship? A day when you didn't think you'd make it to nightfall?'

Taken aback by the force of his words, I shook my head. A hard day for me was when my breakfast was a tad too cool. Or my favorite fashion designer couldn't supply the outfit I wanted instantaneously. Or I overspent my allowance and had to ask for an advance.

'I thought so. Thorn said so too. He called you a moneyed-up harpy.'

'What?' My fist clenched. How dare that overgrown lout talk about me that way? As the captain wasn't there, my eyes narrowed, choosing Slick as my target. 'He had no business saying that.'

I had the dish in my hand.

Slick darted out of the room and my bowl landed in the space he just vacated, the left over sauce splashed up the wall and over the bench. A growl left my throat. How dare that overblown buffoon ridicule me and say those things to someone else. He should try saying it to my face next time.

I was still there glaring and gnashing my teeth when the captain came in. Slick had obviously told tales. A strange calm settled over me.

Thorn stood with arms crossed, glowering at me under lowered brows. 'Clean it up.'

I smiled. It wasn't nice. 'I don't know what you mean. I don't remember household tasks being part of the orientation or the rules.'

'The rules are what I say they are. Rule ten: do not throw plates at the staff. Rule ten B: if you inadvertently toss a plate, pick it up and apologize. Rule ten B, part two: clean up the mess you make, and Rule ten C: always do what the captain tells you.'

'You think this is funny? What right do you have saying nasty things about me behind my back to that boy...or to anyone?'

'Truth hurt?'

I was hurt, but I wasn't going to admit it to him. I clenched my fist and hoped the opportunity to pop him on his smug jaw came soon. 'I'm not a harpy. That's a derogatory reference to me.' My voice went higher and louder. 'I want an apology. Now.'

He turned to leave and said over his shoulder, 'I rest my case.'

There were no more loose items to throw but I felt like ripping the table off its moorings and tossing it. Why did he make me so mad? He knew nothing about me. Yet those words stung. It wasn't my fault I came from money and privilege. I did not act like a harpy. I was not some kind of shrew.

Rattled by the loss of my temper, it took me a while to establish some equilibrium. I was unused to being angry and it was a strange and disturbing emotion. Nothing usually vexed me and life had gone smoothly, until now. My life had been disrupted when Rae appeared on the scene. But as I was in every way her superior, I had softened my attitude towards her and achieved a new balance in my life. I made room for Rae and she tolerated me. We were family.

I had no idea what Thorn's problem was but I was going to get even with him somehow.

5

SOME FINESSE

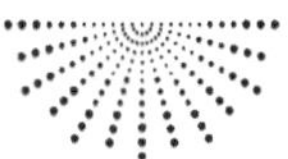

Because I'm a mature and subtle person, I dressed in clean clothes for the evening meal. Slick was nowhere to be seen, neither was there any food in the mess at mealtime. I strode, as best I could in the light gravity, to the bridge. Handrails helped.

Wearing a crossover pantsuit with a modest split to show my cleavage, I was ready to confront Captain Hunk. The absence of gravity made my breasts drift upwards, looking like they were trying to break free. If that didn't tempt him, I didn't know what would.

Thorn was bent over the console, checking screens. It looked like he was assessing the telemetry readouts and making micro course adjustments. I bounced over and ran my hand up his back. He stiffened. I leaned on him and read over his shoulder.

'Nice work. We are on course. Congratulations,' I said breathily in his ear.

Righting himself, he dislodged me abruptly. I flung out a hand to stop myself from sprawling and latched onto his forearm. His eyes flashed. I guessed he was annoyed at me for disturbing him. So much for trying to make peace.

'What do you think you're doing?' he demanded. His eyes drifted lower so I thrust my chest out further.

'Nothing. I was—'

The next thing I knew, I was plastered up against him. I didn't know whether to be thrilled or scared. He glared at me, face pressed close to mine. 'You're ridiculous. Throwing yourself at me? You're just a kid.'

I struggled but he held me tight. 'Let go. I wasn't throwing myself at you. I have better taste in men. And for your information, I'm seventeen.'

The tension left him and he gently set me aside. 'You're practically a matron.'

He turned back to the command console.

My lips pursed as I glared at his back. 'Not that it's any of your business, but I'm experienced.'

He laughed, but it wasn't in mirth. It was a sad laugh. 'Groping with boys most likely,' he muttered, but I caught the words.

'What?' I was riled yet again. He was giving me the brush off.

Turning to face me, he said, 'I'm not one of your toy boys. I'm the captain of this ship. Now get off the bridge and don't try to flaunt yourself at me again. Get it?'

My hands went to my hot cheeks. I'd never been spoken to like that. 'I wasn't—'

'Out!'

Struggling for composure, I bounded over to the hatchway. After sucking in a few breaths, I turned around. 'For your information, I came to inquire about dinner.'

Without looking at me he said, 'It's your turn to cook. Sound the intercom when you're done. Now out.'

I practically threw myself down the companionway. My turn to cook? Was he serious? I. Did. Not. Cook. I returned to the mess and saw clearly that there was a roster with my name on it. So much for the fee I paid to hire the ship. They really did expect me to cook. I squinted at the roster again. And *clean*?

The only solution available was to convince Slick to cook for me. I undid the clasp on my pantsuit to reveal more cleavage. A young man like him would go a mile for these ladies, I was sure. It took a while to locate him, as he was holed up in his quarters. The door opened when I buzzed.

He sprung off the bed when he saw me and flung the eReader he was studying into a corner.

'Is there a problem?' he asked, his eyes focused on a spot behind me.

There was sweat on his brow and upper lip. I made him nervous. That was good. I smiled and sidled closer. 'No. Not a really big problem.'

'That's good. Does Thorn need something?'

I shrugged. 'Not that I know of.'

I was close. Our bodies were almost touching. Suddenly, he became aware of it. Tension gathered in his body. His gaze slid down and stuck on my cleavage. I breathed heavily, the exhale ruffling his bangs.

He looked up, swallowed and licked his lips. 'W-w-what?'

My hand slid up his arm and rested on his neck, my fingers playing with his long, straggly hair, which was slightly greasy. 'I need help in the mess. Would you?'

'Let go of him,' thundered Thorn's voice behind me.

I jerked hard, knocking Slick so he fell backwards onto the bed. Thorn gripped my upper arm and tugged me from the room. He kept on tugging until we reached the mess.

He flung me into a chair. 'You do not get to play with that boy because you weren't successful flirting with me. Get it?'

My eyes widened. He was really pissed. I don't think I'd seen him really pissed before. 'Yes, but I don't understand. You didn't want to play.'

'It's not a game, you spoiled, self-centered brat. Slick has a heart.' He slapped his chest. 'I have a heart and there's no way you're getting your hands on them.'

A chuckle bubbled to my lips. 'I don't want your hearts.'

'Exactly. You're a fake, a narcissistic little girl. You don't care what damage you do.'

I gazed down at my breasts meaningfully. 'I'm not a little girl.'

'Then stop acting like one.'

'Look, let's be honest here. You don't like me. I get it. I was just asking Slick to help me cook a meal.'

'Were you? Looked more like you were trying to cook him.'

'It wasn't anything you need to be concerned about. Do you have any rations I can eat? I'm starved.'

He turned to a cupboard and tossed a prepak meal at me. I caught it with an oomph.

'You can't cook, can you?'

I hated to admit it. 'No, I've never needed to.'

He took a marker from his pocket and crossed my name off the roster in jerky movements. That made me sad. He turned back to me, his sky blue eyes bright. I was beyond thinking him cute. He was a brute who spent his time stamping all over my feelings.

Tossing my prepak meal in the air and catching it, I pretended the altercation meant nothing and returned to my quarters.

Later, I smelled food cooking and heard them talking to each other. The prepak meal was a crappy mac and cheese. I tossed most of it in the refuse chute and tried not to listen to them.

I had to do something about the food. More importantly, I had to do something to clear the air between us. Not that I cared, really, but it was a tad uncomfortable to be at war with those two on a small ship. If only the Robo Chef worked, then there wouldn't be a need to cook. Slick had mentioned that the circuitry or the programming was fried. If it was circuitry it would have been repaired by now, I was sure, but programming? That was a tad more difficult. The thought of playing with some code appealed to me, but I didn't want to let on that I was doing it. Let them think I'm some bratty, low-brained heiress. I may not have culinary skills, but I knew code.

There was an access port next to the entertainment unit. I synced my handheld. The security was way outdated and easily silenced.

Once I was in, I searched for the Robo Chef's software. Pulling up a seat, I sunk into the code. I wasn't an expert on Robo Chefs, but I figured reading the code would tell me something and also help me see if there were any random time bombs or viruses.

The next day, I was in the mess to retrieve another prepak and Thorn came in, wearing a forehead full of thunderclouds.

'Miss me?' I quipped. 'No defenseless girls to pick on?'

The thunderclouds dispersed and he chuckled. 'You defenseless? I wish. You have dangerous written all over you.'

'Something wrong?' I asked, trying to be interested.

'Nothing important.'

I sat down at the table, chewing the inside of my cheek so as not to set off another argument. 'So what happened to the Robo Chef?'

He took the seat opposite. 'You still on about that?'

'Funny.'

'I'll give you a discount on your fare.'

'That's not what I'm after. Tell me.'

He sat back and looked at me. There was a faint widening of his eyes, like I'd surprised him. 'Look, it's broken so let's just drop the subject.'

His right hand closed into a fist as it rested on the table. I guessed the subject upset him. I was hoping my questions didn't set him off. 'They're pretty robust. What happened?'

His eyebrows met. 'An attack. It hasn't worked since.'

'So it was a power surge? Fried its components?'

He slapped his hand on the table. 'Enough already. Drop the topic.'

'But couldn't they fix it?'

He stood up and towered over me. 'I said I don't want to talk about it.'

I stood up and he backed off. I wasn't really up to this. Sparring with Rae was one thing, even twisting teachers into tight balls of confusion was a game I enjoyed. But dueling with Captain Hunk was another matter entirely. He made my emotions churn and that I didn't like. One minute I was incredibly angry and the next sensing that I should pity him. I didn't pity anyone. Then sometimes I wanted him touching me and other times I wanted to stroke his pain away. I usually tried to ignore sympathy if it alighted at my door.

Confused, I backed out of the discussion before it became an argument. 'Fine. I'll stay out of your way, as even friendly, potentially helpful questions are too much for you.'

With a short bound, he was right next to me. I could feel the heat radiating off him and the light spice of his cologne. 'Are you really being helpful or is it another one of your ploys?'

Being this close was seriously disturbing my hormones. I shook my head. I startled at the touch of his hand on my hair.

'You look better without the harness imprinted on your face.'

There was a softness in his expression, a slow burn to his eyes that melted my animosity. He caught a hunk of my hair in a fist and kissed me. At first, I resisted. Control was my thing and this was not coming from me. It was alien and it was scary. Next thing, he deepened the kiss, draping me along his firm body. Then I was helpless, my blood thumping around my body, my will dissolving, letting his kiss dominate. He was all man, muscle, blood, bone and heat.

Alarm bells went off inside my head.

I squirmed and he released me enough so I could break the kiss and push at his chest. He let me step back but I was still within the cradle of his embrace.

'How defenseless do you feel now?' he asked.

I stood there panting, trying to put my head back together. He didn't mean it. He was playing with me. But oh my god, it was amazing. That was scary. I had been totally swept up by that kiss. Yet it was a joke to him.

Rage descended as my hand impacted on his cheek.

His face jerked to the side. He rubbed at his cheek, his eyelids lowering. 'Nice. You're quite strong for a little thing.'

I glared at him.

'You don't like being toyed with, do you?' The corner of his mouth lifted and he turned away. He paused at the hatchway and looked over his shoulder. 'Consider us even. Now you know what it's like.'

'Scum ball.' I turned and fled back to my stateroom, with suspicious moisture in my eyes.

6

LITTLE MISS FIX-IT

'You know, your sister didn't come across like you do.'

I lifted my eyebrow. I was sitting in the mess reading and sipping some mild stim with my leg over the armrest. Despite liking solitude, my quarters were not the most spacious of surroundings and even I needed to see another human being, no matter how odious, occasionally. I could tell from the tone in his voice that he was annoyed but I didn't think I'd done anything to deserve another dressing down. I'd spent the last week not speaking to Slick, who spent his time avoiding eye contact. The way they reacted, it was like I'd raped him or something. If he was from Prima Nova that couldn't be right, could it? Word was that anything went on that planet.

Deciding to fall for this lure, I lowered my eReader. 'How did Rae come across then?'

'She had guts and was solid.'

I scrunched up my face. 'Is that a compliment? You make her sound like she's obese.'

'You know what I mean. She'd come out and say she couldn't cook and wouldn't try to worm her way around to get what she wanted. Straight up, I thought. You though, are gutless. Chicken-hearted.'

161

Slamming down my eReader didn't calm me. It cracked the screen. Not *that* tune again, I thought he'd got me back already. Don't tell me there was more.

Being compared to Rae snapped something inside me. Rae would get on fine with these jerks. She could bounce around like a pro in low grav and talk ship talk. She probably knew fifteen ways to make beans not taste like beans. I hated being compared to her, particularly in a derogatory fashion. It really cut me in ways I found hard to describe.

'I think you've said enough,' I growled like a feral animal as I launched myself at him.

He caught me, controlling my hands before they reached his face. We were chest to chest, him breathing as hard as me. Our eyes met and his head lowered. God, was he going to kiss me again? My heart lurched and I had to fight the impulse to tilt my head higher.

He paused, lips hovering just above mine. 'Like I said. Gutless.'

Seeing red, I surged up and slammed my mouth against his. At first, he didn't react. But then he did. My hands tangled in his blond hair and his rough stubble sandpapered my chin. I was in the kiss before I knew it.

At first I thought I was in control but then this hunk of man who held me took over, possessed me. The moment I felt I'd lost control I panicked and struggled to get out of his grasp. He wouldn't budge. His hands slid into the gap my pantsuit, his thumb teasing a nipple.

Panic stations! This was more than I'd bargained for, considering I hated the man.

Stopping suddenly, he lifted away from me but held me still. 'You see, there's playing and then there's for real. One day you'll work out the difference.'

He put me away from him and left the mess.

Collapsing in my chair, I wiped tears from my eyes. I was crying? What did he mean I'd learn the difference? That kiss was real? Heavens. It made me feel powerless, out of control and also scared. I hugged myself and glanced at the hatchway. He could have taken me all way and I didn't think I could have stopped him, or would have wanted to while I was in the moment. That kiss wasn't like any I'd had before. I'd been the boss in previous encounters. I'd dictated what we did and when.

My quarters would hide me — I didn't want those brutes to see me emotional.

To avoid thinking about the encounter, I buried myself in the Robo Chef's code. I was familiar with it now, could understand the logic of it, the command sequences, the formulae, the dictionary of recipes and biochemical combinations to create proteins and carbohydrates. I read to the end and was puzzled. There was something alien in the code.

Diving back in, I started from the beginning, beginning to understand what each group of commands meant. There in the middle, buried within a huge block of code, were three lines of text.

Using the edit tool, I cut them out and saved them to a separate file, thinking it was a virus. I continued my reading until I reached the end. The lines of text had worked like a time bomb that prevented the Robo Chef from initializing. Leaning back in my chair, I realized I'd been sitting there for hours. The lights had dimmed to imitate the night. My bed looked tempting, so I crawled in.

I was drowsy and tired, but the words Thorn had hurled at me kept rising out of the darkness. I couldn't ignore them. He was right. I didn't like being played with.

Did he feel that way when I tried to play up to him? Was Slick hurt because my flirting wasn't serious? Or was it more that Slick might fall for me and I'd never be interested and he'd end up with a broken heart. There was that, I supposed. I tried to put myself in his position and detected a smidgen of guilt. That had been low, really.

I thought about Thorn some more and realized that his play was to show me how it felt. He knew I fancied him and wanted to give me a taste of the hurt I'd inflicted. I understood a bit better now. I wasn't good at empathy — it didn't come naturally. There was something missing in me, something to do with how I was reared.

Thorn though, his hide was tough. There was no way I'd made a dent. I wouldn't have hurt him at all with my flirt. But he'd hurt me, and that made me think long and hard about my behavior and his. His comparison of me to Rae was awful. What did he know anyhow? He'd only met her briefly, or so I assumed. Maybe he'd helped her out. Why else would he imply I was shallow and Rae was deep?

My thoughts and emotions were in such a tangle and I was getting nowhere. I needed to sleep. Sitting up, I drank a cup of valerian tea, hoping it was enough to put me out.

Eventually I started to drift off. A smile lit my face. I pictured me working the Robo Chef in front of those two and the smug look on my face. I slept for a while and then woke up out of a troubling dream with a start. The valerian tea had worn off. I closed my eyes but Thorn's words kept going around my head. I tried to ignore them and put them out of my mind. My hands fisted and my jaw clenched. I was really riled. Then, breathing through it, forcing myself to relax, the tension in my body eased. When the anger gave way I considered Thorn's words, especially about being gutless. I knew that wasn't true. I had nerve. Hell, I broke into buildings and cracked security systems for money. That meant I wasn't gutless, didn't it? That was because I did it for money, for me, my inner voice said.

I didn't stick up for other people, did I? I didn't even stick up for Rae when she copped slack from others — like that horrible karate teacher. I could have stood up to him, but chose not to. Why was that?

Out of the darkness, the thought came slashing out at me. No one was close to my heart, except maybe my mother and possibly after a year, Rae. Was that what he could see? My lack of emotional commitment? Memories of Thorn's voice mingled with visions of him snarling at me, deriding me and of him kissing me. I had emotions for sure, but they were walled up pretty tight.

But I had good reason. Reason enough to never, ever acknowledge why. The reason was buried so deep I didn't think I could unearth it.

Dark circles ringed my eyes the next morning. I timed my entrance to the mess for when they'd both be there. What was the point of a triumph if there were no witnesses? I strolled past them.

Slick smiled at me. 'There's porridge on the burner. Or a prepak if you like.'

'Thank you, Slick. I think I'll try this.'

I powered on the Robo Chef.

'We told you it isn't working.'

The lights flashed on the console. The ready light blinked green.

'I know you did.' I selected something from the menu — eggs benedict and a soy café latte. The machine whirred as it assembled the ingredients, rehydrated them, combined and cooked them. In two minutes the Robo Chef chimed and I took out my meal.

Thorn was out of his chair, half ready to pounce at me and half astounded. He shut his gaping mouth. 'How?'

Slick ran up to the Robo Chef and keyed in an item. A short ping later I heard him open the door. I sipped my café latte, enjoying the aroma of my eggs.

Thorn slammed his hand down in front of me, making my plate jump. 'I asked you how?'

I'd slipped a portion of food into my mouth so I had to chew then swallow. 'I accessed the Robo Chef's program and analyzed the code. I found some alien text in the program, maybe a virus, maybe a time bomb. I removed it and it works again.'

He shook his head. 'You accessed the ship's systems?'

I nodded.

'You gained access and then edited the Robo Chef program?'

I took another bite, closing my eyes in exultation and nodded.

Slick brought two hot dogs to the table. He glanced at Thorn and offered one. Thorn refused with a swipe of his hand. He was distracted and angry.

'What's wrong?' I said around a sip of café latte. 'I thought you'd be pleased.'

'You accessed ship's systems without my authority? You bypassed the security systems, delved into crucial operating systems while the ship was in flight?'

'It was meant to be a surprise. I couldn't ask you for access.'

He turned towards me, looked down at my plate and at Slick chowing down on his second dog. 'A surprise? You could say that. We're lucky we're not dead. What gave you the right?'

I frowned. How did this get to be a bad thing? 'I knew what I was doing.'

Thorn's complexion had turned dark red and the cords of his neck flexed.

'You knew what you were doing? I don't care. You don't do that, don't you understand? You don't do shit like that without authority, without supervision.'

'I'm sorry. I didn't mean to break the rules. I thought I was helping.'

He leaned closer, hand on the table, mouth poised to speak and then stopped. Backing up, he bounded out of the mess and went to his quarters.

I turned to Slick in mute appeal.

He swallowed a big bit of bun and sauce spurted over his hands. 'You're quite smart for a moneyed-up harpy.'

'Thanks.' I fake smiled. He continued to eat with abandon. 'Do you know it's quite rude to call other people names?'

'Sorry,' he said and licked sauce off his hands.

'It's also disgusting to speak with your mouth full.'

'Sorry.'

'Yeah, well. I've been wanting to say I'm sorry for…you know…flirting with you in your cabin. It was wrong of me. I hope you will forgive me.'

Slick wiped his hands on a napkin and smiled. 'Thank you. You just earned me a fiver.'

'A fiver?'

'Thorn bet me you'd never apologize for anything.' Without excusing himself, he stood up and went back to the Robo Chef. The smell of hamburger with the lot filled the mess.

I couldn't believe this. I'd done something remarkable and neither of them remarked on it. After tossing my plate in the recycler, I headed back to my quarters.

I was disappointed. I'd been hoping for something more. Something like triumph with humble pie on the side. Theirs, not mine. I may not have Rae's guts, but I had something better. I had brains. That Thorn thought me less than her really smarted.

A few hours later, the buzzer to my stateroom went off.
'Come in.'
I looked up from where I sat. Thorn filled the doorway. I'd been playing a game on my handheld. I'd finished a book and hadn't decided what to do next.

He cleared his throat. 'May I come in?'

'Sure. Take a seat.'

All that was available was the bed. He glanced at it and stood.

'I want to thank you for fixing the Robo Chef. I'm sorry I got angry. I overreacted. It's a bit unnerving when someone you never would have imagined could, breaks into sensitive ship's systems. I should have kept better security. You acted in ignorance.'

I stood up, anger flaring. 'There was nothing ignorant in what I did. Your ship's security is about five upgrades behind standard. It was easy to break into.'

Raking his fingers through his hair, he sighed loudly. 'Probably. Look, you're right, I haven't had the spare credit to upgrade things.'

'Captain, I didn't go anywhere near critical ship systems. I'm not stupid. The Robo Chef's program is in a subordinate system quite separate from the rest. I only had to pass through the top layer of security to get at it. To hack the drive or navigation would take a lot more work and knowledge of security keys, which I don't have. There was no danger that I could even accidentally do anything to endanger the ship.'

He studied me. 'You really know your stuff. I'm amazed they teach this in school.'

'I didn't learn it at school.' I puffed out a breath. 'I taught myself, with the assistance of the web.'

Nodding, he rolled his shoulders and sat on the edge of the bed. He rested his head in his hands.

'What is it? What's wrong?'

He looked up at me and wiped his hand across his face. 'I thought the Robo Chef shorted in that attack. How could you have fixed it?'

'Like I said, I removed some foreign coding. I'm not a programmer per se, but I like code. I like its logic and there was something weird in it. Virus maybe, but it looked like text.'

'Text?'

'Yes, three lines of text.'

'You mean like words or a message?'

I cocked my head. 'Yes, maybe. I didn't look.'

'Show me.'

I'd quarantined the file in my handheld, so I passed it over. His olive complexion turned a shade of green.

'What is it?'

He shook his head, his mouth dropping open. 'It's a message.'

'Really? Who from?'

'From my father.'

I sat down next to him. He was shaken and I was careful not to touch him.

'Something happened to your father?' I asked softly.

'Yes. I'm sorry.' He straightened up. 'Can I have this?'

I nodded. He took out his handheld and transferred the file.

'I'll talk to you later.' He rose from the bed and so did I, putting my hand on his forearm to stop him leaving.

When he looked at my hand and then my face, I said, 'Tell me what happened.' He avoided looking at me and made to move away. 'Please.'

Thorn stopped by the hatch and gazed at the ceiling. 'Okay.'

He sat back down and I moved to my chair, giving him space. He wrung his hands and his eyes travelled around the room. Fixing the Robo Chef had upset him. I was worried about what he had to say.

'I'm sorry. I never meant—'

'No. It's okay. I'm just thrown…I never expected—'

I hadn't seen Captain Thorn disconcerted before. 'What?'

'To find a message from him, one that makes me think he's alive.'

I was tempted to launch in and ask questions, but I took a breath and let him speak. This was important.

'I was on the ship when they attacked.'

'Who?'

'Pirates. I'm pretty certain it was pirates. He hid me in the hold when he saw them coming. The ship was shot up quite badly. I still remember the sound, still dream of it occasionally. Lucky my father had launched a distress beacon or I'd never have been found. I'd be dead meat floating in space. When it was over, I crawled out of my hiding space and found nothing but blood and a few smears of flesh. He was gone. Dead, I thought.'

My heart was thumping. Thorn was getting to me. I could almost see him as a boy, hidden and then alone. I could empathize with his loss. What was happening to me?

'What does the message tell you?' I asked softly.

'Rendezvous gone bad. Sorry, son.'

I frowned at the implication. His father had set up a meeting with pirates? Or was it someone else? 'Why do you think he's alive?'

'I always thought the pirates attacked us randomly. It never occurred to me that he was there to meet them.'

'He could have been meeting someone else and they intruded.'

He shrugged. 'Possible, but not likely. It was way off the main shipping routes. Space is huge. It's hard to bump into someone randomly.'

'Do you think he went with the pirates willingly?'

'Yes, maybe. I just don't know. Even ten years ago, a small independent was an easy target for pirates. I knew he'd been pressured and kept refusing their overtures. I thought they killed him in the end. Now…I think he gave in and decided to go with them.'

Thorn was still struggling with what the message meant. He

avoided eye contact and kept his hands clenched. I was tempted to reach out and smooth the crinkles from his forehead, but didn't. If his father wasn't dead then that meant he'd abandoned Thorn and that his father was in league with pirates. I could see how that might be disturbing.

He stood up. 'Look, thanks for listening. I've got to head to the bridge. We'll be coming up on those coordinates any time now.'

'Thanks for sharing.'

'No problem. You know, you could do something with this skill of yours. You have a chance to stop being who you are and make yourself anew.'

Anger stirred. 'What's wrong with who I am?'

'Look, I'm not trying to pick a fight. It's just, you know, you're so much the rich girl, the spoiled brat, but you can be whoever you want to be. You're not bound to follow that crap your whole life. Toss it and believe in yourself. Find out who you really are.'

I was gobsmacked. 'I'm Rayessa Gayens.'

'I know that, but who is Rayessa Gayens?'

He left, leaving me to digest his helpful suggestion. How did he know? How could he read me? I was playing a part. I didn't know anything else...did I?'

I stared at the closed door. I hadn't warned him there were most likely pirates involved with my mother's kidnapping.

With a sigh, I picked up my handheld and then tossed it on the bed. That conversation had floored me. I had sympathy for Thorn, an alien emotion but I liked it and he'd said the most amazing thing. I could be who I wanted to be, not who I was meant to be. How profound was that?

I sunk onto the bed and started ruminating. If I wasn't Rayessa Gayens, who would I be? I was smart. I could be useful if I chose to be.

I was developing emotions and empathy. How did that happen? Was it a sudden thing, or had it been coming on for some time? Certainly seeing Rae struggle had pricked my conscience on one or two occasions. Sometimes I even liked her. At school I kept everyone at a distance, and until Mother had forced me to share with Rae, I'd been alone in the dorm. With boys, I'd only dangled, mostly to annoy my mother. I'd liked them and lusted after them, but only for short spurts of time.

With a sigh, I punched my pillow. This ship was the first time I'd been in close quarters with anyone except my mother and Rae for more than a week. I don't count security or staff because they kept their distance.

I sat up again suddenly. I could be who I wanted to be.

I thought about the list of chores, where my name had been crossed off. I remembered how sad I was when Thorn did that. I didn't blame him. I got up and went to the mess. I pulled down the list and examined my chores. I could do those. I put a tick next to my name and went off to the hold. I'd check that everything was stored appropriately and then move on to check the EVA suits were charged and the oxygen was full, then I'd move on to cleaning the air vents.

The air vents took a lot longer than I anticipated and were a lot harder than I'd ever imagined. I was covered in grime. I detected a presence behind me and turned.

'Oh hi, I'm nearly done.'

Thorn folded his arms and nodded. 'So I see.'

I wiped the last of the muck off the vent I was working on and leaned over to slot it back into place. 'Is there something wrong?'

'No, no. We were having a meal and came looking for you. Slick noticed the ticks. I've been following your trail. Most impressive.'

The last vent slid into place. 'They were easy chores.' I didn't know where to look. Thorn's eyes were shadowed, but I knew he was studying me.

'Yet I appreciate the effort,'

'Well, thanks. I appreciate your patience and your advice.'

His eyebrows lowered. 'Really?'

I didn't like how incredulous he sounded.

I went to move past him but he stopped me, putting his hand on his elbow. 'No. Don't go yet.'

'I've got to get cleaned up. I'm covered in...' I glanced back at the vent and screwed up my nose.

'You have some muck on the tip of your nose.' He reached up to wipe it off.

My eyes widened, yet I didn't pull back.

Slick's voice came over the intercom. 'Where are you guys? I'm starving.'

Thorn rolled his eyes. 'Come on. Get cleaned up and I'll meet you in the mess. Slick has something special planned.'

He let go of my arm and stepped back. I swallowed. 'Yes, well, I'll just go then.'

While heading back to my quarters, I had the distinct impression that I'd just had a moment with Thorn. We'd connected in a way I hadn't ever experienced before — kind of awkward and raw. The way he looked at me when he wiped the grime off my nose was intimate, like a kiss. Hesitant and honest. I was being me and, I guessed, Thorn was being Thorn.

7

SO CLOSE

A day or so later, the intercom buzzed. 'Miss Gayen's. We are coming up to the coordinates. I thought you might like to be on the bridge.'

I didn't answer straight away.

'Essa?'

Flat on my back, the ceiling came into view. I blinked a few times. I'd been dreaming about selflessness, doing for others and enjoying it. God, what a nightmare!

Thorn's voice intruded again. 'Last call for Essa Gayens. This party is going to start without you.'

'Coming!'

Surging out of bed, I hit the san unit double time and was stepping into my most boring ship suit (a onesie) within two minutes. I bounded down the companionway to the bridge.

Slick was at one of the command chairs, checking the scope. Light on the console flashed different colors. My attention was snared by the view screen — it was filled with black velvet space, an ugly backdrop of asteroids and some light from a distant star.

Thorn turned slightly, not quite making eye contact. 'Take a seat.

There's a ship at those coordinates but we can't raise them. We're scanning the area before approaching.'

'Why? Can't you go straight in? That's my mother out there.'

Our eyes met as I took a seat. 'What?'

'The ship is undamaged. Their comms are working normally.'

My eyes narrowed. 'So they should be able to respond to our hails, if they are on the ship.'

'That's right. No signs of life. There's atmosphere, so no hull breach but it's a sitting duck. A trap, maybe.'

A trap? For who? What kind of trouble was my mother in? How close were these pirates to the center of power? I rubbed my chin. 'Perhaps the crew transferred to another ship for a meeting or something.'

Thorn titled his head, considering it. 'Maybe, depends on what your mother was up to out here.'

I said nothing.

'Do you know what she was doing out here?'

I shook my head. I didn't know *specifically* what she was doing out here. I had a feeling now wasn't a good time to mention the possibility of pirates.

'Illegal trade with renegade aliens? Slave trading—'

'I said I don't know.'

Thorn's eyes narrowed.

I didn't care that he was suspicious. 'Can we dock with them?'

'Yes, but we won't.'

'Why not?'

'Because you know something and I'm not moving until you tell me.'

I nodded, my eyes on the ship outside. I swallowed. It was time to come clean.

'My mother was on the trail of pirates who had infiltrated her company. I don't know what's happened or why she is here. I don't know if there are pirates involved, but,' I said with a shrug, 'there could be.'

Thorn swung away and clicked a few switches. 'It's most likely a trap then. We will proceed with caution. Thank you for being honest, Essa.'

Our eyes met and Slick glanced over at me.

'If we dock with that ship, we get caught,' Thorn said.

'But I need to go there. I need to find my mother and my sister, and that abandoned ship is the only clue.'

There was a grunt from Slick.

'You found it?' Thorn asked, spinning towards the younger man.

'Found what?'

Our attention was fixed on Slick.

He looked up, his eyes moving from Thorn to me. 'Debris from your sister's ship.'

The elevator of my stomach descended. 'My sister?' I plonked myself back on my seat. 'How can you tell?'

'Transponder in the wreckage.'

'Keep scanning,' Thorn said to Slick, before swiveling in his chair to face me. 'Don't worry. I'm sure she's alive.'

'But—'

'But the crew of her hire aren't likely to be. Your sister, Rae, fell into the trap. Or, I should say, her captain did.'

It was a relief that Thorn thought she was alive. 'I need to find my sister and my mother and the only way I can do that is to dock with that ship.'

'No, it isn't.'

Seriously, I was having trouble communicating with Thorn. 'Why isn't it? We just float over there, use thrusters to maneuver, align the docking tube. Easy peasy. Then I check for clues and we leave.'

'I'm not taking this ship over there until I know more about the situation. We will wait and see. The only way over there without jeopardizing this ship is by EVA. I'm not quite ready for that option. In the meantime, this ship stays hidden.'

He pointed to the view screen. A large asteroid neared and we were moving towards it.

'We're hiding in the shadow of an asteroid?' I lifted an eyebrow. It made sense in an infuriating kind of way.

'Yes, we are. I bet the people who are waiting to spring that trap are hiding behind one of their own too.' Thorn powered down the ship's systems, while Slick put the ship in alignment with the asteroid.

'So what do we do? Sit here and wait?'

Thorn leaned back in his chair. 'I guess we do. Unless you have a better idea.'

8

SPRINGING TRAPS

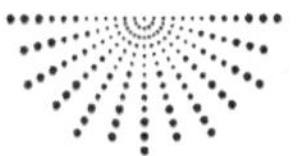

We continued to stare at the screen, watching the abandoned ship surreptitiously until I could stand it no longer. 'We need to spring that trap.'

'Not with my ship. You saw the readout. Your sister's ship was destroyed. She may have gone over there but the crew that flew her here are dead. Is that what you want? Us dead?'

I shook my head. 'No, of course I don't want you dead. But I can't help worrying about them. They could be torturing my mother for access codes — or Rae for that matter, to put pressure on her.'

'And what could you do about that? If we went there they'd capture you too, dispose of us and everything would be the same.'

'What am I supposed to do then? Just wait?'

'For now, yes. I'm mulling over our options.' He lowered his voice. 'Just sit tight, okay?'

There wasn't any point arguing with him. I nodded, and then sneaked a look at the view screen before retreating to my quarters. I found myself wondering what Rae would do in this situation. What came to mind was quite scary. I paced around my quarters, not easy in low grav. I kept bumping into things.

I thought back to what Thorn said about being who I wanted to

177

be. It was terrible. I was wracked with indecision, and confused. If we couldn't spring the trap, why was I here? What did I come for? I couldn't risk Thorn's life or Slick's, I knew that.

The thought of Thorn hurt struck me hard. I found it unbearable. I sat down hard on my bed. I cared about him.

Then I set about wondering how I could care about such an obnoxious person. I realized it was because he'd bothered to look behind my façade and he'd seen what I had to do. I needed to find out who I was and what I wanted. He'd given me good advice. He'd touched the essence of me.

Thorn's voice piped into the room with an update. The sound of it thrilled me, made my skin tingle and my body shiver. There was something wrong with me. I went to the san unit and looked at myself in the mirror. It was still me — brown eyes, brown hair, straight nose, straight teeth, but there was something different, too. A sparkle in my eyes, a softness to my mouth that wasn't there before. I fiddled with my hair, tucking it behind my ears.

His voice sounded again and I held my breath. Thorn reported that my mother's ship was still stationary and they'd counted two bodies in the debris of the destroyed ship. He didn't sound too happy about it. I let my breath out.

I really wanted Thorn to like me, but not at the expense of my mother and sister. To save them, I was going to have to go against Thorn's wishes. He was way too conservative. I thought about the bodies in the wreckage. I prayed that one of them wasn't Rae. Yet, deep down, I knew it wasn't her. My sister had gone onto that ship and set off the trap — just like I wanted to do.

I went over the conversation on the bridge. Thorn said the only other way to get there was going outside using EVA suits. I had EVA training. It was compulsory for us when staying in any orbiting space stations for more than a week, and we'd had orientation on this ship so I knew there was a suit calibrated to me. I'd also checked them while doing my chores and they were all charged up.

But EVA to that ship? It was a bit far. Could I do it? Was I brave enough? If I went, would that spare Thorn and Slick? Could I get back again without them noticing, without the pirates or whoever kidnapped my mother noticing?

I had to think about it carefully. I was prepared to risk myself, but not Thorn, not Slick. I tried sleeping on it but was tormented by what I didn't know. Was my mother okay? Was she suffering? And Rae, silly, ignorant Rae — what had become of her?

All sorts of scenarios went through my head. I could see only three options: stay here, do nothing and leave empty handed, go over to the ship, find a clue to where they were and rescue them, or spring the trap and then rescue them.

But how would I rescue them? If I sprung the trap then I would need to get help.

After dozing for a bit, I put on some clothes and slipped out of my quarters. Thorn was asleep on the bridge. I checked the security code on my handheld and keyed it in. Then I sent off the coordinates and a short message. It would take them a while, but AllEarth Corp security would be better than nothing.

Standing on the bridge, the steady beat of the sensors matched the beat of my heart. Slick was nowhere to be seen, so I guessed he was asleep in his quarters. My eyes traveled over Thorn's sleeping form, sprawled in his chair. His head was thrown back and his blond hair was hanging over his face. With his arms crossed, he looked like he was ruminating rather than sleeping. I was ready to reach out and stroke the hair from his forehead, but I backed away quietly so I didn't disturb him.

My EVA suit hung next to the main airlock. After taking it down, I started to climb into it and double-checked the jet scooter's fuel level. It was full. There weren't any tethers that were long enough to anchor me to the ship and get to the other one, so once I went out there I was on my own. No getting it wrong.

It had been a long night, I thought as I checked the suit's status. I couldn't live with doing nothing, turning around and going home.

If I did, I'd eventually inherit everything when there was no news of my mother, and get on with my life. But that was a random, floating thought. I loved my mother and I didn't need or want her money or the responsibility of running AllEarth Corp. The money was nice to have, but I had enough gumption to earn my own. Even Rae was important to me now. It was a shock to realize it, but it was true. She was the missing part of me. I wasn't going to sit around and do nothing.

I hesitated as I locked the suit down. Was I doing the right thing? Could I get on that ship, find a clue and get off again without springing the trap? I had to try.

I was ready to depart, except for the helmet. Now to slip off the ship without setting off alarms.

My handheld assessed the ship's internal alarm in a flash. I managed to silence and then kill it. Thorn didn't storm down the corridor demanding to know what I was doing, so that was fine. Nor had he changed the ship system's password after I had broken in to fix the Robo Chef. I rolled my eyes. He was a slow learner.

With the alarm dead, I slipped on my helmet and stepped into the airlock. The jet scooter was nestled in front of me. I just had to hold on and steer once I was clear of the ship.

My suit's status showed green, so I punched the lock. The inner hatch snapped shut and a minute after, the outer one zipped out of the way, launching me out into space. I barely kept hold of the jet scooter, the force of expulsion was so strong. I slow circled, which completely disoriented me. Going EVA was my number one fear. I hated it. My stomach knotted and punched, threatening to fill my helmet with puke. Fighting hard to control it, I did a suit check. Everything was sealed up tight.

I breathed hard and then I slowed it down. My heart rate was up, but only keeping calm was going to fix that.

I couldn't engage the jet scooter until I had my bearings. Floating free was the weirdest experience. I fired my suit's thrusters to slow my spin.

The outside of Thorn's ship was dark grey in the shadows and the running lights were dimmed. He really was hiding. If I hadn't known he was there, I would have missed the ship.

As I turned, I saw Mother's abandoned ship and got my bearings. I was upside down in relation to the ship but the jet scooter didn't notice it. I felt so small clinging to the handlebars as it pulled me towards the larger ship.

Actually, it pushed me. Whatever.

I jetted closer, my heart rate monitor going wild and my breath loud in my ears. I looked around for another ship but couldn't see anything. I checked behind me and Thorn's ship was still hidden. I changed direction, slipping behind a small asteroid before darting across to Mother's ship again. Hopefully it would confuse the trail if someone was watching me.

Relief flooded over me as I drew nearer. It wasn't nearly as far as I'd thought it would be. A twist of my wrists and I was aligned with the ship's airlock. This close I could see the scarring from where she had been fired on. So they had been attacked.

My mother was either dead inside or taken hostage. Funny there were no ransom demands. Mind, I wasn't likely to know about them as I was hurrying through space to rescue her and Rae. It didn't matter now. I'd committed myself.

The airlock cycled and the hatch slid aside. I pulled myself and the jet scooter inside. The outer hatch snapped shut and I waited for atmosphere before I released my helmet. I needed to pee. I was still in shock that I'd actually crossed that empty divide and made it there.

The inner hatch opened and I stripped off the suit, leaving it by the airlock. I kneeled down to check the gauges and nodded. There was enough air left for me to get back if I was careful. All the while my ears were peeled, listening for sounds of human occupants. All I heard was the *beep-beep* of messages received and the gurgles and whistles of the active ship's systems.

This ship was Scout Class and could house up to forty occupants. My mother's stateroom was on the next level down. I headed there to use her san unit. One couldn't concentrate with a full bladder.

The atmosphere in the ship was creepy as I pushed myself down the ladder to the next level. My mother's ship didn't carry the full complement of staff. She had Alwin and one other crew member, a senior director, on this trip.

I knew this because I found and cracked Alwin's online diary a year ago when he was staying with us. He was hard to understand. For instance, why did he prefer Rae to me? I was superior to her in every way. Sneaking a peak in Alwin's diary was the only way to learn why. Regular snoops also kept me abreast of his activities. I found all kinds of restricted entries and file notes on his investigation. Last month, I even read the entry on his and Mother's plans. Technically, what I did was an epic breach in AllEarth's security, but because I didn't tell anyone, the information was still secure.

Mother's quarters were four times as large as mine on Thorn's ship. A few things were out of place and there was an incessant beeping. I found the san unit and stripped out of my suit. Why were these onesies so inconvenient?

After relieving myself and checking my hair, I snooped around Mother's cabin. She'd left in a hurry. Her handheld was still there. It was the source of the beeping. I keyed in Mother's password — Rayessa — and a message displayed. It was some sort of code. Had to be. *Inyaface*, it read.

I sat down on the bed. My gaze flicked around the room. Was the clue here? There was nothing obvious. Was it a name? I keyed it into my handheld.

Nothing.

I picked up my mother's handheld again and keyed it in. Then I recollected she was investigating pirates. Didn't Rae say they had funny names? The search came back positive, as Mother had unlimited search and huge storage capacity in her personal database.

Inyaface, alias for Mik O'Dowd, known pirate. Estimated kill date, two years ago, it read. I scrolled down the display. Inyaface appears in communiques. These were linked to Alwin Anton and his investigation.

Further down, I found an old image of Inyaface. It reminded me of something in Al's diary, some kind of biometric assessment of one of Mother's executives. Maybe Inyaface wasn't dead.

There was a noise coming from the bridge. I bounded up the ladder and hit the receive button on the main console.

'Wait till I get my hands on you, Essa. Are you out of your mind?'

'Hello, Captain.'

An inarticulate groan reached me.

'Captain?'

'Thank god you answered. I'm almost there. Meet me at the airlock.' He was very gruff, maybe angry.

'Ooh, I rather not.'

'Essa,' his voice was a growl.

'You threatened me.'

'I was worried.'

Why did he follow me? I didn't expect or want him to. I heard the airlock cycle.

'I'm here. Come down.'

Hastily, I checked the other readouts. There was no sign of another ship, so I slipped out of the chair and made my way to the airlock.

Thorn was peeling away his suit, his pecs straining the thin fabric of his under suit. I raised my eyes. I would have to restrict my fantasies to fantasies. My, but he was built.

'Come here,' he growled at me as he shucked the last of the suit and kicked it free.

I stayed still. Before I could draw breath, he grabbed me by the arm and shook me.

'I ought to paddle your silly backside. What the hell do you think you were doing?'

'I couldn't sit there doing nothing.'

'I wasn't doing nothing. I was thinking about what to do next.'

'Well I didn't know that and I didn't think you'd come after me'

'Why not?'

'I didn't want you in danger.'

That gave him pause. He let out a breath. 'What do you hope to achieve here?' He looked around him.

'I thought there'd be a clue.'

'Was there?

'I found Mother's handheld — I haven't finished looking yet. But it's not safe for you to be here. Go back. I'll be there soon.' I went to climb down the ladder.

'I nearly went crazy searching the ship for you.' I paused and looked back. 'How stupid are you? Do you know the danger you've put yourself in, put me and Slick in?'

'I'm sorry to make you worry.' I looked down the ladder then back at him. He wasn't putting his suit back on. 'I didn't think it was stupid. It was the only alternative that seemed like a good idea.'

'I'm the captain. You should have consulted me first.'

I lowered my head. He was right. 'I didn't want to put you in danger. Please go back now.'

'You overrode my ship's security and then later Slick saw you in the surveillance feed.' I was mesmerized by the soft tone of his voice. 'I think I stopped breathing watching the footage of you spinning, helpless.'

My cheeks were burning. I swallowed, not quite sure how to respond. 'It was a bit unnerving.'

He swept a stray hair off his forehead. 'I called you gutless.'

'You were right.'

'No, I was out of line.'

'No, you weren't.'

He opened his mouth to contradict me. I held up my hand.

'Let's not argue, okay? I was a moneyed-up harpy. You helped me to see clearly, made me decide to change myself, find some "guts".'

He blushed. 'I didn't think you would take what I said to heart.'

'You thought I didn't have one.'

He shook his head and I lifted an eyebrow. 'Okay. I did think you were—'

The blush that flooded his cheeks was wonderful. Maybe I wasn't done with forgiveness.

'Did you find anything?' he asked, changing the subject.

'My sister left me something. A name?'

'What name?'

'Inyaface.'

He paled and stepped back.

'You know this guy? This Inyaface?'

'Only by reputation. I try to stay away from pirates. Inyaface is a key name. If a pirate says it, you ask how far he needs you to go, or how long he wants your services for free.'

I frowned at him, missing the logic. 'If you have stayed out of the way, how do you know this?'

He gave me the I-can't-believe-you-asked-such-a-dumb-question look. 'Independents talk. Word gets around. We all know that name. I've been particularly careful until now.'

'I can understand that, after what happened with your father. There's more to your story, isn't there?'

His bright blue eyes darkened. 'You know I thought they killed my father. That's how I got this ship. Another ship came by after a few weeks in response to the distress beacon. The captain had his crew patch my ship and offered me a berth, even though I was underage. But I was too angry. After that ship left, I flew myself to Prima Nova, as it was the closest inhabited planet. It ended up being a good choice. Because the authorities there were so lax, I was able to claim my father's credit and finish the repairs on the ship.'

I lifted my eyebrow.

He nodded. 'Yeah, the Robo Chef. They said they couldn't fix it. Said it must've shorted during the attack. I guess the lazy bastards didn't even check the software.'

'How long were you on Prima Nova?'

'Three years.'

Heavens, three years in that hellhole. I wondered how he'd come out unscathed.

'That long. So how did you end up with Slick?'

'It was a hard life on the colony. Lots of things failed. The economy, society, families. Slick was one of the homeless. He tried to rob me, but didn't. I took him in and fed him from what I could afford to eat. We grew to be friends. I needed to go but I couldn't leave him behind. I couldn't abandon him to that life.'

I tried to calculate the age he must've been, and Slick would definitely have been underage. 'But Slick would have been a ward of the state.'

'Yeah, right. Like I said, I couldn't leave him there.'

I didn't know that much about Prima Nova but Thorn's account pricked my conscience. There were thousands like Slick left behind. Whole generations of grown humans left to fend for themselves.

Thorn moved to the ladder. 'Come on, let's check out the ship. Bridge first. I need to see what their scanners picked up.'

We headed up the ladder to reach the bridge. 'You were saying about Slick?'

'Right. I had to indenture him so he could get permission to leave. I had no choice. I could have left the spaceport but I wouldn't have been able to avoid the planetary sensors.'

'Indenture? Is that even legal? How old were you?'

'Seventeen, but I had my ID forged so it said eighteen. Because I was from off-planet, a bribe was enough to get the authorization I needed and we took off. I employ Slick as my deckhand and I pay him.'

'You were seventeen and you saved some kid from a life on hell on Prima Nova and have been piloting a ship ever since?'

They had reached the bridge. Thorn spoke over his shoulder as he checked the readouts. 'Pretty much.'

I stood in the doorway, arms on my hips. 'No wonder I annoyed you so much.'

He sat in a chair and looked up from the console, a smile bringing that dimple back. 'Yeah, maybe. I had baggage and you were plain annoying.'

I lifted an eyebrow, sliding my hand up to his shoulder. 'Am I annoying you now?'

He locked gazes with me. I saw his eyes drop to focus on my mouth. My heart rate increased. Was he going to kiss me? Just the thought made my stomach boil like lava.

Sudden impacts on the hull sounded like acorns dropping on the bonnet of a ground car. 'Attack?'

Thorn dived to the ground and took me with him. 'Damn, the shields are down.'

Sparks flew from the command console.

Thorn grabbed my face. 'Put on your suit. Hide.'

I pulled my face out of his grasp. 'I'm not hiding. This is my chance to find my mother. You hide and then follow in your ship. Okay?'

'I can't.'

'You have to. Get your suit on. You can't leave Slick alone.'

He stroked my head. 'I can't leave you.'

'You have to.' I'd had the most horrible thought — I was worth something, Thorn was not. Not to the pirates, anyhow.

'They'll kill you. They won't kill me. I'm a moneyed-up harpy, remember? There's ransom to be had.'

He nodded. 'What if they kill the ship while I'm on it? I'll still die.'

'Look in my mother's stateroom, there's an escape pod masquerading as a wardrobe. Put yourself in there. When I leave, come out and get back to your ship. If the ship is fired on, use the pod to escape. It's rated so it should withstand normal missiles or anything short of nuclear or plasma weapons.'

'Hide with me.'

'I can't.' I got up on my knees. 'I sent for back up. If you are still here and you track the ship attacking us, then can you pass the coordinates on?'

He nodded again. I pushed away to leave and he stopped me.

'Essa!'

I turned back. His eyes had gone soft and a smile lifted a corner of his mouth.

'You should hurry.'

Tugging on my arm, he drew me forward, his mouth capturing mine. There was an urgency and a desperation in his kiss. Too soon, he broke off, leaving me with just the taste of him.

With a nod to me, he walked back down the companionway. I climbed to my feet, clinging to the console.

It wasn't long before a voice came over the comms, all rough and snarly. It demanded me to surrender.

'Who is this? Are you firing on me?' I put on my most offended, imperious voice.

'You bet, sweetheart. What's your name? Quickly now, before I let the big missiles fly and spread your DNA across the galaxy.'

'My, that's original. Been watching too many old vids? I'm Essa Gayens and I take it you have my mother.'

There was a pause, a muffled sound like he was muting the transmission while he consulted with someone else. 'A full house. Prepare to be boarded. Transmit nothing or we'll blow you away.'

'Sure you will. Like you'd toss the money you'd get for my ransom.'

'Look kid, we have the rest of your family. We have all the leverage we need, so don't go over investing in your ass. Take it or leave it. Cooperate or die.'

I pursed my lips. I hadn't thought of that — being unnecessary, superfluous. Before Rae came on the scene, I'd never been superfluous before.

'I'm not going anywhere.'

There were a few more pings as the pirate worked off his anger firing across the bow. I jerked backwards as the main navigation showered me with sparks and ozone filled the cabin.

9

BEING BAIT

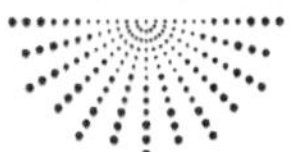

Two obese pirates came through the docking tube, both wearing respirators. I guessed they thought I'd put a hole in docking tube and try to kill them. Hadn't they worked out I was here to get my mother?

Thorn's suit was gone and mine was hanging up next to the airlock. Standing there impatiently, I waited until they noticed me. My pulse was beating fast, but I stood my ground as they bounded towards me. Thorn needed time to hide.

The fattest one darted behind me, grabbed me by anchoring my arms and holding me against his flabby belly.

'Watch it, you creep,' I protested.

The other pirate rocked from side to side, grinning. I thought he looked like a drunken sailor until his slap stung my cheek.

'Where's your ship?' he spoke like a bear, all teeth and gravel.

His body odor hit next and his bad breath. I gagged and then breathed through my mouth. 'I sent it away after I boarded.'

Heavens! I had never smelled anything so gross before. I could bottle it for subversive warfare. I tried to block the smell but my hands were restrained.

Another slap, this once caused a tooth to cut into my lip.

189

'Liar. No way you came on your own. We'll find your friends and we'll fry them.'

My face burned from the impact of his meaty hand. I shook my head to clear it, giving myself time to think. 'I'm a Gayens. We don't have any friends. I came in a single person vessel with auto-pilot. I'm not stupid.'

His gaze narrowed and he leaned in closer giving me a healthy waft of foulness. If he smelled this bad, I wasn't looking forward to being on his ship.

'You look stupid to me.' His gaze centered over my shoulder. 'You got the scanner, Bub?'

Bub? My eyebrow rose. That mountain of quivering flesh was called Bub? Rae was right. Pirates did have funny names. The smelly one grabbed my face, sticking his fingers into my jaw to open my mouth. He stabbed the swab in, shoving my face back with his whole hand over my face. I fell back against the pirate behind me, wrenching my shoulders at the same time. He hadn't loosened his hold on me. The smelly pirate was going to pay for that insult. The scanner beeped.

'Yep, it's a match.' He slapped his comms badge on his shoulder. 'Is the docking tube secure?'

There was a muffle of static and a low, scratchy voice. I saw the receiver in his ear. He nodded. 'Come on, bring her.'

Quickly changing hold, Bub lifted me off my feet, wrapping his huge slabs of meat under my breasts and bounded out of the cabin.

As I was carried horizontally through the docking tube, I panicked. All the things that could go wrong flashed through my mind. They could blow up the ship with Thorn on it. They could kill me. They could disfigure me, which was even scarier. What if my mother and Rae weren't where they were taking me? What if they'd been killed?

I started screaming for all it was worth.

'Shut it,' Bub said and jiggled me until my ribs hurt.

The other hatch opened and we climbed in. The atmosphere

equalized and the tube began to retract. Gravity winked a bit and my stomach felt ready to erupt as Bub put me on my feet.

Smelly pirate grunted. 'Bring her to the main conference room.'

'Sure, Pit.'

'Move it!' Bub shoved me from behind and I stumbled forward. An alarm sounded above our heads.

'What's that?' I asked, not moving after I recovered from the vicious shove from Bub.

'Shut up,' Pit said as he checked the controls on the bulkhead. He talked into his comms unit. 'Just a malfunction with the docking tube retraction. I'll sort it.'

Bub held me by the arm. As he was taller, I just dangled there. 'It happens all the time. Just extend and retract again. That will flush out the airlock.'

Pit nodded. 'Whatever. Get her to the conference room. I'll deal with this.'

Bub swung me around in front of him and shoved. I managed to grab the handrails to stop me falling and then I stepped carefully along the companionway. I had no choice but to cooperate.

The design of the ship was alien to me. The corridors were low and narrow with steel mesh underfoot instead of smooth ferrofoam. Through the grating I could see we were walking above a hold, where crates were stacked and strapped to the hull. It looked like some kind of trading vessel.

How did it overpower Mother's Scout Class ship? She had high-grade, technically illegal weapons. If she surrendered without a fight then there must have been a mole, a turncoat who betrayed her. I discounted squeaky clean Alwin Anton, so that left someone else — the other senior director traveling with them, perhaps.

Bub was none too gentle when he pushed me through the final hatch. My head clipped the table and I dropped. My head spun and I thought I'd bitten my tongue. I was too stunned to move.

'Be careful with the merchandise, Bub Rugby.'

A hand lifted me and plonked me in a chair. I cradled my aching head, feeling sticky blood in my hair from the cut. I looked around the room and dark blurry shapes stood there. I blinked, desperate to get my eyes to focus.

My stomach lurched but I managed to open my mouth and say, 'Who are you? Where's my mother? Where are Rae and Al?'

The sounds I made resembled speech but not the clipped delivery I was hoping for, more like a drunken slur. I rubbed my head again and it didn't help.

A wave of dizziness hit me and I lowered my head into the cradle of my arms. I was going to throw up.

'Put her with the others?'

'Are you sure you want to do that?'

'She's a teenager — a spoiled one at that. There's nothing she can do.'

There was something familiar about one of the voices. I stood up and pointed to where the voice came from. The dark form wavered and blurred in my vision.

'You'll regret this. I'm going to rip out your…your…'

A black wave of nothing swamped me and I collapsed with a *thunk* onto the table.

1 0

REUNION

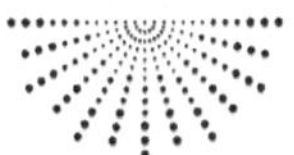

The smell of mother's perfume and the soft stroke of a hand woke me. I opened my eyes, and then shut them quickly as a wave of pain hit. 'Ohh.'

I was nestled in my mother's lap.

'They hit her.' It was Rae's angry, tight voice. A marvelous sound.

I struggled to open my eyes a crack. My vision was still blurry.

'No, I fell.' My words came out globby, like lumps of porridge.

'Essa, darling,' my mother's voice cooed above me. 'Open your eyes. Show me where it hurts.'

I lurched out of her lap to sit on the floor against the wall. My head swiveled, making the world spin. Rae held me so I didn't fall again. My mother rubbed my legs and chafed my hands. I was desperate for a painkiller. I slapped my chest, feeling for my pouch and my handheld.

'No! They're gone.' I was truly naked without my pouch, and more so my handheld. I blinked a few times and rubbed my forehead. My vision cleared. We were in a small room with no furniture, no amenities, nothing. I focused on my family.

'Mother?' Opeia looked tired and grubby but essentially unharmed. I hugged her close.

Rae moved to my side and I slid around to face her. She smiled at me, but I could see a bruise on her jaw. I reached out and ran a finger along it. I'd been wanting to tell her off for being stupid and running off, but as I'd done the same, there was no point now.

'Which one of them did that?' I asked.

Rae lowered her eyes. 'It doesn't matter now.'

My gaze scanned the room, noticing the san unit, a little niche in the wall. Nothing else. Someone was missing.

'Where's Al?' Gaping, I turned to Mother. 'Is he dead?'

She bit her lip before answering. 'No, he's with the pirates.'

'What?' Squeaky clean Alwin was with the pirates? Hang on. I was jumping to conclusions. 'Tell me what's going on.'

Mother sighed and sat down next to me. 'We've been looking to weed out pirates in AllEarth Corp. We had a lead on one that led us to those coordinates, but we were jumped. It was all going to plan but we were betrayed.'

'And Alwin?'

The skin around my mother's eyes tightened, her gaze flicking to Rae quickly before she lowered her eyes to the floor. This wasn't going to be good news.

'When Rae showed up, things got ugly. We tried to get them to let her go, but they wouldn't budge. We didn't expect either of you to follow us. I'm afraid Al took it badly that Rae was also caught in the trap. In the end, they took him away.'

Rae's eyes brimmed with tears and she sniffed loudly. Seeing her hurt wounded me. Surprising myself, I opened my arms. Rae hugged me back.

'I'm sorry, Rae.' I rocked her, and a memory unlocked of my mother rocking me. It was vivid and startling. I cast a puzzled look at my mother. Had she held me like that?

'What do they want? Ransom?' I asked Mother over Rae's head.

Opeia shrugged. 'If it was that simple, they should have let us go before now. They know I won't deal with them, but they want—'

'You to stop hunting them, I suppose.'

If Father had been one of them, then the pirate connection must have gone deep. Alwin's little cyber blitz must have rattled them badly to have gone to such lengths to weed them out.

Mother nodded. 'Yes.' Her mouth pursed up, her fingers held tight against her palm.

'To turn a blind eye to their activities?' I ventured. My mother wasn't that forthcoming, but then, she did think we were children who needed protecting.

She nodded. Yet, there was more. There had to be if she was still held prisoner.

'To be complicit in their activities?' I asked hesitantly.

Mother nodded again and sniffed. Her eyes watered and I could see it was a strain not to give into despair. My mother had a soft side but in business she was tough. She might have inherited her wealth and position, but she'd built them up in her lifetime, quadrupled her wealth and the reach of AllEarth Corp. Now, both her daughters were caught in a trap with her. I knew in my heart she wouldn't agree to any degree of involvement with the pirates.

I sat back, realizing she'd die before she gave in. But now Rae and I were here.

I studied her and realized there was something she wasn't saying, but I wasn't going to push it now. I sighed and looked at them both, rubbing at the wound on my forehead.

'So do either of you have any painkillers? My head is killing me.'

'Let me see,' Mother said, as she examined my head wound. It was a lump with a bit of blood clotting around my hair line.

'We don't have any medical supplies, darling. I'm sorry.'

'That's not very civil of them.'

Mother eyed the door. 'I'll ask them next time they deign to feed us.'

My stomach rumbled. 'So what's the food like around here?'

As if on cue, the door *shushed* open. I saw there were two armed guards outside. A dowdy-looking older woman carried a tray of food inside, kneeled and slid it along the floor. She wore nondescript overalls in a mustard color, which did absolutely nothing for her complexion. Yet, there was something familiar about her.

'Excuse me,' I said, crawling forward. She backed out. 'Could I have a painkiller?'

She caught my eye and shook her head before the door slid shut. Why was that woman familiar? Had we met?

Rae dived onto the tray and lifted lids. 'They only sent enough for two.'

'That's fine. We can share,' Opeia said as she began to divide up the food.

I wrinkled my nose at my serving, which was cold and congealed — some kind of bean stew with dry, undercooked rice. There was a canister of water to drink. Slick's cooking was luxury compared to this.

Shoveling food in and swallowing, I let my thoughts drift to Thorn. I hoped he made it off the ship. I didn't think they had destroyed the vessel, but I didn't know for sure. Sound didn't carry in space, but I'm sure I would have detected large weapons fire through the hull of this ship if they'd fired on the vessel.

Worrying about him made me realize I cared, really cared. I hoped he was free and clear and could give intelligence to AllEarth security when they arrived. I wanted him safe and unharmed. Thorn was important to me. My gaze flicked to my mother and Rae and I smiled, knowing that I did love them.

I hadn't thought it was possible for me to love. It wasn't how I was made. I could fake it, but rarely tried to. Something was happening to me. Some little piece of string that was coiled up inside me was unravelling. When did it start? Was it Rae's arrival or was it Thorn? He definitely made me think, opened up possibilities for my future. I could be who I wanted to be, not who I was, who I thought I was, or what people expected of the little rich girl.

What Thorn thought about me was important. I hadn't thought so at first, but I was realizing now that it did. Did that mean I loved Thorn? I wasn't sure. I think he liked me, despite thinking I was a reckless care-for-nothing. There was a moment there on the ship where we had connected, man to woman, with no filters, no hedging.

I thought of Slick too and hoped he hadn't come to harm either.

Thorn had done a lot to help him. I'd hate to be the one to take it all away. Alwin Anton came to mind, also. I hoped he was okay. Although he didn't care for me, he was important to Rae and part of the family.

I rubbed my head. I was turning into a regular softie with all this hoping and wishing. It must have been a bad head injury.

With the food all eaten, we slid the tray by the door for easy collection. There wasn't much room to walk around or even lie down. The bare floor wasn't comfortable either.

'We should keep the tray,' Rae suggested. 'Then we can hit her over her head and make a break for it when she collects it.'

'Mmm,' I said as I considered her strategy. 'We could, but then we'd get shot by the two guards by the door. They're armed.'

Rae pouted. 'Well we can't just sit here doing nothing.'

'Yes, we can,' Mother said.

Rae snuggled up next to our mother. 'Opi, what about Al? What if...?'

Mother cupped Rae under the chin. 'Shhh...none of that. What did I tell you? Think positively. We know we are worth more to them alive.'

She turned to me. 'So how did you get here?'

'I hired a charter, following Rae.'

'And the charter is...?'

I shrugged. I didn't want to say it was hiding in case our captors were listening, and if Thorn had escaped, I didn't want the pirates chasing after him. So it was best to say nothing.

Opeia leaned her head against the wall and studied the ceiling. I wondered what she was thinking and whether she had a game plan. I knew I sure didn't have one.

'I'm sorry,' I said, and Mother looked at us both and sighed.

A dark thought crossed my mind. What if they let Mother go but kept us, or at least one of us, hostage to make her do what they want? My gaze locked with my mother's and I could tell she had thought of it. She had two daughters to protect now — two interfering daughters. Although, she didn't remonstrate with us at all, I felt guilty for adding to her troubles.

The door slid open. We were expecting the lady to collect the tray, but there was a wrestling match going on outside, with fists, grunts and thumps. After a well-placed punch, a limp body was flung through the door, catching on the tray and sprawling into the room. I shot up, gaping at the body on the floor. I couldn't believe it.

'Thorn?'

DOUBLE THE TROUBLE

Squatting down, I tugged on his shoulder. He had a couple of egg-sized bruises, one on his cheek and one on his head. His blue eyes were unfocused. 'What in stars name are you doing here? Thorn?' I shook him.

Mother and Rae were standing against the wall.

'You know this man?' Mother gaped.

I looked from Thorn to my mother. 'Yes. He brought me here in his ship. He's Captain Thorn Hanover.'

Rae held Mother's hand. 'I met him too. He couldn't bring me because his ship was being resupplied, so he helped me find another charter with a captain who was trustworthy.' Rae looked down and sniffed loudly. 'Captain Milson was very kind. They killed his ship.'

Rae turned her head to mother's shoulder.

Mother patted her head. 'You didn't know.'

'But he died because of me. And his first mate.'

Mother held Rae's face between her hands. 'He brought you to those coordinates, but it was his decision to approach the ship and trigger the trap.'

'Yes, we didn't realise it was a trap.'

'You see, you couldn't have known. It's right for you to feel sorry for what happened, but it's not your fault.'

Rae nodded, but I could tell she didn't believe it. She blamed herself.

'Will he be all right, Essa?'

He was breathing, that was a start. 'I hope so.'

'Why is he here?' Rae asked.

I shrugged.

Rae and Mother shared a look. 'You.'

'Me?' I shook my head. Gently, I ran my finger along his hairline, amazed at the feelings welling up inside me. Touching him made my heart flutter and my gut clench. 'I told him to get away. Now he's put himself in danger.'

The color left my mother's face and she lowered herself down the wall to squat there. 'No, I don't want his blood on my hands.'

I looked at my mother and my sister, letting their words sink in. He'd come for me. The end of my nose stung — I was going to cry. I quickly rubbed at my face and focused my gaze on the wall. I would not blubber like an idiot. Mother was right, now he was in danger too.

Thorn wasn't responding. The longer he was out, the more worried I became.

'Try shaking him by the shoulder,' Rae suggested.

I grabbed his shoulder and nudged a few times, trying not to think of how his muscles had rippled under my fingers when he'd kissed me. I'd been so angry at the time, but touching him brought it back.

Thorn stirred.

'Essa?' he said, struggling to lift himself up.

He squinted at us and, before he lay back down, I edged under him to cradle his head in my lap.

'Thorn, thank heavens you're okay.' I brushed the blond hair from his face. That well of emotion I'd discovered threatened to overflow, but I kept a lid on it. If I let that out now, I didn't think I could stop it.

He smiled up at me and lifted a swollen finger to brush my cheek. 'Couldn't let you go by yourself.'

He had such a soppy look on his bruised face I thought he must have been damaged. He lifted up onto his elbow and took in my mother and Rae. With a nod to them he said, 'You found them?'

'Yes, but we're all prisoners now.'

He nodded and groaned. 'I know, but I couldn't let them take you. I had to make sure you were all right. I thought I could help you escape if I sneaked on board. I'd almost made it, but I was caught in the hold.'

'Is he serious?' Mother asked. 'Escape to where? There's nothing but space between us and home.'

'Don't be negative. It's the thought that counts.'

Both Rae and Mother widened their eyes. I wasn't about to tell them about Thorn's ship or the security force I'd called. Not when we were most likely being monitored.

'Is there any water left in the canister? Thorn needs a drink.'

Rae rummaged on the tray, grabbing a cup. I helped Thorn sip what remained. He lifted a finger and traced the wound on my head. 'They did that. Bastards.'

My mind had calmed, adjusting to the new situation that included Thorn in our little trap. 'I'm okay. Just a headache. The only one they haven't roughed up is my mother.'

Rae sat forward. 'What makes you say that? They took her away for hours and tortured her, trying to get her security codes, access to her bank accounts.'

Swallowing hard, I examined my mother more closely. On the edge of her neckline were little bruises shaped like finger prints and I noticed she shifted occasionally on her behind as if she was sore.

'Show me.'

Mother shook her head and it was then I saw her fear.

'Rae, help her. I want to see what they've done.'

Rae went over to Opeia. Mother was wearing a two-piece suit. Rae unzipped the top and parted it, lifting her undershirt. Her ribs were covered in bruises, and a large hematoma decorated her lower abdomen. Her shoulders had gouge marks and her arms were bruised where she'd been held.

'I'm going to kill them. No one treats a Gayens that way.'

My mother shrugged her jacket back on. 'Essa, while I appreciate the sentiment, this is serious. We need to keep cool heads if we're going to get out of this alive.

I thought of Alwin Anton and looked down at Thorn. This was bad. Having people you cared about in danger was the pits. I had no idea how to get us out of it.

The doors snapped open and we swung around.

'Bring them,' a new voice said.

I couldn't see who it was. The guards turned towards us, guns poised. They jerked the nozzles of their weapons, urging us out. We hunkered out the door, moving slowly. Opeia went first, with Rae and me helping Thorn as best we could. After a few steps, Thorn took his own weight, although he lurched.

Sweat beaded on his forehead. I slowed and Thorn smiled, placing his hand on my lower back. I took comfort in his touch, even though I wished he was somewhere else and safe.

We were ushered into a large conference room. There were a group of people there — some standing, some sitting and one with his back to us. The first sweep of my gaze, as I hesitated on the threshold, missed Alwin.

My second didn't.

Standing along the far wall, he had a fresh scar down his face, temple to jawbone. A chill ran up my spine when I realized he wasn't restrained nor did he appear, in any way, a prisoner. The point of a gun dug into my back and I was forced into the room.

Rae sucked in a breath and she went to take a step towards him before a guard's weapon stopped her.

'Al?' The dismay in her voice clenched my heart. I could feel the betrayal in that one word.

Alwin was one of them. That could be the only explanation for him being free, for him letting this happen.

Mother, Rae and I were forced to sit in chairs. Thorn was left to hover beside us. He swayed on his feet, still dazed from the head wound.

Al's gaze passed over us, but it was as if he didn't see us. His eyes were cold, dark and emotionless. A slight twitch made his eyelid flutter. It was the only thing that let me know he was alive.

The man with his back to us swung around on his chair. He wore a sleeveless vest, and his long, red hair was drawn back into a ponytail. He was clean shaven, looked lean and had heavily inked, muscled forearms. His eyes were very pale blue, I thought, but when I looked again the irises were white.

'Thank you again, Snoop, for delivering this lot to us.'

Al bowed his head, but his expression did not change. Obviously, Snoop was Alwin Anton's pirate name. It fit. He was good at sniffing along cyber trails.

The seated man, who was appeared to be calling the shots, ran his gaze over us. 'Where did he come from?'

All eyes in the room centered on Thorn. I reached up to grab his arm as he looked up, complexion fading to ash.

A tall man with grey-blond hair stepped forward from the back of the room. 'Looks like he broke in when Pit Bull was bringing the other one over. We caught him skulking around in the cargo hold.'

Thorn rubbed his eyes and shook his head. He squinted at the man who was talking. 'Dad?'

A man to the rear stepped forward. His eyes were cyber installs.

Thorn trembled. It must have been a shock to see his father mutilated.

'This your offspring, Ogle?' said the red headed boss.

'Yes, that is my son.' The unseeing eyes glowed eerily red.

My stomach took a dive to my feet, then surfaced somewhere near the ceiling. I really couldn't take more of this. Double trouble, turncoats, backstabbers and Thorn's dead father alive.

'Son,' he replied with a slight nod before turning away.

'I thought you were dead.'

'You were meant to.' This came from the seated man, his inked elbows resting on top of the table. He steepled his fingers before his face, studying us.

Thorn swayed on is feet. Without permission, I slid out a chair and guided him onto it. I glared at Thorn's dad as he retreated to the rear of the room.

Then my words rushed out like a bark, 'You left him alone on a spaceship. You don't deserve to be called a father.'

The head pirate slapped the table. 'He's no worse for wear. Shut your trap. We'll deal with Ogle's little splinter later. Perhaps he'll be willing to join us, seeing as he is so resourceful.'

Thorn's father stayed against the back the wall. He kept his vision centered on the table, lights licking around the edge of his prosthesis. It was ugly. Scars showed around his face, like his eyes had been burned out. Poor man. I shivered at the thought of Thorn becoming one of them. Yet he might. It was his father over there by the wall. A man he loved. I wondered what Thorn was thinking.

The red headed man leaned forward and spoke in a low voice. 'Now, for the record, I'm known as Masher. I don't take shit, so you'd better start cooperating or things could end up being…regretful…'

Alwin leaned down and whispered into Masher's ear. The pirate boss' pale eyes zeroed in on me. 'So, you're the clone.'

My breath stilled and I stood motionless. He'd said it. He'd said the word that had been hanging over my head my whole life. I'd always known — despite mother's stories — what I was. I may have had some of Rae's memories, but I also had memories of the growing case, blurred visions of my father and the attendants who assisted in growing me. I'd never bonded with my mother's touch, or known early laughter or love. Until recently, I didn't believe I could really love or empathize. Not until I met Rae and Thorn.

I closed my eyes. Thorn would not be able to love me now he knew the truth.

'No. They're twins,' my mother blurted, as she leaned across the table, her hands splayed on the table top.

I blinked, released from the spell I was under.

Masher turned to her. 'They share the same name. And you may have fixed the records to get her a birth certificate, but there was a single child on the birth record. The witnesses attest to it. Your husband did a good job on her. Remarkable.'

'I know I'm a copy,' I spat out, relieved finally to get it off my chest.

'Essa no. Don't listen to them.' It was my mother.

Thorn reached out and squeezed my hand. I let it go. They didn't need to know he was important to me.

I turned to my mother. 'It's okay. I've known for a long time, before Rae came back. It wasn't hard to figure out. My father was a geneticist. He cloned people. Why not his family?'

I couldn't bring myself to tell her of my early memories. She'd tried to love me in those early days, just after I was deployed. Did love me now, I had no doubt of that, despite how much trouble I gave her.

I turned back to the pirate. 'What is it to you if I'm a copy?'

He rubbed his chin on two fingers of his steepled hands. His eerie gaze unnerved me.

'You may be useful to us.'

I scoffed. 'By helping you?'

His gaze drifted to my mother and Rae. I swallowed. He had a point.

He sat back and returned his gaze to me. 'We have a clone here we could deploy. Yet she has certain flaws. You could tutor her, show her how you did it, how you imitated the original. For that, I might let you continue your counterfeit existence.'

Mother was moaning into her hands and Rae kept repeating, 'Don't listen to them'.

I frowned at Masher and was about to tell him to shove it where the sun didn't shine, but stopped myself. I could buy time with this. His proposal was ridiculous, I couldn't teach someone else. I had no idea who the clone was meant to be imitating, but if it got me out of the cell, it was worth a shot.

I struck pose, putting my hand on my hip. On the inside, I was laughing. They were ignorant about clones. Except for the memories from childhood transferred from Rae, I did it all on my own. Rae and I were very different. 'Sure, if your clone hass got what it takes, I may be able to help.'

He lifted his chin. 'Bring it in.'

I didn't look at my mother or Rae while we waited. Thorn

slumped forward, leaning his head down. I stepped away, not daring to show concern — not here, not now. They needed to believe I was an ice-hearted clone, reared in the cold gels that nurtured my life, instead of being bathed in warm blood and the comfort of a mother's love.

The door opened and everyone's gaze arrowed to that spot. The dowdy woman who'd brought our food came in, head bowed. She was a clone? I chewed my lips as my gaze flicked back to Masher.

'Meet Gayens' insurance.'

The clone woman lifted her gaze. Now I knew why she was familiar. She was my mother's clone, but not anywhere near as well kept as Opeia. She'd been damaged during her life.

Opeia tried to stand, but the guard thumped his hand down on her shoulder and her knees buckled. Rae's eyes were large, brown and wet with tears. They wanted to replace Opeia with their puppet.

'You want me to betray my family and help you steal my mother's life, her company, her fortune?'

'You are a smart clone, I'll admit that.' Masher lowered his eyelids, but still watched me. His thumb rubbed against his cheek as if he was feeling the bristles there.

I studied the clone and turned back to him. 'What's in it for me?'

I kept my gaze averted from my family. I needed to play it tough now, so tough they believed my loyalty was easily won.

'Besides your life? You get to go free, provided we can ensure your silence. You will be paid well if it works out.'

That was hard to believe. I nodded. 'That sounds interesting. Any sweeteners in there?'

Rae called out. 'Essa don't do this. We love you. You're family. You're my twin.'

I shook my head and looked at her with my sad brown eyes, eyes that exactly matched hers. 'Rae, I'm a copy. I've known all along. Mother pined for you, wanted you. I could never be enough for her. I could do anything, be anything, be the perfect daughter, but it wasn't enough. So I gave up trying.'

Thorn chose that moment to lift his head. Turning to me, he reached out. 'Don't listen to them. You are yourself.'

I dodged his hand. He closed his eyes, obviously fighting pain. I almost teared up.

'No one can take that from you, Ess.' He ceased trying to reach out to me and swallowed. 'And you're not a copy. You're an original. You see, you're taller than your sister. You've a scar here.'

'Listen to him, Essa. You're not a copy of me. Not really. We share the same DNA for sure. But you're a better model than me. I studied the process Dad used. You're smarter than me. Way smarter. Your brain was nourished by nutrients. The formula was scientifically balanced. I had a deficiency in my diet. I can never be as smart as you. Or as strong. You're strong, Essa.' Rae dropped her gaze to my legs and then lifted her gaze to me. 'That's why the cloning ended. Not because people wanted them to have equal rights, the world just didn't want stronger, smarter people. They were afraid.'

My mother patted Rae on the shoulder and when she sat back, I had Opeia in my direct line of sight. 'You choose what's best for you, darling. Know that I have loved you since you have been in my life. You are mine, part of me, no matter how you were created.'

For some strange reason, I felt moved. Tears pricked my eyes. My biggest weakness was the fact that I was a copy, that I was less worthy than anyone else. It was the chip on my shoulder that made me hate the world, made me treat everyone with indifference. It's what drove me. It was my foundation.

Only Rae had penetrated my defenses. Thorn had crumbled them. I wished the circumstances were different. I wished I wasn't who or what I was. I never wanted anyone to know, but being a copy made me feel less than I was. Now that secret fear had been ripped out of me by these pirates and exposed.

The reactions of my family, of Thorn, surprised me. I thought they'd be shocked, recoil — hate me as much as I'd hated myself over the years. But it didn't matter to them. They said it didn't and I believed them.

I remembered Thorn's words, 'You can be who you want'. Having the fact that I was a clone out in the open liberated me from a lie.

I surveyed the pirates. Their eyes were glued to me, waiting for my answer. I was going to play this game — I needed time out of the cell. I wasn't sure what I could accomplish, but it was better than being locked up with no ability to do anything. 'I need time alone with your clone before I can tell if I can help you. She looks worn out, used. She may not pass as my mother no matter what I do.'

Masher nodded. 'I'll give you an hour.'

'They stay unharmed until I give you my assessment?'

He nodded. 'Snoop, take her and Vee to quarters on level two. Pit, see this lot goes back to the holding cell.'

Although groggy, Thorn resisted the guard, shaking off the grab for his shoulder. 'Dad?'

His father looked back as he was leaving the room. 'Later,' he said and the door shut behind him.

Thorn shared a look with me before he was shoved into the corridor. Vee stood by the door. The look of hate I leveled at Alwin made him squirm.

He lifted his shoulders. 'This way, ladies.'

TURNING THE COAT

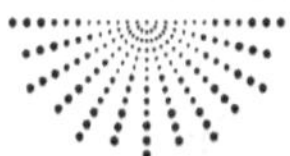

'Keep your betraying, turncoat hands off me,' I hissed at Alwin when he tried to hold me by the elbow.

'Shut up and keep moving, Essa.'

Opeia's dowdy clone said nothing as she walked ahead of us head down. Already, I could tell that she was a lost cause — she was so dispirited, lacking energy. It was hard to imagine her copying my mother, with her drive and intellect. As I descended the stairs, sandwiched between Vee and Alwin, I looked at his feet and had the urge to cut them out from under him. I couldn't do it. It was hard to imagine Alwin turning on us, turning on Rae. Mother had given him a big promotion after he'd found those counterfeit pirate payments. What if it was an act, part of a bigger plan? I just didn't know what to think. The scar, for example, wasn't fake.

The pirates were a pretty vicious lot. Thorn's father came to mind. I'd bet he hadn't been mutilated before he joined them. Once they'd changed him, he couldn't go back to his old life, not with that kind of prosthesis.

Thoughts of Thorn made my gut clench. I sympathized with his predicament. His father had betrayed him big time, left him alone in space and pretended he was dead. Yet, the old man had left a distress beacon allowing Thorn to be rescued, and had hid a message for him. So he did care about Thorn. The pirates had obviously maimed him, so maybe he wasn't a willing participant. Who knew what was going through Thorn's father's head, particularly now he'd seen his son.

We reached level two. I must have been daydreaming as Alwin shoved me unexpectedly, and I nearly fell.

'Keep moving. I don't want any trouble from you.'

I gave him a filthy look, straightened my shoulders and then laughed. 'Trouble is all you're going to get, traitor.'

He punched the control that opened the doors to apparently empty quarters. The clone walked inside, hung her head and stood still in the middle of the floor. I turned to Alwin. 'You've done your lapdog chore, now leave.'

'Essa.'

I put up my hand. 'I don't want to hear your excuses. You're wasting time. I have to assess this clone and I only have an hour. Now, if you don't mind.'

Alwin sighed. 'Fine. I'm locking you in. Anything I can get you?'

Not one to knock back an offer like that, I said, 'Sure, painkillers, a decent meal and my handheld. If you can manage that for the others too, that would be great.'

Alwin shook his head. 'I can't get near them, but I'll see what I can do.'

The door slid shut before I could answer. I moved to the bed and crossed my legs. 'So, clone, what's your name?'

'Vee,' she said without looking up.

'Look at me when you speak. Is Vee your whole name?'

Vee looked up. She had my mother's eyes and the same shaped face, yet there was something fundamentally different. 'Yes,' she answered before lowering her head again. She'd obviously been maltreated. She'd been beaten, I was sure. The shape of one of her cheekbones was out, like it had been broken and badly repaired. Generally, there was an absence of spark, an absence of personality.

I patted the bed. 'Take a seat and let's talk, clone to clone.'

Vee said nothing but sat down as instructed. This wasn't going well. There was no way I could turn this person into my mother, not unless I could get to the bottom of what was bothering her.

'So have you been with the pirates long?'

She nodded. I glanced at the ceiling, schooled my patience and tried again. 'Do you enjoy being with the pirates?'

She shook her head.

'Tell me?' I lifted her face using my finger under her chin.

The eyes that met mine were desolate. I could imagine her life in that one look and I didn't really want to. I sat for a few minutes more, waiting, but she sat in silence and I let her.

The door swooshed open and a guard walked in with a tray. I spied painkillers and the aroma of the food was heavenly. There was enough for both of us.

The guard left and I pounced on the painkillers. A bottle of mild stim was on the tray and I downed a few mouthfuls to wash down the pills.

I lifted the cover on a plate and handed the food to her. Under the next cover was my handheld. Vee was focused on her food, so I slipped my handheld out of sight, trying to keep my breathing calm.

I was surprised he'd given me that. There was more to Alwin than first appeared.

'Yummy food,' I said, as Vee hunched over her plate. The food was disappearing at a fast rate, like she was used to it being taken.

While she was distracted, I took the chance to slip my handheld into my pouch and secure it in my suit before forking some of the meat into my mouth.

As I ate, I remembered my mother had said she'd destroyed her copy, but it looked like my dad had made another. This one didn't appear to have mother's memories or her personality. That didn't explain the rest of her behavior though. My bet was she'd been abused, used as a slave. Maybe this was what would have happened to Rae if she hadn't been found — or to me if I hadn't been swapped into Rae's place.

Appalled, I digested that realization. I cast a surreptitious glance at Vee and knew that her fate could have easily been mine. Clones had rights and lives, but obviously it didn't apply to all of us. Some slipped through the fingers of the law, particularly if underhanded, low-life criminals were in control

I shook my head. What was I doing? I was identifying with clones. Why, for heaven's sake?

Because I was one.

I wasn't used to acknowledging it, but I was a copy. Not the real deal. I've known for an age and hid what I knew. Now it was out there. Rather than addressing my inability to bond or empathize, I'd squandered my privileged life. But, at least it had been privileged, not like Vee's.

I watched Vee closely. Despite what my father was and the things he'd done, he had nurtured me well when he grew me, he made me into a superior copy. Compassion arose in me as I realized that had not been Vee's fate. Mine wasn't even a hard life, Vee had been abused and used and never valued.

After she ate her food, I reached out to Vee and touched her shoulder. She jerked and looked up at me with eyes that held wildness. 'You don't have to do anything you don't want to. We can work something out.'

Her gaze held mine and she nodded before picking up her bottle of stim. I regretted being away from the others, even though it was only an hour. Despite the painkillers and the food, I fretted.

'You can rest if you want. I won't hurt you.'

Vee slid off the bed, leaving her bowl on the tray. She sat on the chair and curled herself up into a ball. She faced the door and although she closed her eyes and appeared to sleep, I knew she was alert. Vee had lived in fear for too long to relax. There was no way I could make her into my mother. It would be hard enough if Vee was willing and able. I shook my head and lowered it. The painkillers were working and I felt drowsy.

The sound of the door opening roused me. Had I fallen asleep? Vee stood hunkered down by her chair. Alwin was there.

'How did you go?'

My gaze slid to Vee. 'You've seen her. What do you think? A no-brainer. How do they think they can treat someone like that and expect her to be…well pretend to be someone she isn't.

Alwin lowered his brows, causing his scar to twist. He gasped and raised a hand to touch it. I wondered how he got it, but wasn't going to ask. 'I'll take you back to the cell and let the boss know.'

I wanted to rant at him, to tell the boss pirate what I thought about how they'd treated Vee, but bit down on it. I had my handheld secreted away. There was no point in risking what I'd gained by being out of the cell.

I headed out, Vee hovered there.

Alwin noticed. 'Stay put until someone calls you.'

The door slid shut and we walked down the corridor.

Facing Alwin I asked, 'So Thorn's dad—'

'I don't know anything.'

'What happened to his eyes?'

He shrugged as he gestured for me to precede him. 'You're so smart. You figure it out.'

I turned and nearly stumbled when he shoved me from behind. I sneered at him. 'Feel better now that you can beat up a defenseless woman? It's what you pirates are good at.'

We neared the guards, holding their weapons as they stood in front of the now-familiar door.

Alwin leaned in close and hissed into my ear, 'You're not defenseless, Essa. You should listen to Rae sometimes.'

The door of the cell slid open and Alwin shoved me inside. It was so unexpected I barreled into the room and sprawled on the floor.

The door slid shut.

Picking myself up, I looked around the room and sucked in a huge breath. 'Where's Thorn?'

13

SECRETS AND LIES

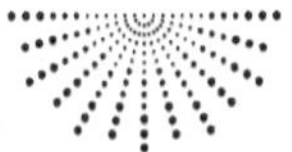

The room was too small to pace, but I was too anxious to sit still.

'What are you going to do, Essa?' Rae asked. 'If you can't train the clone, what will happen?'

I shook my head. Thorn had not returned and I was worried for him. He was in trouble because of me.

'Essa, are you listening?'

Swinging around, I saw two sets of anxious eyes staring at me. 'What can they do?' I asked, thinking out loud. 'Make you cooperate with them?'

My gaze centered on my mother. 'That might mean more torture or...' I had a nasty thought.

Opeia nodded. She'd known all along what the options were.

My gaze shifted to Rae. 'Leverage. They'll use one or both of us to force her cooperation.'

Without voicing my next thought, I sank down on my haunches. They only needed one of us to keep our mother in line. The other would be killed to show they meant business. I was the expendable one.

My stomach dropped to the floor and I had to kick my legs out to sit down before I toppled. The realization that I would be killed was quite calming. In fact, I had to volunteer. It only seemed right. I had the life that Rae should have had, now it was time to let it go.

My head dropped to my chest. The next thing I knew, arms enfolded me.

'We'll work something out, Essa. We'll all get out of here. Don't you worry.'

I turned into my mother's shoulder and sobbed. Her words didn't comfort me. They only confirmed my worst fears. My mother may not have given them the codes they wanted while under torture, but she would not stand by and let them hurt one of us. And I couldn't let her throw her life away.

When I quieted, I shifted away from my mother and stared into space. Eventually, my brain kicked in. My handheld was pressed against my chest. I could use it. I scanned the room, looking for some kind of access port. I had a means to get us out. I'd just climbed to my feet when the door zinged open.

Thorn was tossed through it, colliding with me. I grappled with him but we both ended up on the floor in a tangle.

Opeia and Rae were on their feet, calling out enquiries. 'Is he all right?'

'What happened?' I asked him.

Thorn had a bandage on his head and his sky blue eyes met mine. 'You're okay?'

The fear fled out of me like air through cracked hull plating.

He nodded, giving my hand a squeeze before we both climbed to our feet. 'I've had the head seen to and was given some top-of-the-line pain meds,' he said, looking me over. 'How did you get on with the clone?'

I shook my head. 'A bit of a lost cause.' My hands balled into fists just thinking about Vee. 'Did you learn anything from…Ogle?'

I wasn't about to call him 'your dad'.

Thorn's eyes widened and he rubbed his chin, which was now covered with stubble. 'A little.'

Opeia came forward. 'That's informative. Is there anything concrete you can tell us?' This was the Opeia from the boardroom, used to dealing with executives that gave her all the information she wanted, on demand.

Thorn turned towards her, eyes darkening. 'Make an escape plan and be quick about it.'

'I agree,' Opeia said. 'What are our assets?'

Rae held up her hand. 'What if the room is bugged?'

'Good point.' I turned away, stretched a thumb into my pouch and pressed a small button on my handheld. It broadcast interference to any electronic listening device. It was the deadliest heavy metal cross gangster rap in my database. It was an antique but it did the job. 'Okay, let's talk.'

Thorn eased his neck and rubbed his shoulder. 'If we can get to an escape pod, my ship should be able to pick us up. Slick had orders to follow.'

My mother's eyebrows raised and then she titled her head to look at me. 'And?'

Damn my mother was perceptive. 'I have my handheld. If I can find an access port, I can get us out of here.'

'How did you get that?' asked Rae and Thorn simultaneously.

'I asked for it,' I replied with a shrug. It was the truth.

'Sure you did,' Rae responded.

Mother nodded. 'With the handheld you could scramble some critical systems, but I think internal security and de-linking the escape pods from the alarm takes priority.'

'I can do that with this,' I said, tapping my handheld.

My mother's eyes narrowed, but she closed her mouth. I figured she knew about my side operation and had kept her mouth closed. Interesting. My mother was a clever woman. Not that I'd ever doubted it.

'Essa and I can handle logistics,' Rae said, putting her hands on her hips.

Thorn's eyes widened. 'What logistics?'

Rae looked him up and down. 'If you're up to it, you can help. It's called beat the dumb pirates at their own game.' One of her fists slammed into the other.

She did know martial arts and she wasn't bad in low gravity. My gaze assessed Thorn. He did look better. Maybe he'd had the same painkillers I had. His father owed him that much.

'Will your father come with us?' I asked Thorn.

He shared a look with me and then shook his head. 'No. He can't. Won't.'

'It would be good to have inside help, someone to watch our backs,' Opeia said as I went to the wall, looking for a small hatch that hid the room's security, and maybe a passing conduit to ship's systems.

I thought of Alwin and I wasn't sure. He did get my handheld. Alwin may not know what I could do with it, but still, he wasn't that stupid. I tried to recall everything he'd said. He told me to listen to Rae. And what was that about my strength? I couldn't say anything though. I couldn't give Rae false hope, and if Alwin was on our side, I didn't want to jeopardize his life too.

Thorn took out a small piece of foil and held it out to Opeia. 'I brought you this. Sneaked it off the med tray. It's a painkiller. Works like a dream.'

Opeia took the foil and opened it.

'Take it, Opi,' Rae urged. 'We need you in the best condition. We may have to fight and run.'

With a nod to Rae, Mother put the small tablet on her tongue. 'Look for something we can use as weapons. The water canister, for instance. The tray.'

Thorn and Rae dived on those items, while I continued to scan the walls. The logical place for the hatch was by the door, but there was nothing there. Thorn lifted me so I could run my hands over the top of the doorway, near the ceiling. There were no ceiling grates, as it was just one piece of metal. It was possible to blast through but as we had no weapons or explosives, so that wasn't an option.

I continued to search, worrying at the back of my mind that we might get interrupted. For that reason, I kept my handheld hidden. I thumbed the switch and turned off my music broadcast. It could make them suspicious if I left it on too long.

Opeia was pacing and Rae leaned against the wall with her hair hanging over her face. I could sense her despondency. I wished there was some way I could alleviate it, but I couldn't. Alwin had betrayed us all and even if I had the slightest doubt that he was actually a traitor, there was no point in me voicing it. Things could turn out ugly.

As much as I accepted that I was the one who would die, I'd rather matters didn't get that far. If I could get Mother and Rae off the ship with Thorn then I could die happy. I shook my head at my thoughts. Thorn lowered me down and I then crawled along the floor.

'Found one.' The hatch was tiny and well hidden. I ran my hands around the join, looking for a press point to spring the cover. It hadn't been sprung in quite a while and it took a bit of jiggling. Thorn hovered above me.

'You're in my light, do you mind?'

Thorn hunkered down beside me and ran his hand up the back of my leg. 'Better?'

A shiver passed over my skin. I glanced at him over my shoulder. 'That's distracting.'

He moved away. 'Better?'

'Slightly.' I lowered my voice. 'How are they holding up?'

The little hatch sprung open and I slid my handheld out of my pouch.

Thorn turned towards them and chewed his bottom lip. 'Okay, I think. Your mother needs medical attention.'

'Internal bleeding?' I asked

His eyes met mine. 'I think it's likely.'

My mother was holding up, but that hematoma on her abdomen was bad news. If she didn't get help, she could die. Then the pirates wouldn't have any use for us. Their plans would be wrecked.

I tried to get the handheld to sync with the room's security, but it couldn't engage. I could see there was a larger conduit in there but it was too hard to access without ripping out more of the circuitry.

Thorn leaned in closer so he could talk privately. 'I'm no expert, but I have some training. She's sweating. Although the painkiller is helping for the moment, it won't help the underlying problem.'

'Good. I think she'll hold up.' I prayed she would hold up.

'Essa…'

My gaze flicked to Thorn's and my heart clenched. 'Yes.'

'If we get out of this…'

My app synced to the room's security. 'I'm in.'

Thorn stopped talking and I was glad. I didn't want to think about the future, the future where I would be dead. But as my app analyzed the security system, I did let a slight sliver of a possible future unfurl in my mind. In that future, I was with Thorn on his spaceship, living our lives how we wanted.

I stamped down on those ideas and focused on busting us out. 'I can open the doors. If you give me a bit longer, I can try to disarm the internal alarms but I'm afraid it won't take them long restore it. There are too many variables.'

We shared a look. 'Do we break now and try to disarm later?' I asked, my eyelids lowered so my mother couldn't read my expression.

Thorn's gaze flicked to the others. 'I think we have to risk it. We might get separated.'

'Get ready then.'

Thorn called to the others. 'Rae, Mrs Gayens…'

The door snapped open. Thorn and Rae bounded out, taking the two guards by surprise. Rae bashed one repeatedly with the water canister. Thorn wrestled with the other one for the gun. Luckily, the guard hadn't had his finger near the trigger. Mother raised the tray and brought it down on Thorn's guard's head. It was enough to stun him.

'Shove them in here.' I was still on the floor, synced to the room's security, keeping the door open. Thorn nodded, then punched Rae's quarry in the face, sending him sprawling into the room. It saved us time. Rae helped drag the other guard into the room.

'Wait outside. I've got to time this right.'

I had to make sure I didn't leave any trace, except a few minutes of blank space in the audit logs. I prepared to disengage the sync and readied myself to bolt for the door. Because the handheld's range was limited, I had to be quick.

Thorn stood in the doorway, hand out ready to grab me. I climbed to my feet, crouched to maintain the connection.

'Now,' he called.

I bolted, snatched Thorn's hand and was tugged out as he dived clear of the door.

'Which way?' Rae asked, panting heavily. She had grazed knuckles and a bruise forming under her left eye.

Opeia had the metal water canister and was tapping it against her palm, looking absolutely feral. She was really pissed. I lifted an eyebrow. I didn't realize Mother had it in her to smash heads. They really must have hurt her bad when they tortured her.

'This way,' Thorn said as he bolted.

I sighed as I jogged after him. 'Come on. Best stick together.'

Thorn's feet stamped down the stairs to the next level. I checked around the corner to see if anyone was about. As there wasn't, I waved Rae and Mother ahead before bringing up the rear. Sounds of an altercation reached me. I wanted to push the others out of the way and get to Thorn.

Mother leaped from the step in front of me. A dull thud resounded as the canister met skull. Mother stopped to kick the downed pirate in the ribs. He looked young and thin and reminded me of Slick. Mother's boot didn't make the pirate twitch. She was pretty lethal with that canister.

Thorn checked the wall. 'This way.'

As I jogged past, I saw he was looking at the safety notice, which pointed out the nearest escape pod.

A shout behind me made me turn back. Three pirates were heading down the companionway, running as they held the handrails.

'Rae?' She was behind me. 'Thorn, get Mother to the escape pod. We know the way. We can catch up.'

Silence greeted me. I turned slightly. 'I'm staying.'

Thorn's eyes were pleading.

I shook my head. 'Please, it's her they want. Get her to safety.'

Thorn's eyes darkened and he nodded. He and Mother kept going. I deflected the punch of the first pirate. He was a bit surprised by my block and counterstrike. I heard his nose crunch and he fell to his knees. The next one leaped over the first and was greeted by a kick to the groin by Rae, who then punched him while he was down.

'Not bad,' I said. 'Those extra karate lessons paid off.'

The third pirate was going for his weapon — not as dumb as the other two that lay senseless on the companionway. I leaped up, scissor-kicked the gun out of his hands and it sailed over the rail to the level below. Rae finished him with a roundhouse kick to the head that slammed him against the bulkhead. I stood on his out-flung hand and heard a satisfying crunch of bones.

'Run.'

Rae didn't need prompting. She was good on her feet, hardly needing the assistance of the handrails. Me, I clung for dear life. Rae stopped suddenly and I barreled into her.

I recognized the corridor. This was where I left Vee. Suddenly, I couldn't see myself leaving her behind. I could have been her and I had to save her.

'Wait here.'

Rae swung around. 'What are you talking about?'

'Give me five and then go without me.'

Rae's face turned red and her fist curled.

'Please. It's important.'

Rae nodded and hid in a wall niche. It wouldn't hide her, but it did make her less noticeable. I ducked down the corridor and used my handheld to open the quarters where I had assessed Vee. She was still there and jumped to her feet when I entered.

'Come with me.'

Vee stood still, shook her head.

'We're getting out of here. Come with us.'

Again she shook her head, her eyes wide.

'Come and live life away from here, Vee. We'll take care of you. Trust me.'

I held out my hand. Vee looked at it. 'Please hurry,'

Something moved behind her eyes, some instinctive sense of survival. She grabbed my hand and ran with me.

Rae joined us at the corridor. 'You're brining Opi's clone?'

'Yes. It's a long story.'

Rae nodded to Vee. 'Stick with me then. Essa's got work to do with the ship's systems before we leave.'

We ran down the corridor, nearing the bay holding the escape pods. But a mountain of flesh stood in our path. It was Bub Rugby.

Rae looked at me sideways as we backed up. 'Remember what I said, Essa. You're stronger than me.'

'Sure.' I pushed down the fear boiling in my gut. This was one huge man and I was pretty sure I couldn't stop him if I tried. Yet Rae was with me. She lashed out, aiming to cut him down at the knees. I aimed for the face. He leaned forward as Rae's hit unsuccessfully tried to down him. He blocked my gouge, but missed my punch to his stomach. He doubled up, my hard fist penetrating his soft flesh. Rae thumped down hard on the back of his neck with her bare hands. I went for it too, and mine slammed him down.

'Quick,' Rae said, leaning around the corner. 'Coast is clear.'

She grabbed Vee's hand and tugged. I kicked the hulk on the ground in the family jewels, before diving around the corner. He wasn't out, as he cried out like he had tears in his eyes. He'd be after us in a couple of minutes, although he might be limping for a while.

We reached the gantry where the escape pods were. Thorn was waiting, waving at us to hurry.

'I have to disengage the alarms first.' I didn't have time. Bub Rugby or some other pirate would be after us soon. We'd left a number of injured pirates in our wake. 'Rae, take Vee and go strap yourselves in. If we're interrupted eject the pod anyway. You too, Thorn.'

He shook his head. 'I'm watching your back.'

I was in luck, the bulkhead had a thick conduit running along it with secondary ones snaking in different directions. I kneeled down to access one of the secondaries, hoping to come into the system by a back door. The secondaries were there in case the main conduit was damaged during an attack.

My handheld synced quickly but it took a while to identify the escape pod systems. They were rather complex, being connected to a number of systems.

I heard a shout. Heavy boots reverberated along the metal grating I was crouching on. A quick glance told me it was Bub Rugby and he looked really pissed. He limped and I smiled. At least I got him where it hurt. I couldn't deal with him and the ship's security systems.

'Thorn,' I said with clenched teeth. I was high in the back end of the ship's systems where I wouldn't be noticed and it was working. These pirates were scum — I could do all kinds of things while in these sensitive ship systems but, with so many lives at stake, I couldn't do it. I thought of Alwin, and even Thorn's father. I couldn't have their deaths on my hands.

Thorn charged for Bub Rugby and was swatted away, rolling as he hit the rail. He shook his head, stunned for a moment. Bub was heading for me — the girl who'd stamped on his balls. I left my handheld there, hoping it would diagnose which code I needed to alter.

Thorn called out, still trying to pull himself up. A ribbon of blood curled down his neck. 'Watch out.'

I stood up and faced off with the big guy. He growled and lunged for me with his arms spread wide. I ducked, using his momentum to push up as his body tipped over me. I pushed for all I was worth. He was one heavy pirate. Yet I had power in my legs, fed by desperation — and maybe something else I'd never tapped into. I had hidden strength. Perhaps there was conditioning there that prevented me using it, but now that I was desperate, power surged through me.

Jumping, I raised my foot to hit him in the jaw when he landed, but he was quick and moved, blocking my kick and sending me sprawling.

'Thorn?'

Thorn had inched over to the handheld and checked the readout. 'Not yet.'

Bub was moving but I was faster. I grabbed him from behind around the throat. I squeezed and Bub tried to pry my hands off, at the same time using his weight to crush me. I screamed, squeezing for all I was worth. I just had to hold on and he'd pass out.

Thorn called out. 'It's got it.'

'Hit engage.' I called through gritted teeth.

Thorn stood up, looking for something. He wasn't leaving.

'Get in the pod,' I shouted through gritted teeth.

The strength was leaking out of Bub. He still fought me, but his movements were sluggish and had less force. After what seemed like an age, he went limp.

Thorn nodded and entered the pod.

Struggling out from under the mountain of flesh, I dived for my handheld and checked that the three ways the escape pod eject sequence would alert the bridge had been blocked. I was weakened. I was breathing hard and my arms and legs felt like lead.

Crawling, I reached the pod and saw everyone was inside and strapped in. I used the hatch to help pull me upright. When Thorn's face changed, I knew Bub was up again.

Turning, I saw him looming large. Rage exuded from him, quivering his excess flesh. I had nowhere to go. Our escape was ruined, we weren't going to get away. Bub had his arms outstretched, his lips tight over his snarling teeth. A feral growl filled my ears.

I stumbled back into the pod just as the sound of a shot echoed in the corridor.

Bub crumbled.

With the last of my strength, I hit the eject button and lunged for a safety harness. The hatch snapped shut. I prayed that it all went to plan as I tried to buckle in. A face appeared in the hatch window.

'Alwin!' Rae yelled, fighting her harness.

I gaped at him, wondering if he would set off the alarm and wondering what would happen if he didn't, how he could explain it all. Stay safe. He banged on the window as if he was beating it in frustration.

As the thrusters fired and we pushed away from the ship, Alwin's face grew smaller and then faded.

Rae screamed as we plummeted away from the ship. There was no more time to think about Alwin. If he set off the alarm, our trip would be short. If he didn't, we still ran the risk of being picked up by the ship's sensors.

'Can we maneuver this thing?' Mother yelled at Thorn. 'We're sitting ducks out here.'

Thorn was near the navigation console. He ran his gaze over it, hit a few buttons. 'It only has some thruster capability to avoid debris or an orbit. We can't go anywhere.'

'What if they come back?' Opeia asked. 'We need to be away from their trajectory so we won't be so easy to find. Can't you use the thrusters to change our direction?'

'Yes, we can do that Mrs Gayens, but that would make it hard for Slick to pick us up.'

I closed my eyes to sort through the competing thoughts in my head. I breathed slow and deep.

Thorn unstrapped himself and floated towards me. 'Are you hurt?'

I shook my head. 'No, I'm thinking things through. Alwin must have shot Bub to help us get away.'

'I knew he hadn't betrayed us,' Rae said. 'We have to go back for him.' Tears had left a trail on her cheeks.

Both Thorn and I turned to her. 'How do you suggest we do that? We're not even sure we've got away.'

She shook her head and then turned to Mother. 'Opi?' Rae pleaded.

Opi held Vee, who sagged when released from the straps. 'You're as safe as we are, Vee. No promises just yet.'

Vee looked at her original and there was a light in her eyes. 'Thank you.'

'Do you know who I am?' Mother asked.

Vee nodded. 'You are the template. The original.'

Opi touched Vee's face. 'I'm sorry for what has happened to you. I'll do what I can to help you. I can't undo what has happened in the past, but I can help you have a better life. Do you trust me?'

Vee nodded. 'Thank you for not killing me.'

I'd never seen real rage on my mother's face before. She swallowed once and the expression faded. Turning away from Vee, she said, 'Alwin has his own path. We don't know for sure he helped us. He could raise the alarm and they'll be here to pick us up any minute.'

'Mother! How can you say that? That's Alwin. My Al...he wouldn't...couldn't.'

Mother kept her face impassive. No wonder the pirates couldn't get information out of her. I couldn't tell if she thought Alwin was a traitor or a hero.

The pod jerked. Thorn looked out the view screen. 'I can't see who has us.'

'It's a bit soon for Slick, isn't it?'

'I don't know. How long have we been arguing?'

'It's not too soon for the pirates to have come back and found us if Alwin raised the alarm.' Mother delivered that deadpan.

Rae sucked in a huge sob and wiped tears from her eyes with her forearm. Vee backed up against the wall, a bit overwhelmed by all the voices, all the action. I caught her eye and nodded, hoping to appear confident. Her life had been crap so far. I didn't want her possible death to be worse than that. It wasn't why I rescued her.

Clamps grabbed the pod and drew us inside a dark hold. Thorn readied himself to pounce on whoever opened the door. If it was the pirate ship, I wasn't looking forward to meeting Bub, given how mean I'd been. Rae was a mess, half anxious to see Alwin again and half scared to be back into the hands of the pirates.

Mother sat calmly, wasting no energy on fretting. I considered that. No wonder she was a successful businesswoman. Now I understood where I got my nerve from. I was like my mother. I was a Gayens.

Then there was nothing. No one came to open the pod. We were left in a dark hold, not knowing if we were recaptured or rescued. I didn't like waiting and neither did Thorn. He thumped the hatch.

'Should we open it?' Rae asked, a touch hesitant.

Thorn shook his head. 'We don't know if there's atmosphere out there. There are no sensors in here.'

I unstrapped my harness, went up to Thorn and massaged his shoulders. He glanced at me, a flash of hope in his eyes.

I shook my head. 'My handheld is full of useful apps, but not one that can detect if there's atmosphere out there.'

'How much do we have in here?' my mother asked.

Thorn glanced around the interior of the escape pod. 'It's rated for two weeks for one person.' He studied us, doing some mental calculations. 'A few days.'

'I hope whoever picked us up figures that out.' I sat back down in my seat and folded my arms. It had seemed such a good plan. All that excitement about escaping and now we were back in limbo, as we had been in our cell.

'No point in stressing about it,' Thorn said. 'Maybe we should take a moment and rest up. I must admit the painkillers I took are wearing off.'

He came up beside me and took my hand. 'You?'

A headache had been growing behind my eyes. It wasn't debilitating but I felt tired too as the drug left my system. 'Yes, it's wearing off.'

'May I?' He indicated the spot next to me. After a nod from me, he was there beside me, a warm, large body.

'I'm sorry I got you into this,' I said quietly. Mother was comforting Rae and organizing Vee. Thorn's strong arms embraced me. I gasped and he grinned, which helped me relax. It was so right to be in his arms.

'I'm glad we're safe. I'm glad you're safe,' he said softly in my ear.

My heart beat erratically at the sound of his voice. 'I never meant for you to get caught up in this.'

'I know, but you've been marvelous at getting us out. You know, I saw my father again and as confronting as it was, it was worth it. And you got your mother and your sister back. There's nothing scabby about that.'

I nodded, liking the soft look in his eyes. 'So, do you still think I'm a moneyed-up harpy?'

'Oh, definitely.'

I pulled back, my face showing all my shock.

He laughed at my expression and leaned in close to whisper in my ear. 'What I want to know is will you be my moneyed-up harpy?'

He drew back to catch my expression. Tears pricked in my eyes. He knew I was a clone. I'd been a right pain in the butt, but still he found something to like. 'I'm not sure in what capacity.'

He smiled. 'The thought occurred to me that I could use someone as handy as you on my ship—'

'And?'

I watched his eyes, the slight flare of nostrils before he leaned in to press his lips to mine. His kiss was gentle and sweet. I liked it, but wanted more. We separated.

'Not very convincing,' I said.

He came in again and captured my mouth, his arms tightening. His kiss possessed me, took me on a journey where my heartbeat thumped in my ears and my breath was stolen away. His tongue engaged with mine and it was divine.

When we separated, me still within his embrace, he asked, 'Better?'

I smiled, closed my eyes and rested my head on his chest. It was like being home. 'Definitely.'

The tapping from outside woke me. Thorn lifted away from my side, instantly alert.

Rae had her arms around Opeia and they both turned their heads to the hatch. Vee lifted her head, her gaze still desolate, face expressionless. It was like she was ready to be taken back and had given up hope.

'It's opening,' I said to the others.

Thorn stood by the hatch, concealed from view. A head appeared. I saw greasy hair and a lopsided grin.

'Slick,' I yelped.

Slick screwed his face up as he looked left and right. 'Where's Thorn?'

'Here,' Thorn said, coming into view. 'You did it!'

Thorn launched himself out the door and picked up the younger man and swung him around.

I climbed out and smoothed my ship suit. 'What took you so long? We were out of mind with worry.'

Slick swept hair from his forehead. 'Patience is a virtue, little harpy.'

'You'll regret that, little greenhorn.' I grabbed and hugged him.

'So if you lot are in here, who is in the other escape pod?' Slick asked, shoving a hank of greasy hair out of his face.

Our eyes swung to the other escape pod that Slick had retrieved.

I swallowed. 'Not Bub Rugby?'

As I spoke there was a bang on the escape pod's door and I jumped. Palpitations signaled my unease.

'What's going on?' Rae asked, climbing out the hatch.

'There are two escape pods,' I replied.

I saw a light leap into Rae's eyes. 'Alwin!'

Thorn shook his head. 'We don't know that.'

'But you can't leave whoever it is in there.' Rae made puppy-dog eyes at me and Thorn.

I grabbed Rae's arm to stop her running over and getting in the way. Thorn assessed the round metal contraption, his top teeth biting his lower lip. 'Slick, get my weapon.'

Slick ducked out of the hold and came back carrying a pulse weapon. A nasty thing that burned deep into flesh. He locked gazes with me and nodded. He and Slick went to the hatch. The banging grew louder. Whoever it was, wanted out.

After a nod from Thorn, Slick keyed the control that would open the hatch. I held my breath and Rae squished my forearm, her nails digging deep, her eyes riveted to the dark hatch. A bloodied hand flung out and a dark head appeared. We stood there like dummies.

'Doesn't look like Bub Rugby,' I said.

Rae let out a cry and bounded off, nearly pushing me over. Alwin's head lifted up at the sound, his scar livid on his face.

Rae leaped through the opening, nearly smothering Alwin.

Thorn and I shared a look, then a grin, which turned into a laugh. 'Looks like he wasn't a baddie after all.'

Opeia had climbed out. 'Of course he's not.' She peered around me, and then let out a relieved sigh.

'Give me a hand,' called Rae. 'He's injured.'

Thorn went over to help extract Alwin. He nodded when Rae gave him instructions, clucking over Alwin as if he was fragile as broken glass. Both of them bore it well. My heart rate had dropped back to normal and I turned back to our pod just as Vee climbed out, her eyes wide. Slick stood beside me.

'This is Vee. Be nice to her, she's had it tough.'

Slick nodded. 'Welcome aboard.'

He looked over his shoulder at Thorn and Rae assisting Alwin and then turned back to me. 'Not bad going for a moneyed-up harpy.'

My hands went to my hips, my eyelids narrowing. Someone was going to pay for that comment.

Alwin was able to walk. He called out from where he leaned on Thorn. 'My, he has you pegged.'

I sneered at him, and then let a smile soften my face. 'Well, it's good to see you too.'

Rae draped his arm over her shoulder and Alwin let go of Thorn to lean on her. The smile on Rae's face made her tear-filled eyes glisten. We'd been through so much and I really couldn't believe that Alwin was with us, that we'd made it.

Thorn gestured for us to follow him out of the hold. Mother, Vee, Rae with Alwin followed him.

Slick held back for me. 'Sorry it took so long to open up for you all. I had to get us away first and then once I'd set the course, I needed to re-pressurize the hold so I could open the pods. I couldn't do it any faster and I had to be careful because there were two and I didn't know who was in which, or whether you had split up.'

'You did great. We just didn't know if it was you or the pirates that had snatched us, so we were a little anxious.'

'I didn't think about that part. I'm sorry.'

I stopped walking and threw my arms around Slick and hugged him. 'Thank you, thank you, thank you. You were brilliant.'

Vee and Opeia slowed to wait for me. Rae had stopped too, looking back as Alwin rested.

Slick gaped at me. He looked from Rae to me. 'Are you Essa?'

'Yes, of course I am.' I punched him in his skinny arm. 'Rae would never let you get away with calling her a harpy.'

A stupid smile transformed his face. 'Well I never thought…thanks and you're welcome.'

14

ENDINGS AND BEGINNINGS

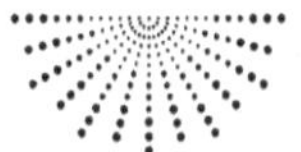

Mother resisted letting me tend her in the med bay, until Thorn raised his voice at her. 'Just get in there and get seen to woman. I won't have any peace until you do.'

Vee was in her quarters, resting. Her rehabilitation, if that was possible, would take a while. Whatever spark she'd been born with had been beaten out of her. Well, Mother could pay for the best therapists, and she had taken to her clone like a long-lost sister. It comforted me to know I'd done the right thing in going back for Vee.

Rae was quiet but there was a calm stillness to her. She had her Alwin back. He'd refused to let us treat his injuries, saying nothing on this ship could heal his scar and, as the rest were superficial, he could deal with them later.

'Rae said I'd never pass for a pirate.' He'd run his forefinger along his scar. 'Well, she was wrong.'

Rae had replied. 'I take it back. You were a very convincing pirate.'

Then Rae was there beside me, helping me look after our mother. We were still to get the full story from Alwin about what happened. Rae sent me a smile and I understood how she felt. I'd never cared for anyone before, not like I did for Thorn. Somehow, Captain Hunk had maneuvered into a position where he ranked equally with my family.

Alwin was using the computer terminal like he'd never had a break from it. I ignored him as Mother needed my attention more. Rae ran the scan over our mother's upper abdomen, while I checked the read-outs. The huge hematoma had turned purple and streaks of red ran from it.

'There was a small bleed, but it has stopped. The system recommends oxygen, monitoring for shock and maybe a blood transfusion until we can get her seen to.'

Rae went to the cabinet and brought out a pouch of universal blood. Mother saw it and shook her head. 'I don't need that. I'm okay.'

Opeia tried to get off the bed. I whacked the oxygen mask over her face. 'Stay still. Humor us, please.'

I read the instructions to set up the IV to get the blood into her. It looked simple enough.

Her gaze flicked between us. 'All right.' She lay back down and folded her hands over her chest.

'You need to clean your hands first,' Rae said.

There was a san unit niche in the wall. I waved my hands under it until the indicator flashed green. I was looking forward to inserting the IV. I'd never done that before.

'You'll feel a bit of a pinch.'

I slid the cannula in and hooked up the IV. All seemed to be going steadily. Mother's vital signs improved. Her blood pressure rose and her heart rate steadied.

'So.' My eyes locked with Rae's. 'Spill.'

Opeia glanced over to Alwin, who was busy at the computer terminal. As if he sensed we were looking at him, he looked up.

'Mrs Gayens?'

'Did you get it?'

Alwin nodded and held up a tiny button.

'What's that?' Rae asked.

'A tiny camera. I took a picture of the man in charge and a few others besides.'

'You took photos?'

My mother noticed my puzzled expression. 'AllEarth Corp is a large corporation. There are employees, some in high places, who I've never met. The images Alwin has managed to take could help us find out who they are and whether they work for me.'

'So you let Alwin get hurt?' There was a catch in Rae's voice and a look of disbelief on her face.

Alwin came over and rubbed her shoulders. 'Your mother tried to protect me. I took the risk. It was my plan. There was a risk that, as we were compromised, the pirates would strike. They did. That only proved that it was someone high up, someone with a means to get information.'

'And what does it show?' Mother asked, nodding at the console.

I checked her vitals and they were within normal range. Her pallor was improving and there was a healthy shine to her eyes. She was going to be okay.

Alwin went back to the terminal. 'I'm running the images against the company's database. They disguise themselves, some have even had facial refits, but there are some biometric indicators that can't be changed.'

He stared at the screen and rubbed his chin. 'Mmm interesting. Inyaface is your outer planetary chief of operations. Hector Guilford.' His eyebrows rose. 'A few of his henchmen work for you too. One in security, which is how information about our trip was leaked. All up, five of them work for you.'

Opeia sighed and shook her head. 'Do you think that's it?'

'I think it's the head of it. We'll just keep cleaning up as we go.'

Opeia nodded. 'Take that IV out now, girls. I'm feeling much better.'

I shrugged and Rae nodded so I started to slip it out.

'Al can you get an order ready for me and I'll authorize it. By the time we get back, they should be rounded up.'

Thorn chimed in over the intercom. 'No sign of pursuit. We are almost back at your ship, Mrs Gayens. There appears to be a number of vessels waiting there.'

'I think that must be the security force I sent for,' Rae quipped.

You? I sent for them.' I insisted.

Alwin grinned. 'That must be why there are so many of them."

Rae went over to drape herself on Alwin, who smiled as he gazed into her eyes. I sighed heavily. Seeing them happy after so much despair filled me with joy. Everything was going to be all right.

Mother sat up and called out so she could be heard on the intercom. 'I'll talk to them. They can recover my ship. I'll stay on board if that meets with your approval, Captain.'

Mother was staying aboard? I wondered what she was up to.

'Roger that and you're most welcome to stay. We're about to hit the accelgates next. You want Earth or Jupiter station?'

'Earth,' Opeia said and looked at Rae and me. 'You two need to get back to school and I'm sick of space for the moment.'

'About the school thing,' I began. 'I'm not going back.'

'Oh yes you are, young lady.' She tried to get up but I pushed her back down gently.

Rae came over and held Mother's hand, her wide dark eyes assessing me.

'No, I'm not.'

'If you think you're going to live off your inheritance and not work, you have another thing coming.'

'I'm not after the inheritance. I have my own money, my own business, in fact.'

My mother screwed up her face. 'But you could achieve so much more with your life.'

'I want to make my own way.'

Thorn walked in and stood there on the threshold of the med bay. I glanced over to him and nodded. We'd barely had a chance to speak. My pulse was rather ragged and I had a strange feeling in my stomach, like there were seven dwarves in there all packing their suitcases ready to rush out the door.

'But...but—'

I ran my hand over my mother's head, smoothing her hair. I slipped the oxygen back over her face. 'I'm going to stay with Thorn, if he'll have me.'

Her gaze slid to Thorn's and then back to me. 'You don't love me?' she asked yanking the mask off again.

'Of course I love you. I love both of you. But I've known for a while that I didn't need school to get me anywhere. I have smarts already. And as much as I admire you and what you do, I don't want to go into the company and follow in your footsteps. You have Rae for that — Rae and Alwin, actually.'

Rae patted Mother's hand and wiped a tear from her eye. We shared a look, Rae and I.

'I'll look after her,' Rae said. Turning to Thorn, she said, 'You better look after her or I'll be coming for you.'

'That's a bit full on, Rae,' I said, rather taken aback. 'Like I said, I hadn't even spoken to him yet. He's only hinted that I'd be welcome, not the particulars.'

She turned and smiled at me. 'I don't want him abandoning you.'

She went all teary, not quite over the emotional journey of losing Al and getting him back again. I grabbed her to me. Opeia sat up and enveloped us both in her embrace.

'Right,' Rae said after a while and went back to the counter. 'You need to lay still, Opi, so I can give you this shot. It will help with the bruises. We can't have you turning up home looking a fright, can we?'

'Darn, I took the IV out,' I said. 'It would have been able to deliver the dose, unless the shot is meant to be intramuscular.'

'It is,' Rae said and prepared the shot and jabbed it into Mother's thigh. She took it like a trooper.

Opeia took Rae's hand and lay back down. Thorn still loomed there. I needed to speak to him, but first I had to give something to my mother to help her sleep, and for the pain. Now that she had answers and could cut the pirate cancer out of her company, she was much more compliant. After the pain meds, Mother authorized the round-up order for the pirates Al had identified, then she dosed off.

Slick had taken some food to Vee and reported back that she was fine. Rae had curled up on one of the mess chairs, her hand on Alwin's knee as he sent through the instructions. As Alwin hit the console decisively, Rae's head jerked up. Alwin swung around, tugged her over to him and settled her in his lap. Rae's smile was wide and they started kissing.

I sighed. I couldn't believe it turned out so well. I left them alone so they could have some privacy.

Thorn followed me to my quarters. He stood with his arms crossed by the door after the hatch closed.

'We could have both spoken to your mother.'

I folded my arms. 'There wasn't time. We had to get her seen to and it just came up. I would have loved to talk to her together.'

'When were you going to tell me about giving up your inheritance?'

'Look, if you don't want me for who I am, that's fine. I can find a life of my own.' I sniffed as my nose started to run and my eyes watered. 'I thought you wanted me to join you.'

He was silent so I chanced a look at him. He cocked his head to the side, his blue eyes traveling all over me. 'You're pretty handy at breaking into security systems — and in a fight too.'

He changed position, as if his family jewels were hurting. My lips lifted in a smile at his joke. 'And I thought you were an heiress.'

A laugh escaped me. 'I'm not without means.'

'Yes, I heard that too.' There was a smile on his face. I was pretty sure money wasn't what the issue was.

'So is it because I'm a clone that you don't want me?' I lifted my eyes to his.

He shook his head and then had me in his arms within two strides. 'I'm just sassing you. I want you with me so bad it hurts.' He kissed my forehead and held me at arm's length. 'I want you to be sure, though, because I don't think I could deal with a broken heart on top of every-thing else I've been through. And living on a ship like this is not the life you are used to. And you're used to the best. Are you sure you could take slumming it with me and Slick?'

'I'm as sure as I can be, Thorn.' I stepped in close to him and ran my fingers through his hair. 'There are no certainties in the universe. We can only live in our moment and a moment can be just a minute or one hundred years. You told me to be who I want to be, not who I am. Well, I want to be this person, the one who choses her own destiny, who flies away with the man she loves. If you can deal with that, deal with me on that basis. You have a new shipmate.'

'Not shipmate.'

I paused, my mouth dropping. 'What?'

'Not shipmate, I was thinking maybe something a little bit more intimate.'

'I like the sound of that.'

Thorn's arms encircled me and he lifted me up so our faces were close together. 'Kiss me,' he said, his voice low and sexy.

And I did.

ACKNOWLEDGEMENTS 2014

It is wonderful to bring you more in this world setting of Rae and her sister, Essa. I have to thank Kate Cuthbert and Escape Publishing for liking *Rayessa and the Space Pirates* in the first place.

I owe gratitude to my writing buddy and great friend Nicole Murphy, who read and loved Essa, but also gave me valuable feedback. So thank you, Nicole. I also want to acknowledge my partner, Matthew Farrer, for his unstinting support and his assistance to find the right words, even when he's busy writing himself. A special thank you to Tim Murphy for going over Essa's computer geekery. Any glaring errors are entirely my own.

Thank you also to my audit buddies!

ACKNOWLEDGEMENTS 2019

It's 2019 and five years since *Rae and Essa's Space Adventures* was first published by Escape Publishing, an Australian Digital Imprint of Harlequin Enterprises. I have had fun playing in Rae and Essa's world. If you get to peek at *Opi Battles the Space Pirates* then you see I'm still having fun, albeit with an older heroine.

Harlequin gave the rights to this work back to me and also let me purchase the wonderful covers. I love science fiction and to have such swanky, outer space covers brings me much delight.

Here is hoping that those new to Rae and Essa's world have a load of fun.

Best wishes

Donna Maree Hanson

October, 2019

ABOUT DONNA MAREE HANSON

Donna Maree Hanson is a traditionally and independently published author of fantasy, science fiction and horror. She also writes paranormal romance under the pseudonym of Dani Kristoff. Her dark fantasy series (which some reviewers have called "grim dark"), Dragon Wine, was first published by Momentum Books (Pan Macmillan digital imprint) in 2014. *Shatterwing*: Part One, and *Skywatcher*: Part Two, are now re-published independently in digital and print-on-demand formats. The next two installments of Dragon Wine, *Deathwings* and *Bloodstorm*, were published in 2017. The final installments in the Dragon Wine series, *Skyfire* and *Moonfall,* were published in 2018.

In April 2015, Donna was awarded the A. Bertram Chandler Award for "Outstanding Achievement in Australian Science Fiction" for her work in running science fiction conventions, publishing and broader SF community contributions. Donna also writes science fiction romance/space opera, with *Rayessa and the Space Pirates* and *Rae and Essa's Space Adventures* out with Escape Publishing. *Opi Battles the Space Pirates* was published independently in 2017. In 2016, Donna commenced her PhD candidature researching feminism in popular romance at the University of Canberra. Also available is her epic fantasy series The Silverlands: *Argenterra*, *Oathbound* and *Ungiven Land*. The Cry Havoc series is a steampunk-themed fantasy, with romantic elements, starting with Ruby Heart and Emerald Fire. It is based in Victorian England and features magicians and a very precocious Jemima Hardcastle. Another book, Amber Rose, is planned in the series.

Donna lives in Canberra with her partner and fellow writer, Matthew Farrer.

You can contact Donna or find out more about what she is doing on her blog http://donnamareehanson.com

Or sign up to her newsletter, Wing Dust

Or on Twitter @DonnaMHanson and www.facebook.com/donnamareehanson

www.ingramcontent.com/pod-product-compliance
Lightning Source LLC
Chambersburg PA
CBHW050843190726
48286CB00007B/2201